THE CHRONICLES

OF

TITTSWORTH

The Black Hand

by

John S. O'Connor II

Paperback ISBN: 979-8-218-99897-4

Contact information: J. O'Connor Books

Website: joconnorbooks.com

Email: jsoii@cox.net

Phone: 480-854-9955

Address: J. O'Connor Books
                PO Box 20341
                Mesa, AZ. 85277

Contents

The Beginning..5

College Days..10

Becoming A Soldier 42

Okinawa Days..53

A Taste of War...69

Mike Force Commander 105

A Warrior in Bangkok 160

Return to War 182

The Last Patrol...192

The Beginning

On a quiet Sunday in January, 1944, James A. Tittsworth was born in Emmett, Nebraska. It was a sunny winter morning, the kind of unseasonably warm day that makes the American plains a peaceful calming place to live. It was a day that belied the fact that the nation was still mired in combat around the world. James was delivered at home by his father Tom and his grandmother Rosaline, the second child of Claire and Thomas Tittsworth. Even though James was a large baby at 10 lbs. 6 oz., it was an uncomplicated birth, thankfully so, since there was no medical care available and the closest doctor was twenty miles away in O'Neill. Folks in the middle plains of Nebraska are a hardy folk, conservative in their ways, deeply patriotic, and used to taking care of themselves. Delivering babies was just another chore and Jim was born into the right family.

Jim's mother Claire was a strong woman in every sense of the word. Of Scottish descent, she was a first generation American. Her family had immigrated to the US from south of Glasgow, Scotland in 1899. Her father, William McStyver, was an ironworker and brought his wife Ann and two young children to America hoping to find work on the railroad. Being ambitious, and not seeing much opportunity back in the north of England, William wanted to see the American west and buy land, the hallmark of wealth in Scotland. America, the land of opportunity, seemed like the logical place for William to find his fortune. Working their way west, by 1906 the McStyvers and their two children had ended up in St. Louis, Missouri.

William's wife died of the flu in 1915 and he remarried a second wife in 1917. The last of his two American children – Claire – was born in 1918.

The youngest of four, Claire was tall, fair-haired and outgoing. Probably spoiled, as the youngest child often is, she had a sharp mind and was instilled with a strong work ethic. If there had been women's sports back then, she would have excelled in them. She was agile and strong — she could out run most of the boys in her school until tenth-grade. She had a toughness about her that belied her tall slender frame. She never complained. After high school she found work as a seamstress with Holman Outfitters in St Louis. If she wasn't good looking she was certainly handsome and not short on suitors who recognized a good woman when they saw one. Everything about her upbringing seemed to prepare her for life on the American plains. When she met Thomas Tittsworth in 1938 at the age of 20, she was smitten by the handsome, athletic Missourian as much as he was with her. They wed in less than a year.

Thomas Tittsworth was a third generation American, the prodigy of Abner and Rosaline Tittsworth, born in St. Louis in 1916. His family was of British stock, his grandfather Harold had come to America as a 16-year-old in 1865 landing in Boston via Liverpool. He somehow made his way to Chicago following the dream of many immigrants to "Go West!" He took a job in the Chicago stockyards as a delivery man until he saved enough money to buy his own team and wagon and start a livery and freight hauling business of his own. His last son Abner was born in Chicago in 1892. By 1912 the Tittsworth owned three stables, twenty wagons and the teams to pull them. In 1913 Harold moved his clan and business to St. Louis, Missouri. He figured there was a lot more work hauling freight off the Missouri and Mississippi Rivers than there was on Lake Michigan and in the stockyards of Chicago. The newly married Abner and his wife Rosaline followed the family west.

Abe, as Abner was called, was a strapping six-foot five hulk of a man. It was said he could lift a full-grown steer by himself — which was probably not too far off. In WWI's call to service of 1917 Abe joined the US Marines and as an infantry private served in France with the Allied Expeditionary Forces under General "Black Jack" Pershing.

World War I was a transitional war, where tactics and technology were evolving from the Civil War/Napoleonic tactics to modern warfare.

6

The technological sophistication of combat was also becoming much more lethal. Corporal Abner Tittsworth distinguished himself at the Battle of Belleau Wood in June of 1918, America's first significant engagement of WWI. He courageously assaulted a German machine-gun by charging directly into the German line killing three Germans, the last in hand-to-hand combat. His daring action saved the lives of several of his comrades and enabled his unit to reach their objective, ultimately turning the tide of the battle. His selfless bravery earned him the Navy Cross - the nation's second highest award for valor. Abner was wounded three weeks later by a sniper round that severed a tendon in his left leg. He would walk with a limp for the rest of his life. The carnage of his time in France, he was one of four survivors of his platoon, left a mark on Abe Tittsworth and he returned home a changed man. He never talked about his time in France and only said he was one of many who served their country and did what he was supposed to do. He passed his firm constitution on to his children.

Abner Tittsworth's son Thomas, James' father, was also a combat veteran. Drafted into the Army at twenty-six in early 1942 following the attack on Pearl Harbor his military service was cut short, when he was severely wounded in Morocco, North Africa in December 1942. His initial wound occurred while his company fought a German mechanized infantry unit during the final days of the allied attack near Fes. Wounded by shrapnel, Private Tittsworth continued to fight, knocking out a German halftrack and allowing his unit to capture the main road into Fes. He was awarded the Distinguished Service Cross for his unselfish valor. A few weeks later he was more seriously wounded, again by artillery fire, and returned home to convalesce. In early 1943 Thomas was mustered out of the service on a medical discharge. Shortly after returning home to Claire and his daughter in St. Louis, Thomas moved his family to Emmet, Nebraska where he bought 800 acres. He wanted the independence of farming where life mostly depended on an individual's work ethic and initiative, along with a little luck from Mother Nature. Thomas was determined to raise his family to be respectful citizens and earn their own way in the

7

world. It could be truthfully said that James A. Tittsworth came from a family of American patriots who, when the country needed them, they answered the call.

Emmett, Nebraska ain't much of a town, just a grain elevator, family run feed store, a small grocery/general store, a one room restaurant-bar that served food Thursday through Sunday, and a three-pump gas station. The population was less than 100 when James was born. Because he was such a big baby his grandfather called him Big Jim and the name stuck. He was a fine child, seldom cried and seemed from an early age to understand that you had to earn your way in the world. Like most farm children, as soon as he could talk he was assigned chores and learned the value of work.

Big Jim's adolescence was mostly uneventful, that of a boy growing up on a farm. There was one incident, however, when he was eleven. Jim and two neighbor boys were fooling around at a neighbor's large pond. The pond was about three acres and had a floating dock anchored in the middle. It was about 16 feet deep and the water was Nebraska muddy. The boys were kinda fishing, but mostly just horsing around like carefree kids do. Ted, one of Jim's buddies, took a canoe out to the middle of the pond by himself and for some reason stood up. He quickly lost his balance and tipped the canoe over. Ted couldn't swim and to make the situation worse banged his head on the side of the canoe as it capsized knocking him senseless. Jim was on the shore watching his friend and skipping stones in Ted's direction when the canoe tipped and Ted plunged into the water. As he fell Ted yelled, thrashed around, and then quickly sank out of sight. Jim realized right away there was a problem, kicked off his shoes and swam out to where the capsized canoe was and Ted was last on the surface. He dove down in the murky water and found his friend, who was still struggling and still sinking, and pulled him to the surface. A strong swimmer and half a foot taller than Ted, Jim swam to shore dragging Ted with him as Ted coughed up pond water and tried to catch his breath. On the shore Jim laid Ted on his stomach and smacked him between the shoulders several times. It seemed to work and after a few gasps and coughs and spitting up muddy pond water, Ted caught his breath. The third member of the pond trio, Bob Grimly, just stood there in shock as Jim rescued his friend. After several minutes and Ted regaining his senses, the three boys walked back to the house. Tragedy averted, but just another day on the farm.

School was a pleasant diversion from the constant work of a family farm for Jim. He was a good student, when he wanted to be. Mentally sharp, he liked to read and had no problem with his studies when he applied himself. But that was the issue, applying himself. He would rather be outside hunting or fishing, or roaming around than hitting the books. But he managed to plow through with decent grades. His mother Clair saw to that and demanded her children pay attention to their studies. She was determined that they would go to college and give themselves options beyond farming.

Jim liked school and for the most part thought learning as fun, even though his real love was sports and the outdoors. As he grew in size and strength, so did his athletic abilities. He was a physical specimen: strong, fast, and agile — all the physical attributes that allowed him to excel in every sport he played. Football was his favorite sport. As a freshman in high school he was one of the bigger boys in his class and started on the county high school football team. By his senior year in high school, Jim was on the watch list for several colleges and with his decent grades going to college was a lock if he wanted to. He knew if he wanted to play sports beyond high school he had to maintain himself in the classroom. Being a Nebraska boy, as luck would have it, when the University of Nebraska offered him a full ride scholarship to play football for the Cornhuskers, he quickly accepted. It was a dream come true and he hoped perhaps a first step towards playing professional football. Three weeks following his high school graduation Big Jim Tittsworth was off to the big city, Lincoln, to attend the University of Nebraska and play for the Cornhuskers.

College Days

When Jim got on campus at the University of Nebraska in the summer of 1962, it was like he was in a different world. To characterize him as a "country hick" would not have been far off, he wasn't a dummy, just without experience in a "city" and all the distractions it offered. Emmett, Nebraska was hardly a metropolis and farm boy Jim had traveled outside his county only a few times since he was born. Like most hard working rural folks, he had a positive view of people and mostly took folks at their word. He was friendly and outgoing and a bit naive about city ways and unaccustomed to the constant churning-life on a big, diverse college campus. But he adapted, and quickly latched on to a few of his football teammates who, like him, had more interest in football than school, but being from St Louis and Kansas City, knew their way around a "big city."

Jim was wowed by the constant bustle of campus activity and even more so of the campus nightlife. He found it intoxicating in a number of ways. At Nebraska football players were the Gods of campus life and Jim and his buddies took advantage of their high status at the local bars and restaurants. On his first night out, carousing with his buddies in the week before Fall football practice began Jim learned he wasn't a big drinker. After a few beers, and feeling no pain, with his compatriots egging him on, Jim was sent up to the bar to inquire if the good-looking girl sitting by herself would be interested in meeting a Nebraska football player. Fortified with liquid courage, Jim wasn't really a lady's man, he sauntered up to the bar next to where the girl was sitting, his partners in tow behind him, and sat down. He ordered a beer and looking at the girl who had turned to look at him said, "Hello, my name is James Tittsworth. What do you think my friends call me?" The girl, realizing it was a game with Jim's friends standing behind him snickering as they sipped their beers, said, "Oh, I don't know - tits?" Jim in a staggering mock surprise replied, "No, they call me Jim!" And the half-inebriated football players howled in laughter.

The girl, unimpressed by three wobbly football studs, stood up and said, "Boys, you're not in high school any more, don't you think you should try to grow up?" Then she turned and exited the bar. Chastised, Jim and his buddies shrugged their shoulders and continued to laugh. "Gee, she was no fun," said the running back from Kansas City. Then they all went back to their table to finish their beers. Luckily, their sometimes drunken and inappropriate behavior was overlooked. This was fortunate for the immature Jim who was a bit reckless after a few beers. As one might expect he soon lost interest in his studies. Football and partying became his focus.

Back in the early '60s freshman couldn't play varsity sports at Division I colleges. This was a benefit to both a university's teams and the freshman players. Their first year in school freshmen had a chance to adapt to unchaperoned college life and the academic requirements of school. Scholarship athletes also had a chance to adjust to the demands of big-time college sports, which was essentially a full-time job. Jim while displaying his football potential managed to meet the requirements to stay eligible to play. He was also successful in steering clear of any off-campus disciplinary problems.

On the football field, Jim was one of twenty-seven new recruits to the football team that year brought in by new coach Bob Devaney. Recruited as a linebacker he made his bones as a tough player with a nose for the ball. In the five games the freshman team played Jim was a starter at right outside linebacker and the team's second leading tackler. While he dressed out for the varsity games as a freshman he never saw playing time. Nebraska varsity had a 9-2 record that year and won the Gotham Bowl against the Miami Hurricanes, the program's first Bowl game and winning season in several years. Outside of the intensity and pageantry of Nebraska football, an incident at a gas station in Lincoln in March of his freshman year was the most memorable event of Jim's first year in college.

On a late Thursday evening, Jim and his friend Ralph Evans, another football player and one of his two roommates, were at a gas station filling up Ralph's car. On the opposite side of the line of gas pumps a long silver Lincoln Continental pulled-up with three guys in the front seat. The driver was a black male, the guy in the middle was a white guy and the third person sitting by the front seat passenger door was another black male. As Jim was filling Ralph's car he could hear the three men in the Lincoln arguing about something. When he looked over to see what was going on he saw the black guy on the passenger's side was holding a big knife on the leg of the white guy in the middle. The guy was clearly in distress and scared. Then the guy with the knife smacked him yelling, "Shut-up and stay still," and then handed the knife to the driver telling him to, "cover this Honky while I get some gas and take a leak." He got out of the car, closed the door, and headed into the gas station as Ralph was coming out. When Ralph got to Jim, Jim motioned to the car on the other side of the pumps and said, "Man I think that guy is holding the white guy hostage," and pointed towards the Lincoln as he put the nozzle back in the pump. Ralph took a step towards the pump to get a better view of the Lincoln and could see the driver had a knife tightly held against the white guy's leg pointed down as if he was going to stab him. "Holy shit," Ralph said and moved around to the other-side of the pump and said into the partly open window of the Lincoln, "Hey, what's going on here?" The driver with the knife yelled back at Ralph, "Nothing asshole, mind your own business!"

As Ralph confronted the two in the front seat of the Lincoln, Jim walked to the rear of the long car and was moving towards the driver's door when another car pulled into the gas station. As the arriving car pulled up to the gas pumps its headlights beamed into the Lincoln and the black guy with the knife, startled, turned and looked out his window at the arriving car. At that moment the white guy pushed the knife away from his leg, punched the black guy in the face, simultaneously opened the passenger door, and jumped out, and headed towards the gas station store. But he stopped next to Ralph. The black driver, stunned, took a minute to regain his senses, and then he too jumped out of the car where he saw Jim standing behind the Lincoln. He quickly raised the knife and said, "What do you want fucker, some of this?" and he held up the knife in a threatening motion toward Jim. Jim for some reason was not intimidated and replied. "What the hell are you doing? You better back off and get out of here." The guy with the knife then lunged at Jim with the knife extending his left arm. Jim deftly dodged the attack and grabbed the guy's knife arm and slammed it into the car trunk, while pulling him forward and kneeing him in the groin. The skinny black jerk let out a scream and went down holding his crotch, his testicles smashed. Jim, still holding his left arm, began banging it into the Lincoln's trunk until he dropped the knife. Fight over, as the ex-knife holder was totally in pain and couldn't even stand-up.

As Jim was dealing with the punk with the knife, his partner came out of the gas station and saw the white guy standing by Ralph. He yelled, "Get back in the fucking car Earl!" and started toward him. The white guy, shook up at seeing his other captor coming at him, ran around to the far side of the Lincoln where the black driver was still on the ground holding his crotch with Jim now standing over him holding the knife. He quickly moved behind Jim. When the other black guy got to Ralph, Ralph confronted him. "What are you guys doing? Let that guy alone and get out of here. The cops will be here in a minute and you'll be in big trouble." The advancing black guy replied with, "Fuck you punk, you're the one who better get out of here if you know what's good for you," now turning his attention to Ralph and moving towards him in a menacing way. When the guy tried to grab him, Ralph deftly parried his lunge and punched him. The black guy stepped back, gathered himself and said, "OK punk you asked for it," and charged at Ralph again. Ralph no wimp at six-foot two and 240 pounds and as a football player no stranger to violence. When the guy came at him, Ralph latched on to him and flung him into the Lincoln and pounded him with a few punches. The guy tried to fight back but was outclassed and soon was in a heap next to the hood of the car just as sirens could be heard in the distance.

The gas station attendant had called the cops when he heard the yelling at the pumps and saw Jim fighting with the first black guy.

13

Tittsworth

Ralph grabbed the defeated guy and held him down until the police car arrived and the cops took over. They cuffed up the two hoodlums. They also cuffed up the white guy after interviewing everyone as it was his car and they had found a bale of dope in the trunk and a bag with some pills and packets of white powder in the glove compartment. The whole incident was related to a drug deal gone wrong with the black guys trying to rob the white guy who was their dealer — well known to the police.

Two weeks later both Jim and Ralph received Letters of Commendation from the Mayor and President of the University for being good Citizen Samaritans. When the coaches called them out at practice praising them for their heroic actions they both received good natured ribbing from their teammates.

The first week of April spring football practice started, fifteen days of meetings, drills and scrimmages that left all the players and coaches exhausted and longing for the end of the semester, so they could relax. Jim did well in "Spring Ball" and positioned himself to earn playing time in the fall. But the end of the semester and summer couldn't come fast enough, Jim was tired of school and even all the football requirements that never seemed to end. He managed to salvage his grades and had a relatively decent year academically, but he was burned out. When he finished with final exams in mid-May he headed home to unwind and get in a little fishing and just relax. He kind of looked forward to the farm chores too, they would keep him outdoors for most of the summer. His plan was to go back to school for the second summer session and take two classes so he would have a lighter course load in the fall and could concentrate on football. He'd also be able to use the athletic facilities to get in tip-top shape for the fall.

When Jim came back to campus in early July for the start of the second summer session, he had concluded that farming was not something he wanted to do with his life. He loved the rural countryside, but he had also grown to like "big city" life and its conveniences. He wasn't sure what he wanted to do, but it wasn't to go back to the farm. Little did he know that the coming year would be life changing.

The second Summer session started after the Fourth of July and was five weeks long. Jim planned to use it to get in the best shape of his life and be prepared for football practice when it started the second week of August. He resolved that he would go to class every day followed by a gym session. For the first few weeks of Summer school things went to plan, and then there was an incident at the university gym that would impact Jim and his college career.

After a workout one early Tuesday evening in late July, as Jim walked into the two-story parking garage next to the university gym where he had parked the '55 Pontiac he had brought back to school, he heard a muffled scream and a lot of yelling from two people clearly arguing. One sounded like a girl. The screaming seemed to be coming from the floor above. Assuming something was wrong Jim ran up the stairs to see what was going on. Just outside the second-floor stairwell a girl was struggling to get away from some guy. As Jim exited the stairwell and started toward the fighting couple the guy slapped the girl and she screamed and fell to the floor. Jim moved quickly in their direction and yelled at the guy to stop it and leave the girl alone. The guy quickly turned towards Jim and said for him to keep out of it, it was none of his business. Jim replied, "I'm making it my business! Now leave her alone and get out of here!" The assailant replied "Fuck you!" Instinctively Jim punched him landing his fist squarely on the guy's jaw and knocking him down. When the guy got up he yelled at Jim, "I know who you are asshole and you'll pay for that. You think you're some tough guy. But we'll see about that. I'll be seeing you!" Then the guy ran off.

Jim was glad the incident seemed over and turned to the girl and asked if she was hurt. She said that she wasn't really, just shaken up. Jim asked, "Who was that guy, what a jerk. I hope he's gone, he had no right to grab you or hit you. I'm glad that I came by when I did. Are you sure you're alright?" The girl stood up and other than her red swelling cheek seemed okay and was gaining her composure. She replied, "I'm okay, really. My name is Sharon Davies, I'm a sophomore from Olathe, Kansas. Unfortunately, that nut-job was a guy I dated for a short time last fall. He was still angry that I broke up with him, he was just too weird for me. He's been calling me and bothering me off and on since then, but I won't talk with him or see him. This is the first time I've even seen him since April and he surprised me as I was heading to my car. I'm just glad you showed up when you did. No telling what he might have done." "Well, I'm glad I was here too. My name is Jim Tittsworth and I'm a sophomore as well. I think you should report him to the university or the police, what he did was criminal." "He's not a student and I don't think that will do much good, his uncle is a cop." "Well, I think you should tell someone anyway, so you have a record of it. He may try to see you again and next time it could be a lot worse." "You're right, I'll report him, perhaps that will get him to stay away from me." "Well, you're sure you're all right? Do you need me to take you anywhere?" "No, I'm fine really, I'll just head home." "Fine, I'll watch you get in your car and make sure you get going." "Thanks for saving me, perhaps if I see you around I can return the favor," Sharon said with a smile. "Sure, that would be nice," Jim replied. She then turned, walked to her car, got in and drove off. Nice looking lady, maybe I'll see her around. I could use some female companionship, Jim thought as he headed to his dorm.

About a week later on a wonderfully lazy July afternoon, Jim and two other football players were at the local watering hole just off campus, McGillys, having a sandwich, discussing how their training was going and their prospects for the upcoming season when Ms. Davies and two of her girlfriends walked in. At first, she didn't notice Jim with his buddies and Jim didn't notice her or the two cuties that she came in with. But when the three good looking women passed by the football players' table Jim recognized Sharon. She and her friends took a table just across from them. A few minutes later when Sharon got up to go to the bar to order she saw Jim — who was looking her way. She smiled, walked over and said, "Hello Jim Tittsworth, good to see you again, but under these better circumstances."

Jim was a little taken back, both that she had come over to say something to him and at how good she looked. He didn't remember her to be as beautiful and well-built from the dim light of the parking garage when she was dressed in sweats. Gaining his composure he said with a smile, "Hello Sharon, good to see you again too. I hope no one is following you!" "No, I got my body guards with me," she replied with a chuckle pointing to her two friends. "I'm headed to the bar to get some beers." You could legally drink 3.2% alcohol beer in Nebraska at age 18. "Can I get some for you and your friends? I owe you from our last meeting," she continued, and gave a flattered Jim and his astonished cronies a mischievous smile. It's not every day a good-looking sweetie walks over uninvited to a table of grubby looking football players and asks if she can buy them a beer. "We could go for that, but you don't have to," Jim replied, trying to act cool and nonchalant. "No, I'd like to, it would be returning a favor," she said with a smile. "All right then, we're drinking Coors." "Great, be right back," was Sharon's answer.

When Sharon turned for the bar Jim's two table mates immediately jumped on him and asked where he had met such a great looking chick and what he had going on with her. Jim replied, trying to sound like mister cool, that she was just a friend that he had met at the gym. Neither believed him.

When Sharon returned with two pitchers of Coors and six glasses under her arm, Jim jumped up and helped her as she set one of the pitchers down. One of Jim's buddies suggested that Sharon and her friends join them and he would give them an update on Nebraska's upcoming season and get the next pitcher. Sharon thought for a second and said, "Sure, why not," and motioned to her friends to come over and join the guys.

The six of them spent the rest of the afternoon discussing Nebraska football and the inconsequential things college students talk about in their leisure time. Later, when Sharon and her friends got up to go Jim got up to leave with them. The other two guys stayed at the table. On the way out, Jim asked Sharon if she would like to go out that weekend and maybe take in a movie. Sharon was warming up to Jim. He seemed to be a good guy and a gentleman and thought it might be fun to go out with a Husker football player. When she said yes, that would be great, Jim asked where she lived and for a way to reach her. She was in a dorm not too far from his and Jim suggested he come by and pick her up about five on Saturday afternoon and that way they could make the six o'clock movie. "Done deal, see you down stairs at Robinson Hall at five on Saturday," Sharon said smiling. Jim smiled back and replied, "Great, see you then!" And turned and headed to his car. Neither saw the dark '57 Chevy parked across the street at the end of the block watching them.

Jim was on a high as he walked to his car, a two-tone blue and white '55 Pontiac he had purchased while at home earlier in the summer. That girl was something, he thought as he walked. She was good looking, well built, fun to be around — definitely someone he'd like to see more of — but he'd have to wait until Saturday. Who knows where this might go? he thought as he fired up his car. Saturday couldn't come soon enough.

Saturday afternoon as Jim prepped for his date with Sharon he ran through his mind the circumstances of when he had first met her, when she was being assaulted in the parking garage by the gym. Who was that freak who had been attacking her? Jim had never seen him before and didn't even know his name. He wondered if she had reported the incident as she said she would and if he was still stalking her? No matter, Jim hadn't seen him again, perhaps he got the message and was finished being a problem. Oh well, it appeared things were turning out nicely for him, but what a way to meet a girl. He finished getting ready and headed out on his date.

Sharon Davies was a midwest girl from Olathe, Kansas. She had gone to Nebraska because her mother was a legacy and she wanted to be somewhat close to home, but far enough away so she could be on her own. Her father was the owner of Davies Aviation, a small manufacturing company that made after-market parts for civilian aircraft. She was a typical midwest girl, and had attended Olathe High School where she played basketball and ran track. She was level headed and knew she was attractive, but was careful about who she hung out with, especially the guys. How she had misjudged the knucklehead who had been harassing her these past several months continued to amaze her. She had only gone out with him once and never even kissed the guy, but somehow, he latched on to her. When she tried to cut him loose gently he refused to believe she was through with him. She hadn't seen him since the incident in the garage and was hopeful he finally got the message and would be out of her life for good. But she was wrong.

Jim showed up at Sharon's dorm just before five and she was already in the lobby when he walked in. "Jim," she called out as he walked in the door. It was hard to miss the six-foot three football player who looked every bit the athlete he was. When he heard his name, he looked in her direction and walked over to where she was sitting. She looked great in jeans and the blue crewneck sweater she was wearing with two slim white stripes running across the chest. A small gold chain with a gold cross hung down on the sweater. She looked just how Jim had fantasized she'd look, he was smitten. This girl is beautiful and she's going out with me, he thought. "You look great," he said, "my buddies are going to be jealous!" "I doubt that," Sharon replied with a smile. "If you like we can head to the Regent now, Dr. No is playing with Sean Connery," Jim said, laying out the plan for the evening. "Sounds good, let's go," was Sharon's reply. "If we get there a little early we can get a coke at the coffee shop next door. I'll buy the tickets early and that way we don't have to wait in line for our seats." "That will work, I don't like to sit in the theater a long time before a show starts. You can't talk," was Sharon's reply. "Ok, we're off," Jim said and pointed to the door falling in behind her as she headed out to the parking lot.

At the coffee shop, after Jim bought the tickets, they exchanged stories about themselves filling in the highlights of their lives before coming to Nebraska. They were reserved, kind of feeling each other out, and letting the conversation wander. Jim didn't want to be overbearing or play the big football player guy trying to swoon the pretty coed. He kept football stories to a minimum. They each seemed to be genuine and interested in the other while enjoying each other's company.

The theater was only about half full and little was said during the show. Both thought Dr. No was entertaining, even if the special effects were a little goofy. Following the show, they went to a Big Boy drive-in not far from campus for something to eat. After a hamburger and a coke and some small talk Jim took Sharon back to her dorm. As they sat in Jim's car each expressed that they had enjoyed the evening and Jim secured a promise that they could see each other again. Both felt comfortable together, and without commitment, thought they would see where their new-found relationship might take them. It was about nine forty-five when Jim, ever the gentlemen, walked Sharon into her building. He thanked her for a great evening and she replied in kind. He then put a hand on her cheek and gave her a sweet thank you kiss on the other cheek. Sharon wasn't really expecting a kiss, after all it was a first date, but she was taking a liking to the big guy from Emmett. She appreciated his gentleness. Jim looked her in the eyes after the kiss and said, "Thanks again for a great night, I'll be in touch." "I look forward to it," she replied. Then Jim, with a wide smile on his face said, "Good night," backed away, turned, and headed towards his car. Sharon didn't respond, she just stood there with her own happy grin and watched him until he was out the door. Quite a guy, she thought to herself as she hit the elevator button, I could see a lot more of a guy like him. When the doors of the elevator opened she stepped in and punched the button for her floor still with a happy smile on her face.

When Jim walked out to his Pontiac there were two guys standing by the trunk of the car parked beside his. One was about his size and the other a head shorter and skinny. When he got closer he could see the skinny one was the dirtbag punk he had punched in the face in the gym garage a few weeks before. Trouble here, he thought to himself and went to full alert.

As he got closer he prepared himself to fight, zipping up his jacket as he quickly sized up his opponents. Neither seemed to amount to much physically. Jim could see the two were watching him with scrawls on their faces. When he got to the rear of his car the skinny dirtbag punk, whose name was Donnie Aaron, stepped in front of him and snarled, "Tough guy football player, remember me?" "Ya," Jim replied looking directly at him, "I smelled you when I got to the parking lot, you're the dirtbag I knocked out at the garage. You come for another smack in the face?" As Jim stared at the punk his partner moved to Jim's left side and took up a menacing stance. "Well, Mr. tough guy, I think it's time I repaid you for your punch and for taking out my girl. Let this be a lesson to you asshole, and you stay away from Sharon." Then dirtbag Aaron took a wild roundhouse swing at Jim. Aaron was no athlete, nor really even a fighter, just a big mouth wannabe tough guy. His awkward swing left him off balance and, Jim ready for a confrontation, easily caught his right arm as he swung and pulled him forward and flung him into his partner knocking them both off balance. Jim now in full attack mode followed up with a hard kick that landed on the right thigh just above the knee of Aaron's friend with a smashing thud. The guy let out a yell and went down in a hep holding his wounded leg — he was out of the fight.

When Aaron stood back up and lunged toward Jim, Jim smacked him right in the face with a left fist and followed it up with a powerful right-hand punch that caught him on the neck. It was a one-two Joe Lewis would have been proud of. The punches ended the confrontation as dirtbag Aaron hit the deck with a bloody nose. It was over in less than a minute, with Jim's assailants both on the ground and out of commission. Jim stood over both the knuckleheads and said, "You two punks get the fuck out of here, and if I ever see either of you again or Sharon tells me either of you dirtbags are still harassing her, I'm going to come looking for you and when I find you it won't be pretty. Now get gone and leave me alone or do you want your asses kicked some more?"

The two punks knew it was all over but the shouting, quickly picked themselves up and scampered into Aaron's '57 Chevy. "Fuck you, this ain't over asshole," the dirtbag Aaron yelled from the safety of his car as the two would be assailants pulled away peeling out of the parking lot, Aaron holding a handkerchief to his dripping nose. Jim watched them drive away and then got in the Pontiac. He sat there for a minute to calm down. Damn, those two assholes ruined a perfectly good evening, he thought and tried to shift his thoughts back to Sharon.

Over the next three weeks Jim continued his daily routine: morning class, afternoon workout. Added to his schedule was spending time with Sharon whenever she was available. The two rising-sophomores were slowly falling for one another. Sharon was really the first time Jim had such strong feelings for a girl. He had dated a few girls in high school and liked a few, played a little touchy-feely with them out in the corn fields, but never really felt serious about any of them. His experience with the opposite sex was limited, even at Nebraska where his main focus had been on football. But now he found himself thinking about Sharon whenever he wasn't engaged with something else. Somehow it was more than just wanting to jump her lovely bones, although she was extremely attractive and alluring. She just seemed special; kind, easy to talk to, fun, and acted like she cared about him, even kissing him back when he kissed her. No, this was someone he thought he could take home to mom.

Sharon too was growing more and more fond of Big Jim and perhaps falling in love. She wasn't sure, she just knew she liked being around him. And although she had had a boyfriend in high school her last few years and dated a few guys the past year in Lincoln, this was different. Jim was tall, extremely fit, very strong, and handsome in a manly sort of way. And, he was always kind and a gentleman with her. He treated her with respect. It didn't seem he was just interested in sleeping with her like most of the immature guys she had gone out with at Nebraska. It seemed they just wanted to use her as arm candy and get in her pants. She was comfortable with Jim and more and more over the past few weeks she was physically attracted to him, especially when he kissed her and held her close. She always felt safe when she was with Jim and it didn't hurt that he was a Nebraska football player.

When the second summer school season ended August 1st Sharon and Jim stayed at school for a few days before heading home to recharge before the start of the fall semester. Jim only had ten days before fall football practice started while Sharon was off until the week before Labor Day. Their past few weeks of dating had blossomed into a real romance and both felt that strong emotional attachment that comes from loving someone. They had been dating about three weeks, kissed and made-out a bit, but hadn't slept together yet. Both assumed they would consummate the relationship, when the time came, but Jim was in no rush to press the issue, even though he wanted to be with her more and more as their emotional bond tightened.

The day after the last summer session ended Jim proposed that they go camping for a few days. The weather was spectacular for August in Nebraska and Jim had a trunk full of camping and fishing gear in the Pontiac. Branched Oak Lake was only about twenty miles north of Lincoln and had a nice recreation area. They could pitch a tent there, hike around the lake, rent a boat from the marina and float around, and just enjoy each other's company. And if Sharon played her cards right he'd even teach her to fish. Sharon was game, she liked the outdoors, but had only been camping a few times with her dad when she was quite young. She thought it might be fun to spend a few days just relaxing without all the hustle and bustle of campus and Lincoln. And she'd get to spend some quality time with Jim. She reserved judgment about the fishing.

They were both excited and a little apprehensive the next day as they drove up to Branched Oak Lake. It would be good to be alone, doing something different, and out of town where they could just be by themselves. Once at the recreation area, Jim registered for a camp-site. He got one on the West side of the lake and they made their way there and set up Jim's three-person tent. He had all the necessities, camp stove, lantern, two sleeping bags with air mattresses and of course fishing gear. Jim was Mr. Camper - what else was there to do in Emmet?

They blew up the air mattresses and Jim teased Sharon saying she was really good at that. The innuendo taken, she laughed at his attempt at humor and told him to get his mind out of the gutter. They laid out their sleeping bags and Jim also had a large nylon poncho liner that he laid over them that made the floor of the tent essentially into a double bed. Once they had their shelter squared away they went for a walk along the lake just as the sun began to drop.

As they walked along the trail Jim took Sharon's hand and held it softly. When she looked up at the big guy from Emmet he said, looking directly at her, "Sharon, I gotta tell you I'm in love with you. In the short time I've known you I see in you everything I've dreamed about in a girl. I hope my telling you doesn't upset you. But I can't help how I feel." Sharon was a little surprised Jim was so forward with his feelings, she hadn't expected it — but she had been thinking about him a lot the past few weeks as well. The more she was around him the more she liked him. In fact, she concluded she must be in love with him because she couldn't stop thinking about him when she wasn't with him. She never felt this strongly about anyone in the past. He had become the center of her life. "Oh, Jim," she replied softly, "it's so wonderful to hear you say that. No one had ever told me they loved me before and it's especially good to hear that from you. You're such a great guy. I'm lucky to have found you. Or that you found me

I guess. From day one when you saved me I knew you were special and since then I have fallen in love with you too." "Well, I just wanted you to know - I was hoping you felt the same way. There are so many things I want to tell you and so many places I want to take you and things I want to do with you. Sharon, I think you're perfect. I promise you I will always treat you with respect and be good to you. I consider myself the lucky one." Then he pulled her towards him and kissed her. After a long embrace he pulled back and said with a smile, "Now that we have that out of the way, you want to go to the marina and have dinner?" "Wow cowboy! You really know how to treat a girl," she replied. "How did you know I was hungry?" Then they both laughed and headed back to the camp hand-in-hand.

When they returned to the campsite from the Marina they took off their shoes and crawled into the tent, and laid down. Jim lit the lantern and they lay on the sleeping bags talking for a while about their dreams and the silly things two young people in love talked about when they're alone. They both knew what was coming but were in no hurry, they had all night. After a while Jim reached up and turned out the lantern and took off his shirt. When he laid back down he looked over at Sharon who was watching him. He leaned over, gently brushed the hair from her face, and kissed her. It was a warm kiss and unlike any she had felt before, although he had kissed her a number of times. It was a kiss that was tender, had passion, but it wasn't a selfish kiss. It had meaning. It meant I love you. He pulled Sharon close and held her in a warm embrace as she snuggled up close to the big guy fitting perfectly into his powerful arms. He just held her for a moment. Sharon felt warm and comfortable. One thing led to another and shortly they were both undressed, naked in front of each other for the first time. Jim had little experience in the art of love — he was still a virgin. Like most amateurs, he kinda just did what came naturally and tried not to fumble around or be greedy. He wanted Sharon to enjoy the encounter as much as he knew he would.

Sharon that first night was the teacher. She had lost her virginity as a junior in high school and had shared herself with her then boyfriend a number of times. But this was different. This was love making and not teenage sex. She guided Jim to all the right places and showed him that tenderness and passion could reside in the same place. She touched him in ways that he had never been touched before and took him to the height of passion. After they spent a good while exploring each other they both climaxed and fell back exhausted. They both realized they had just experienced what real love was all about — giving yourself completely to someone because you wanted to because you wanted to share your intimate-self, the most precious gift a person can give to another. They fell asleep in each other's arms. The next day they slept late and when they finally did get up and dressed, Jim drove them to the marina for breakfast. They didn't talk much about the previous night, but each savored it in their own way.

The two days at the lake were the most wonderful of Jim's life. They were idyllic, the two love birds walked around the lake, took a boat ride, and fished, although Sharon didn't like to bait the hooks. And of course, they made love in the afternoon and fell asleep each night in each other's arms. To Jim, it was like a fantasy come true. Sharon too relished the two days with Jim. She now knew what it was like to be totally in love with someone who loved her back and placed her happiness before their own. Jim was a special guy.

They didn't talk much on the ride back to Lincoln, they just listened to the radio and were each lost in their own thoughts, replaying in their minds the best and most romantic two days of their lives as they cruised by the golden ripe wheat fields that lined the road. Jim just tried to stay in the moment and not think about getting back to the real world. Sharon, ever the worrier, wondered what the future would bring now that she had fallen in real love. Time will tell, she thought to herself, no sense tempting fate.

As they approached Lincoln the news came on the radio. The lead story was about a police chase of two burglars the prior evening that resulted in a car crash that killed the driver, one Donald Aaron, and seriously injured his partner Thomas Grantson. Aaron in his attempt to escape the police ran his '57 Chevy into a utility pole. Upon hearing Aaron's name Sharon gasp and let out an, "Oh my god!" Jim asked, "Did you know that guy?" "He was the guy in the garage that day when you saved me. I can't believe I had anything to do with him. I knew something was wrong with him." "Well, I guess that won't be a problem now," Jim replied. He had no sympathy for the little dirtbag. Sometimes you get what you deserve, he thought to himself. He didn't tell Sharon about the encounter in the dorm parking lot.

When they got to Lincoln Jim took Sharon to her dorm and after a sweet kiss and a sad goodbye he drove over to his dorm to pack for his trip home to Emmet the next morning.

Sharon was headed home to Olathe the next morning as well, her father was coming up to Lincoln to pick her up. Jim wouldn't see her until school started and as soon as he dropped her off knew it would be a lonely few weeks without her. But maybe it was good she would be away the next few weeks that way he could concentrate on football. The stay in Emmett would be a short one, he had to be back in a week for the start of fall ball.

Back home in Emmett Jim was lonelier than he anticipated. He found himself calling Sharon at least twice a day and became upset when he couldn't reach her. Mainly during the time in Emmett, he just hung out with a few of his high school buddies who had stayed in town to farm and didn't have any interest in college. He didn't tell his mom and dad about Sharon; his plan was to introduce them to her at Parents Weekend when they came up to Lincoln for the football game.

While he was home Jim worked out every day and helped his dad with chores around the farm. He found the farm work relaxing, he liked the physical nature of farming and being your own man. But after meeting Sharon and enjoying life at the University and the many amenities of the "Big City" he knew he didn't want to spend his life in a small town in the middle of the Nebraska plains. He also realized that if he was going to make it somewhere else, if football didn't pan out, he best apply himself in school and choose a major that would land him a good job with a lot of opportunity.

Jim got back to campus the day before football started. He was rooming with two of his football teammates at an apartment complex that had mostly football players as tenants. For the first two weeks practice would be two-a-days: conditioning and skill training drills in the morning, chalk talks after lunch, and in pads late in the afternoon. Sundays would be off days.

Big time college football is a full-time job, especially at a nationally ranked school. Those that couldn't keep up the pace quickly were shown the door. Jim started camp in great shape and that gave him an edge. He was a standup edge rusher and outside linebacker. Things went well and the coaches liked his smarts and speed and his improvement from his freshman year. However, he was just a sophomore and there were a few upperclassmen ahead of him on the depth chart. It looked like other than on special teams — primarily kick-offs — he wouldn't see much playing time unless they were killing another team or a few guys got hurt — always a distinct possibility.

Two-a-days ended ten days before the first game and a week before school started. The players were glad as pre-season practices were intense and a grind. During the preseason Jim stayed in touch with Sharon, sometimes calling her at lunch and the again in the evenings. He also managed to write her a few letters, as he thought it was romantic and knew everyone liked to get mail. She got back to campus the Thursday before the fall semester started.

When Sharon got back to school she and Jim picked up their love affair where they had left off. Jim had missed her greatly and she him. Both were relieved they could now see each other in person whenever they wanted. Sharon's second night back they stayed in a hotel just off campus. However, there was the season's first football game Saturday, four days after Sharon's return, so they didn't get to spend as much time together as they would have liked as Jim had practice and endless meetings. But the few hours they managed to be together affirmed their relationship. Sharon was Jim's girl and Jim was her man.

The season's first football game on the first Saturday of September. A home game against Western Illinois. It wasn't expected to be much of a challenge, just a warm-up game, but the coaching staff was leaving nothing to chance. Jim was the number three outside linebacker and only slated to play on the kick-off team. He got tickets for Sharon and a girl friend to watch the game in the team's family section where she got to meet a number of the other players' girlfriends. She would join Jim and the rest of the families after the game at the season's kickoff reception. The game was a rout, Nebraska winning 42-14. Jim played on all the kick-offs and several series at left outside linebacker. It was an uneventful game, he had one tackle. But the coaches were pleased and everyone was in a joyous mood at the kickoff reception.

When school started on the next Monday classes and football went along smoothly, until the second week in October. The game that Saturday was away at Kansas State, perennial losers in the Big 8 Conference and not expected to be much of a challenge for #7 ranked Nebraska. But things turned south quickly for Jim.

Nebraska scored the first time it had the ball. On the ensuing kick-off, as Jim assisted on the tackle, one of the K-State players fell on him from behind, and broke his ankle. The loud pop at the contact let everyone know that something bad had occurred. When the players rolled off the pile, Jim lay there grasping his distorted ankle. He was carted off the field and taken by ambulance to the local hospital where they discovered he had broken bones on both sides of his ankle that would require surgery and four pins to repair.

Jim's season was over. He made the two-and-a-half-hour ride back to Lincoln sedated in a team van after Nebraska beat up on K-State 56-6. He didn't inform Sharon of his injury until the following day when he was in the hospital awaiting surgery. When he did she quickly came over to the hospital and gave Jim the comfort only someone that loves you can.

For the next six weeks, Jim was on crutches limping around campus to get to class and just sitting on the sidelines at practices watching his friends and the other players out on the field. With his injury Jim was becoming depressed. Even getting around to be with Sharon was a hassle. He hated the crutches and cast on his foot and people coming up to him and saying how sorry they were. He felt like he was a spectacle for pity. It was hard duty for an almost 20-year-old college football player. With his set-back Jim began losing interest in school and looked forward to the season being over so he wouldn't have to show up at practice and stand around as an afterthought. It didn't help his mood that Nebraska was playing well and highly ranked. They would go on to win the Big-8 Conference, and then on to Miami to play in the Orange Bowl against Auburn. But as an injured guy on the sidelines the season was quite unfulfilling for Jim.

During Thanksgiving break Jim had gone home to Emmett to be with his parents. His older sister came home from Kearny State where she was a senior majoring in biology. Her boyfriend also spent Thanksgiving with the Tittsworth's. He was an agreeable guy who also attended Kearny and was in ROTC, anticipating entering the Army when he graduated in the spring. His plan was to be a Special Forces officer. It didn't help Jim's mood that he was away from Sharon and only had a chance to speak with her occasionally by phone.

Thanksgiving is a big celebration in farming communities and over the four days he was home, Jim had a chance to catch up with some of his high school pals, only a few of whom had gone on to college, and those that did were home. Most of his high school buddies had stayed in Emmett and taken up farming on their family spreads. While Jim envied them in a way, their lives were simple and uncomplicated, he knew for sure after his visit that Emmett and farming were just not where he wanted to be. Exactly where that was he wasn't sure, but knew it wasn't in tiny Emmett.

Back on campus, there were three weeks until Christmas break. Jim's cast came off the first part of December, but he still walked with a limp. He put a lot of effort into his rehab with a goal of earning a starting position during spring ball. The football team had a week off after its last game, a drubbing of Missouri 31-14 before it started to prepare in earnest for the Orange Bowl game. The team would travel to Miami the week before the game and would only have three days off for Christmas then needed to be back on campus to prepare for the trip south. The coaches wanted them to get to Miami a week early to be sure they adjusted to the time change and the warmer weather.

During the last few weeks of the semester, Jim and Sharon's relationship seemed to cool. Jim was still in a lousy mood and uninspired in school. While they enjoyed each other's company, the spark that they enjoyed before Jim's injury was waning. Neither could see it, but both felt their emotions growing stale. Jim's focus was on getting healthy and he missed the signs that Sharon was drifting away. The day after her last final of the semester Sharon kissed Jim goodbye and headed home to Olathe for break. It would be the last time he would see her.

After finals Jim stayed on campus with the team as they practiced for their bowl game. Lonely and depressed, he just hung out on campus until he headed home for Christmas. The three-day break didn't soothe his mood and he was happy to go back to Lincoln and join his team even as just an observer.

The trip to Miami was an adventure for Jim, he had only been out of Nebraska three times in his life before he joined the football team and never to Florida. Miami is a vibrant city with lots going on, especially during bowl week. Jim and his fellow Huskers enjoyed the run of the city and the celebrity that came with being on a team that was playing in the Orange Bowl. Things went a little easier on Jim now that he wasn't in a cast or limping. But he wouldn't be suiting up for the game.

The Orange Bowl game was played on New Year's Day and was a slug-fest. Auburn was built much like Nebraska, a run first team that wore down opponents with a punishing ground game. It was the kind of hard-fought football game that leaves even the coaches exhausted at the end. Nebraska ended up winning 13-6 as they capitalized on two Auburn fumbles. While Jim was happy and proud of his team and friends, he was still unfulfilled as a non-playing athlete relegated to the sidelines. Following the game, the team stayed in Miami three days before returning to Lincoln so the players could enjoy the offerings of the warm beachfront city, a drastic contrast to the snowy cold of winter currently descending on Nebraska.

Jim had called Sharon several times from Miami and missed her terribly. She said she had watched the game on TV and even saw Jim on the sidelines a few times during the telecast. He said he'd like to come see her in Olathe, when he got back to Lincoln, but she was noncommittal and Jim wondered why. He didn't find out that her father had had a heart attack just after Christmas until he returned to Nebraska. Sharon and her mom were devastated her dad's illness. The only saving grace was that Sharon was home when he got sick and was there for both her parents. Sharon told Jim it wouldn't be the right time for him to come to see her and so he went back to Emmett for the eight days before the spring semester began.

When Jim returned to Lincoln in mid-January his mood was better. He had promised himself that he would work hard and earn a starting spot in spring practice. He also wanted to improve on his mediocre performance in school. Jim wasn't a driven student, he was bright, but to date only excelled in classes he cared about. In the others he just did what he had to do to get by. Football and Sharon were his main concerns, but both were soon to take drastic turns.

Back in Lincoln Jim hit the gym and did his running every day. He had eight weeks before spring camp started and he wanted to be in tip top shape when it began. When he didn't hear from Sharon when he got back to school he called her home. That's when he found out her father had passed away. He could tell Sharon was upset and she seemed withdrawn. He asked what he could do, that he'd come to Olathe immediately to be with her. He was perplexed when she said she didn't want him to come. Then she told him she wouldn't be returning to school, that she was taking the semester off to take care of her mother and sort things out. Jim immediately realized he probably wouldn't see her for a while. Perhaps she just needs time to deal with her father's death and to console her mother, that must be it, he assumed, she was sad, confused, she needed space and time. He wouldn't push it, but in the back of his mind, he felt there was something more. This was way wrong. But he'd let it play out, and focus on school and football. There was nothing he could do if she didn't want to see him, but that realization stung.

Spring football practice started the last week in March and would last three weeks. The team, by rule, had twenty-one days to get in 15 on field practices. Video sessions and off field work didn't count. Jim's goal was to earn a starting spot for the fall and he was determined to shine in every aspect of camp. The first week went well, the coaches liked that Jim was in great shape and demonstrated good quickness and a nose for the ball. At six-foot three, 215 pounds, his agility made him hard to block and he hit like a ton of bricks, both positives for an outside linebacker. At his weight he was also fast enough to be an effective pass defender. He could run with most of the receivers and any of the tight ends on the team. His knack for quickly moving to the ball was another asset. Things were on track for him to land a starting job come the fall if he continued to progress.

On Saturday, the 2nd of April, there was one more week until the Red-White game that traditionally ended spring practice. That weekend was a full-dress scrimmage, the last before the spring finale that usually attracted thousands of fans to Husker Stadium. It would be a turning point in Jim's life.

During the third quarter of the scrimmage one of the defensive linemen stepped on Jim's left hand and broke it and two of his fingers. That ended Jim's spring ball. His hand would be in a cast for two months followed by several weeks of rehab. He was again relegated to watching his teammates from the sidelines. His chances of securing a starting position for the fall, what he had worked so hard for, were probably squashed. It seemed the football gods were against him. With the competition for the outside linebacking spots fierce with some of the upperclassmen who had played ahead of him last year, and the studs they were bringing in as new recruits, he was again on the outside looking in. The reality of his injury sent Jim into depression. But things would only get worse.

The following Tuesday Jim received a letter from Sharon. Unusual, he thought, as normally they just talked a few times a week, they hadn't exchanged letters the entire semester. As he stood in the door to his apartment and read Sharon's letter his heart broke. The letter was a classic "Dear John" kiss-off. Sharon wrote that she wouldn't be seeing him anymore, that she wasn't coming back to Nebraska and that she had taken up with her old high school boyfriend. She still cared for him, but didn't see it going anywhere and wanted to be honest with him. Jim was crushed. He didn't know whether to cry or shout. He was wounded as only you can be when someone you love tells you they don't love you. His world had just come to a full stop, first football and now Sharon. How could it get any worse, he thought. He didn't leave his apartment for two days trying to get over his hurt, and then anger. It wasn't fair, he was a good guy, tried to do things right, he worked hard, was honest, and now he gets fucked by fate. It just wasn't right. He never felt more alone.

There were six more weeks of school and Jim went through them as a zombie. He was just going through the motions, doing the tasks, just trying to finish out the semester, so he could go home and figure things out. Maybe football wouldn't be his life, school was okay, but now he felt he was just passing through. Nothing interested him. Sharon was now gone. The two things he really cared about were no longer the center or even part of his life. He knew he had to move on, he couldn't give up, but what the hell was the point? He needed to find himself.

Mercifully the coaches told him that he still had a place on the team, but he knew he was being passed by. He had been hurt the past season and now was injured in spring ball and knew the team wouldn't stand still. Coaches were focused on the players that were playing and not those that were standing on the sidelines. He'd clear his head over the summer and see where things were and try to figure out what he wanted. His head was not in a good place now and he wasn't even sure if he wanted to continue with football or school or what he wanted to do.

The semester ended the last of May and Jim did well in the four classes he took. Hell, he didn't have anything to do in the last month of the semester but study. He was glad school was over so he could go home and sort things out. The truth was he was losing interest in school. He knew he had to get re-energized, but he wasn't sure how to do it. Nothing he saw in his immediate future was of interest. At least school was out and it was one less thing to worry about. He left for home the day he finished his last final.

Summer in Emmett, Nebraska can be pleasant — but it can also be miserably hot and humid. It also rains a lot in May in Nebraska and did so during Jim's drive home further dampening his mood. Jim didn't have a job lined up, he figured he'd help around the farm and if he had the chance maybe make a little money helping neighbors, or if he was lucky get on with one of the various construction crews that always seemed to be doing some project in the county. Several of his old pals were still in town and so he'd have someone to hang out with. He'd figure things out, he also intended on speaking with his dad once he cleared his head, he was sure he would have some words of wisdom that might help him get over his melancholy and help him find his direction again.

The first week he was home Jim settled in and picked up many of the chores around the farm. His mom and dad, even at their ages, usually handled things themselves. They were glad he was back to lend a hand. Jim was comfortable with physical labor, loved working with his dad, and he didn't mind the chores — he'd been doing them most of his life. But he knew that in the long run he didn't want to be a farmer.

On that first Friday home, after dinner when Thomas Tittsworth and his son were sitting on the porch enjoying the lazy summer sunset, Jim told his dad how he was feeling, that he wasn't sure he wanted to play football anymore or even go back to school. He was just at a crossroads — nothing seemed to interest him and he felt like he was just drifting through life. He also told his dad that he and Sharon had broken up — to which his dad replied he was sorry to hear that as she seemed like a fine young girl.

Tom Tittsworth told his son that he was proud of him and all that he had accomplished, but that life was full of setbacks and you had to figure out a way to get past them. His dad suggested that he just relax this summer and think about things, there was no rush to immediately figure out the future. He would find something in due time that interested him. When something caught his interest, he should explore it and determine if it was something he might want to pursue. He was young and had time for a little trial and error until his calling revealed itself. Until then, Jim could stay on the farm as they could always use another hand. Jim thought that was good advice, he knew he would always have a home so it was not like he was desperate. He felt better after just speaking with his father as he knew he would.

Over the next few weeks, Jim worked the farm and helped one of the neighbors build a new barn. It was satisfying work and he started to feel good about himself again. In the evening he'd sometimes meet up with some of his buddies, crack a six-pack on someone's porch, and tell lies about how well their lives were going. It was easy living and upon reflection he understood why some wanted to stay in Emmett and avoid the hustle and bustle of a fast life somewhere else.

On the 1st of July a neighbor's house caught fire. Jim and his dad saw smoke from their porch and sped over to the neighbors to see what was up. When they pulled into the driveway of the Schreiber's property they could see the back of the house had flames and smoke billowing out the bedroom windows and that the fire had reached the roof and was spreading in the gentle wind. As Jim and his dad ran to the house they called out, but no one answered. There didn't seem to be anyone home. Knowing there was little they could do on their own to fight a house fire, his dad told Jim to find a hose and start spraying the fire and the roof. He would go call the Sheriff, who controlled and coordinated the county's emergency services department. Then he jumped back in the truck and raced back to their house to alert the Sheriff. The county fire department was a volunteer organization and when called took a while to assemble then respond to an emergency.

Jim stayed on scene and turned on the hose from the pump in the yard and began spraying the roof and tried to knock down the flames that were licking out the windows in the back bedroom. He also searched around looking in the windows and calling out. He didn't get any response. As he was spraying the back-porch roof, he looked through the bathroom window and thought he saw a figure lying in the hall inside the house. He quickly kicked open the back door that led into the kitchen and tried to enter, but the smoke and the heat came rushing out, it was too intense to run through. As the smoke was billowing out around the top of the door. Jim wasn't sure what to do, but he knew he had to do something. He had to see if there really was someone inside before the whole place went up in flames. He spied some blankets on the wash line, took the large wool one and soaked it with the hose and put it over himself. He then crawled low through the back door staying below the smoke and through the kitchen to where he could see the hallway. It was smoky and hot but most of the smoke was high near the ceiling of the kitchen and the wet wool blanket protected him from the heat and allowed him to crawl forward.

When he got to the end of the kitchen he could see Ed Schreiber lying on the floor in the hall, he wasn't moving. Jim crawled over to him and grabbed him by the collar and started to pull him into the kitchen. He was hot and a dead weight, but with his strength Jim could still drag him. When he got him out of the hall he glanced back and saw that behind him his wife was on the floor and not moving. Jim yelled, but neither of the Schreiber's answered. Jim quickly pulled Mr. Schreiber through the kitchen and out onto the back lawn, then dashed back into the house while throwing the soaked blanket over himself again, then crawled quickly back across the floor and down the hall to Mrs. Schreiber. He pulled her out of the house as quickly as he could. When he had both of the Schreiber's safely away from the house he sprayed them both down with water as they were both hot to the touch and he thought the faster he cooled them off the better. Mr. Schreiber started to cough and spit and breathe trying to clear his lungs and catch his breath. At least, he was moving. His wife just lay still. Jim focused on the wife. He tried to get her to respond, but she didn't. She was badly burned on her legs and arms and her whole body was still quite hot to the touch. He wasn't sure what to do next as he didn't have a first aid kit and really wasn't trained to deal with burn victims. Nothing he did could get her to move or breathe.

It took Jim's dad about fifteen minutes to race home, call the Sheriff's office, and get back to the Schreiber's house. When he arrived, Jim's mom was with him and had a first aid kit the family kept at the house in the kitchen. Jim was still tending to Mrs. Schreiber when they pulled up, and his mother came running over to him. When she saw Mrs. Schreiber burned and silent she instinctively knew she was gone. Jim stood up and explained what he tried to do to help Mrs. Schreiber as his mother knelt down and tried to find a pulse. There was none. Jim's dad was with Mr. Schreiber and he was coming around, still coughing and spitting — suffering mostly from smoke inhalation and with some second degree burns on his hands and face. He would recover. It was a tragic event and not the way Jim anticipated the summer to go, but life is life and he knew that you had to deal with things, many of which were not planned or pleasant, you just did the best you could. Still it was an ugly scene and sad and Jim felt terrible.

About 20 minutes after Jim's dad and mom came to the Schreiber's the Volunteer Rescue Squad, a fire truck pumper, an ambulance, and three Sheriff's cars arrived at the Schreiber home. The volunteer crew jumped into action and within a minute had a high stream of water on the fire and began ventilating the roof and windows. The two paramedics took over the tending to Mr. Schreiber after a quick assessment of his deceased wife. It took the volunteers only about ten minutes to extinguish the flames, but by then the entire back of the house had burned and the entire structure was a total loss.

The incident was just one of the risks of rural living — being away from emergency services. Most farm families lived with the risk of injury, accident and disaster on a daily basis, with the knowledge that they had to be self-sufficient. The safety net of public emergency services was just not available and the vast majority that serviced rural communities were volunteer and seldom close by. Fire was a farmer's greatest fear and the Schreiber fire was a worst-case scenario.

The Schreiber tragedy was disturbing to Jim. It heightened his concern for his own mother and father who were not getting any younger. Perhaps he needed to stay on the farm and look after them. Farming was a simple, straightforward way of life, where you were your own boss and with a little luck and some good weather, could make a decent living. Perhaps he was too hasty in his decision to leave. He'd have to reassess things after the Schreiber incident.

Several days after the fire a service was held for Mrs. Schreiber in Emmett's Presbyterian church with a reception after. Jim and his family attended along with many in the close knit community to extend their condolences. Mr. Schreiber had mostly recovered by then, except for his burns but they were on the mend. His son and daughter came home for the service. His son lived in Denver and worked for the phone company as an engineer, he was several years older than Jim. The daughter, also older, was married to an Army Special Forces officer and lived in Ft. Bragg, North Carolina. The Special Forces captain had just returned from an assignment in Vietnam and wore his uniform to the service. Everyone was impressed with him, including Jim, he appeared to be highly decorated.

During the reception, Jim had a chance to speak with the captain whose name was Joseph Spencer. He had met and married Maria Schreiber at the University of Kansas while they were both students. Spencer was a commissioned Infantry officer who had volunteered for Special Forces duty when he was assigned to the 82nd Airborne Division at Fort Bragg, North Carolina. Jim was intrigued with the captain and during their conversation asked him how he liked the Army. Spencer told him about Special Forces training and some tales about his tour the previous year as a trainer and advisor in South Vietnam. He told Jim he loved the Army and especially the Special Forces community. It was the cream of the crop when it came to warriors and like a brotherhood. He suggested that if Jim had any interest to check it out, but if he was going to join up he ought to see about coming in as an officer. Spencer earned his commission through ROTC while he was in college and he thought Nebraska had a program. Jim told him that it did. The other option might be going to Officer Candidate School (OCS), and since Jim had some college under his belt he might be able to enlist as a "college option." He told Jim life as an officer was much preferred to coming in as a private. Jim left the reception impressed with Spencer and thought he might check out Special Forces.

A week after the memorial service for Mrs. Schreiber, Jim called the recruiting station in Norfolk, Nebraska and arranged for an appointment with one of the recruiters. He shared with his dad that he had some interest in the military and his dad told him it was an honorable profession, and reinforced Captain Spencer's words that life in the Army as an officer was much preferred to that of an enlisted man. Further, his dad reminded him that if he left school he would be subject to the draft if he didn't get a deferment of some type. This closed the deal for Jim. At this point he really didn't have any interest in going back to school or being a substitute on the football team. He could transfer to another school where he might have a better chance of playing, but he'd have to sit out a year to regain his eligibility and that wasn't very attractive. No, he'd look into the Army and if he could get a Special Forces position he'd give that a go.

Becoming A Soldier

On 10 July 1964 young James Tittsworth walked into the Army recruiting office in Norfolk, Nebraska and sat down at the desk of Master Sergeant (MSG) Burwood Yost. MSG Yost was an 18-year combat veteran from Kentucky. Having joined the Army in 1947, he was a two-war veteran, serving in both Korea and Vietnam. He wore two Purple Hearts, one from Korea where he was wounded by artillery fire and a second from Vietnam where he was shot in the leg during his 1962 tour as an advisor. Yost was also one of the first enlisted men to graduate from the US Army Ranger School and had served in some of the country's most elite units. Well decorated with several medals for valor, he was ramrod straight and there was a no-nonsense air about him.

When MSG Yost greeted Jim, Jim knew immediately this was a job interview and not a sales pitch. MSG Yost wasn't going to accommodate any snotty-nose college kid trying to avoid the draft or some sniveling momma's boy who was looking for a place to grow up. No, Bud Yost was the real deal, a soldier in every sense of the word, who saw himself as a warrior looking for other potential warriors to join his Army.

When Jim sat down MSG Yost got down to business straight away. Point blank he asked Jim, "James, what brings you all the way to Norfolk to speak with me?" "Well, sir, I wanted to talk to someone who could let me know about the opportunities the Army had to offer. Specifically, I'm interested in the Army's Special Forces." Jim figured there was no sense beating around the bush with MSG Yost. "You're interested in Special Forces?" MSG Yost replied, thinking that in the six-foot three, 215 pounder before him perhaps he had a good prospect. "Good choice if you can make the cut. Special Forces soldiers are some of the world's most elite warriors — fit, tough, smart. They don't take just anyone, you have to earn the Special Forces flash — and most of the people who try don't make the grade. Still interested?"

"Yes, sir," Jim replied. "I know a few guys who are Green Berets and they suggested I find out about them since I'm thinking of enlisting. They think I could make it. I'm no dummy and not afraid of hard work." "That's a good start, cause the training is intense and not only physical, but you have to think clearly, especially when the going gets tough." "I think my time with the Huskers might have prepared me for that," Jim replied, wanting to show confidence. This caught Yost's interest, he was a die-hard Husker fan. "You play for the Huskers?" He asked. "Yes, sir, I was an outside linebacker these last two years," Jim informed him. MSG Yost was starting to really like Jim now. "Well, well, you just might have what it takes. Why aren't you still in Lincoln?" the warrior recruiter asked. "I got hurt, first an ankle and then my hand was broken. While they are Ok now I thought I might try something different that would give me a chance to travel and see the world. My dad and grandfather both served." "Really, who were they with?" Yost asked, becoming more and more interested in this stud of a young man in front of him.

"Not sure their units, my grandfather was a Marine in WWI and fought at Belleau Woods and was awarded a Navy Cross. He doesn't speak much about his war, but he's a good man. My dad was in North Africa and wounded there and won a DSC. I think I might want to carry on the family tradition, I don't plan on going back to school right now, although that is an option. I had a 2.8 grade point average and was studying history. One of my friends, Captain Spencer, the Green Beret, suggested I see a recruiter and find out about the College Option program and also see if I can get a slot for Special Forces training. My dad agrees it might be a good move." "God Bless your grandfather and father for their bravery and service, you come from good stock, and just might be the kind of young man I'm looking for." Yost was impressed with Jim's lineage. He knew only real warriors had a Navy Cross or a Distinguished Service Cross and that they could only be earned for gallantry in combat.

"Do you have a criminal record? Are you a dope smoke'n hippy kinda guy?" "No sir, never even had a ticket and never smoked anything,"

Jim replied. "Ok, good! Here's the deal, I have a few Infantry ascension slots for 1 August that will send you to Basic Training and then Infantry Advanced Infantry Training (AIT). If you do well there I can send you on to airborne school. I have three allocations for that. It's three weeks and you learn to jump out of airplanes. Second most fun I ever had! If what you're telling me is accurate, cause we'll check you out, and you do well in your initial training, I can get you a slot for Infantry Officer Candidate School (OCS) via the College Option program. Again, assuming your grades are acceptable and everything checks out. If you go to airborne school before OCS it will give you a fallback option if you can't get into Special Forces right away. You don't have to do that, but I recommend it. If you do well in OCS you can request to go to the Q-Course, the Special Forces Officer Qualification Course. I can't guarantee that, but if you're as sharp as you appear there is a good chance it will work out for you. Worst case you'll probably be assigned to one of the airborne divisions and you can apply again after a year. To make all this happen you'll need to sign a four-year enlistment contract. If you don't cut it in OCS you'll be assigned as a private to an infantry division for the remainder of your enlistment. That work for you?" Yost was impressed with the young man and hoped he would take the offer. "That sounds like it might be something I'm interested in, but before I sign anything I want to talk it over with my dad." "Not a problem, I'll give you a draft contract and some information you can take home and discuss things with your father. But I need to fill the two slots I have left for August ASAP, not sure when I'll get others for OCS and Airborne School. If this sounds like something you want to do, become one of the Army's elite, then you need to let me know and sign up by the 15th." "I can make a decision by then," Jim replied. "Ok then, let me get you the brochures and some paperwork," and MSG Yost got up and left the room. The interview was over.

Back in Emmett Jim shared the information he received from MSG Yost with his dad and told him he thought he wanted to enlist and go into Special Forces. His dad wasn't keen on the idea that he would be leaving school where he had a full ride scholarship to play football. But Jim told him he was bored and not interested in school and that football had passed him by. He was impressed with Captain Spencer and thought he could enlist, go to OCS and then Special Forces and perhaps even make it a career. And if he enlisted and it didn't work out he could go back to school on the G.I. Bill.

Thomas Tittsworth was proud of his son and knew if he put his mind to something he would be successful. He also knew he wouldn't be coming back to take over the farm. If he wanted to try the Army, well it was better than a lot of other choices — at least he would be serving his country. He gave Jim his blessing. Jim called MSG Yost the next day and agreed to come back to Norfolk and sign an enlistment contract and take a physical. He'd give the Army a try.

On the 4th of August 1964, Jim boarded a bus in Norfolk and took the four-hour trip to the Armed Forces Recruiting Station in Kansas City, Missouri. After an oath ceremony and a buzz haircut, Jim shipped out to Fort Benning, Georgia with 47 other infantry recruits to basic training and the start of his military career.

Basic Training was eight weeks of military drills where Jim learned the rudiments of being a soldier. He excelled at the physical aspects of the training and was a crack shot, one of the best in his unit — a carryover from his hunting days back in Nebraska. He also made sure that every day his bunk area was made up according to standards and that he looked sharp in his uniform, both of which endeared him to the Drill Instructors (DIs). Discipline and effort were rewarded in Basic Training, while slacking and complaining were a fast way to ensure a rough ride. Jim quickly learned to keep his mouth shut and do as he was told without question. In Basic there were a lot of make-work tasks and a demand for attention to detail all designed to instill discipline. Jim thought it was not unlike farm work, but the tasks were quite different. Soldiering wasn't too difficult if you didn't try to fight the system. Jim was astounded that there were a number of his classmates that couldn't understand that and continually landed on the bad side of the DIs who controlled every aspect of the new recruits' lives. If you crossed them or made them or the unit look bad they were on your case like white on rice.

In his basic class, there were several other College Option recruits from the midwest. One was a little guy, maybe 130 pounds, named Peter Hunter. He had a small head and broad shoulders and quickly earned the nickname Peanut Head from the DI's. Not a particularly endearing term. Hunter was a bright guy, book smart, but with delusions of being a warrior. He lacked practical common sense and the physical toughness to be a combat soldier or a real leader of men. He tried, but he just didn't have what it took. While several of the other recruits teased him and made him miserable, Jim felt sorry for the little guy and looked after him. What really caught the attention of the DI's was during a 12-mile road march back to the barracks from the rifle range — successful completion is a graduation requirement — Hunter fell out at about mile eight. He was just too exhausted to carry his load the rest of the way to the finish. This was an issue not just for himself, but it would have made the platoon look bad. Jim stepped up and took his pack and carried it to the finish. He told the rest of the platoon that they were a team and teammates looked out for one another. This kind of performance leadership is revered in the service as it binds men together. This particular incident established Jim as the platoon's go to guy when things got tough.

Following Basic Training Jim matriculated to Advanced Individual Training. This is where branch skills, in Jim's case infantry specific knowledge and skills, are taught with small unit tactics and weapons the primary training emphasis. Jim's reputation preceded him and he was made a squad leader in AIT. This basic leadership position put Jim in charge of ten men and gave him the responsibility to ensure they were squared away, another way of saying that they were meeting the Army's personal standards and at the right place on time and ready for training. He took the position seriously, his squad was always near the top of every evaluated team task, and his squad-mates met every individual standard required. Needless to say, this made the DIs look good and quite happy with Jim.

There was an incident during the fourth week of AIT that marked Jim as fearless and someone special. Following a six-mile road march to the training area, Jim's unit was divided into two groups for training on the M79 Grenade Launcher and use of the M26 individual hand grenade. The M26 grenade, the US Army standard anti-personnel grenade, has a 5 second delay after the fuse is activated (safety clip released). On the hand grenade range two soldiers and an instructor are positioned in a reinforced fox hole and each trainee throws a live grenade. Following the instructor's demonstration, it became Jim's training partner's turn to throw a grenade. A meek and nervous guy, he was exceptionally anxious and uncomfortable on the grenade range. The instructor stood facing Jim's partner and gave him direct instructions on what to do: hold the grenade in the throwing hand against your chest, grasp the safety pin with your index finger of opposite hand, pull the safety pin while still grasping the grenade and safety clip, take the grenade to a throwing position while still grasping the grenade and the safety clip, make a two second count, throw the grenade in an arc down range, duck down after the throw until you hear the grenade's explosion. All went well until the trainee took the grenade to a throwing position. In his nervousness he let go of the safety clip and dropped the grenade to the floor of the fox hole. In his frenzied state he bent down to pick up the grenade at the same time as the instructor and smashed the lip of his helmet into the bridge of the instructor's nose sending both backwards — with a live grenade on the floor of the fox hole. Jim standing behind both of them quickly reached down, picked up the grenade and tossed it over the foxhole berm just as it exploded — tragedy averted.

When the instructor stood up he was bleeding from the bridge of his nose and the hapless student was shaking uncontrollably. Jim's quick thinking and quicker reaction literally save all three of their lives. Needless to say, the DIs and all of his platoon mates were in awe of Jim's quick reaction and bravery. For his selfless action, the Training

Brigade Commander awarded Jim the Army Commendation Medal. He graduated from AIT as the Honor Graduate.

On 30 November, Jim reported in to the Airborne Training Brigade which was also at Fort Benning. The airborne course was three weeks long. It was a simple school where the majority of the course work was physical training and learning about the T-10 parachute. It was an uneventful three weeks and the Black Hats, as the drill instructors were called, were in as big a rush as the students to finish the course and head out for Christmas leave. The school was easy living for Jim and the day after his last jump and the Wings Ceremony he headed out on a three week leave as an airborne trooper.

Following a quiet Christmas in Nebraska Jim reported into the holding unit for Infantry Officer Candidate School on the 4th of January 1965, just shy of his twenty-first birthday. Taking the advice from a fellow Cornhusker he met in Jump School, when Jim reported in, he already had his uniforms properly prepared with the unit patch and his rank removed. In OCS you don't have rank, you are a "can-di-date". Jim only brought the required number of uniforms and gear and one set of casual civilian clothes with him. The civvies he kept in his car so he wouldn't have to prepare them for the daily inspections that started off each day in OCS. He also arrived with a buzz haircut. No sense giving the cadre anything to harass you about when you showed up. Jim's practice of always doing your homework and being prepared served him well in OCS and would become a characteristic of his entire time in the Army. It was a wise habit that payed numerous dividends as he was seldom caught short or surprised.

Infantry OCS was 22 weeks of intense training that covered a gamut of topics on leadership, military tasks, weapons and small unit tactics. The school mission is to train, assess and evaluate candidates and prepare qualifying individuals to serve as combat officers. Candidates are placed under constant stress both physical and emotional while continually being evaluated on academic and mission performance and especially their leadership. Jim's class had a strength of 90 candidates with about 30% from the College Option Program. The remainder were prior service non-commissioned officers, mostly E-5s and E-6s. The prior enlisted candidates had an advantage over their classmates as they had military experience and were often familiar, if not experts, in some of the tasks and knowledge that were core parts of OCS. Infantry OCS was not a school for wannabes or pretty boys. It was harsh and demanding by design and only 62 of the 90 candidates who began the course with Jim received commissions.

Jim was a quick learner and motivated. He excelled on all the physical requirements and also placed high in the military skills. On inspections he never received a single demerit during the entirety of OCS, an unusual occurrence. And he was particularly adept at land navigation and had the highest score and fastest finish time on the land navigation course. His serious but quiet disposition and willingness to help his fellow candidates earned him the respect of his classmates. His preparedness made him someone they could count on when they were placed in leadership positions to lead training missions. OCS reinforced to Jim that the Army was a team sport and if you're a team player you have a good chance of doing well.

Jim finished near the top of his class in all the physical requirements and did equally well on the academic lessons and skills. When Jim was placed in leadership positions he ably led his platoon to accomplish their assigned missions and tasks and received high marks. Because of the respect he earned by his performance and the support he gave his peers, Jim received the highest rating in his class on the peer reviews. His high overall standing in the class order of merit placed him among the top five in his class and he was commissioned a 2nd Lieutenant of Infantry on June 20, 1965.

His performance during OCS not only earned him a commission as a 2nd Lieutenant, but allowed him to request and be selected for Special Forces training. Since he was already airborne qualified he met all the prerequisites for the Special Forces Officers Course (SFOC). He was well on his way to meeting the basics for an interesting if not exciting Army career and could hardly wait to get to SFOC and enter the brotherhood of Green Berets.

The Special Forces Officer Course is a twelve-week school that focuses on training young officers to lead A-teams, the basic element of American Special Forces. The course teaches officers to plan and lead unconventional warfare forces — clandestine guerrillas who operate behind enemy lines and, as a result of the war in Vietnam, to conduct counter-guerrilla operations in a host country. Included in the instruction are special small unit clandestine tactical missions such as long-range reconnaissance patrols (LRRP), sabotage, raids and prisoner snatches. Jim was somewhat surprised to find that most of his class was made up of inexperienced 2nd lieutenants just like himself with a few seasoned 1st lieutenants and captains to round out the class. The course began with 80 candidates on July 10, 1965.

The first part of the SFOC was mostly garrison academic work where students learned how to conduct area and country studies. These are extremely detailed reports on all aspects of a country from climate, population demographics, languages, culture and customs, political organization and government, and detailed descriptions of their military, especially weapons, force distribution and operational capabilities. A country study makes a college term paper look like a high school freshman essay.

Following the academics students spend time with the various Training Committees where experts give them mini-courses in operations and intelligence, weapons, field medical techniques, combat engineering, and field communications. The students are not expected to become experts in these areas as NCOs in Special Forces units are the technical experts in their assigned fields. The SFOC delivers in-depth familiarization in each of the primary topic areas and students are expected to be knowledgeable and competent in each, allowing them to lead their teams of experts with competence.

The last two weeks of the course are the exercise Gobbler Woods, the student's trial by fire. During Gobbler Woods students are expected to put their training into practice in a simulated tactical situation. The students are divided into teams and individuals rotated through different leadership positions to gauge their leadership ability, planning and problem-solving capabilities while conducting missions common to Special Forces A-Teams.

For Gobbler Woods the teams deploy by parachute into the fictional Republic of Pineland, located in the mountains of North Carolina. Civilians and military personnel act as both friendlies and opposing forces to provide as real a tactical simulation as possible, emulating what the students can expect on actual deployments. SFOC required Jim to apply himself and he actually enjoyed the academic learning as well as the physical nature of the small team operations. The more he was around the Special Forces community the more he liked it. He viewed an A-Team as much like a football team with each member having a special skill that needed to be applied as required for the team to have success.

Following the last mission of the Gobbler Woods exercise, the sabotage of a railroad bridge, Jim's team moved cross-country to an empty Boy Scout camp to clean up and prepare for movement back to Fort Bragg. The evening was just for relaxing and packing up to depart early the next morning. Just after dark a 1959 Chevy station wagon with four girls in it pulled into the camp. They immediately caught the eye of the team when they exited the car and started sashaying towards the bunk house.

A big brunette seemed to be in charge and sauntered over to the lead cadre who was clearly familiar with her. "Hello Carol," he said as she came up close and gave him a hug. "Hi Eddie," she replied, "how you boys doing tonight?" she inquired with a mischievous grin. Clearly these local girls had experience hooking up with teams at the end of the exercise. "They're doing great," Master Sergeant Edwin Davis replied. "Carol, you and your fillies looking to show these boys some local hospitality?" "Well, that's why we're here Eddie, thought they might like to grab a few cold ones down at The Barn and celebrate the end of Turkey Week." It wasn't Carol's first rodeo and there was nothing like some new hot-blooded Special Forces males to brighten up the lonely backwoods of North Carolina. "I suppose there might be a few stallions to take you up on your offer," Eddie said. "Any of you guys want to make a trip to The Barn with these ladies and sample some Hillbilly hospitality?" The women were attractive ladies and most of the team had been without female company since the course began. Five of the guys, all single, said they were game and asked what the rules were. "Well, there aren't any rules, except you need to be back and ready to make movement by 0700 tomorrow," was MSG Davis' reply. He added, "and, just don't cause any problems with the local dudes, some can be pretty protective of the local women and don't much cotton out-of-towners hitting on them." "Not a problem," said the 2nd lieutenant from Ohio. Five minutes later the five SF students and the four girls were crammed into the Chevy station wagon and headed off to The Barn. They all had hopes of getting lucky in a biblical sense.

Fortunately, Jim was exhausted after the exercise, he and the rest of his team members remained behind to look after the gear. The party boys on the team just made it back to camp before dawn after a whirlwind night of drinking and carousing. The team made movement back to Fort Bragg and the conclusion of the course with three hungover lieutenants. Three days later, the day before graduation, the two stallions who got to enjoy the favors of the mountain women required a trip to the dispensary for a shot of penicillin to address the infections their partners left with them. Jim and the non-partiers had dodged a bullet and didn't let their compatriots forget the cost of their amorous adventure.

Jim did well on both the academic and operational parts of the SFOC course and graduated number three in his class. After graduation he received orders for an assignment with the 1st Special Forces Group in Okinawa. He was pleased with the end of his training and felt ready to join the Special Forces community and anxious to get to his unit and get to the real army.

Okinawa Days

The 1st Special Forces Group (1SFG) was headquartered in Fort Buckner, Okinawa, Japan and had a storied history. First activated in the mid-1950s at Fort Bragg, North Carolina, 1SFG was sent to Okinawa in 1957 and oriented toward the Asia-Pacific theater. Initially the 1SFG was assigned the mission to work with the various American allied countries in Asia to help train their military and develop their special operations capabilities. However, almost immediately after arriving in Okinawa 1SFG began to deploy its teams to Vietnam on a temporary basis to train and advise the South Vietnamese Army. Early missions included establishing a Vietnamese commando school at the 1SFG forward headquarters in Nha Trang, Vietnam. The South Vietnamese commandos eventually evolved into Vietnam's own Special Forces Command. In 1961 the 5th Special Forces Group (5SFG), a sub-unit of 1SFG, was stood-up and became the controlling headquarters for all Special Forces operations in Vietnam. 1SFG supported the 5SFG by sending teams on temporary duty to Vietnam to conduct both direct counter-insurgency operations and special reconnaissance missions. By late 1962 the Special Forces training mission in Vietnam fully focused on standing-up regional and local militias known as the Civilian Irregular Defense Group (CIDG) program. Part of that focus was the establishment and train-up of Mobile Reaction Forces with soldiers drawn from Vietnam's indigenous tribes. These units became known as Mike Forces. Eventually as the US mission in Vietnam grew the 5SFG became its own independent command.

When Jim arrived in Okinawa in November 1965 as a 2nd Lieutenant he reported into the 1SFG personal office (S-1) at Camp Buckner. When he entered the group personnel office he was greeted by a lovely Japanese woman, Kiko Matsuyama. KiKo was a twenty-three-year-old porcelain beauty. Tall for a Japanese woman at five foot eight, she had gone to college in Arizona and spoke perfect English. With her long black hair, wide dark eyes and perfect smile she was captivating and immediately put Jim at ease, as she did everyone who entered the S-1 Shop. Kiko was secretary to the group Adjutant who would make Jim's assignment within the 1SFG.

Kiko welcomed Jim to Okinawa and the 1st Special Forces Group and asked if he needed anything. When Jim replied that no, he was just reporting in, she told him that if he did need help with his in-processing she would be pleased to help him. Jim thanked her and said he would just like to see the Adjutant and get his assignment so he could get to his unit. Kiko said, "Sure," she would get Major Johnson right away and got up and went down the hall to Major Johnson's office. As she walked down the hall Jim enjoyed the gentle sway of her long lean body and thought that she took small steps — just like the Japanese woman he saw in the movies. Pretty woman, I wonder if she has a boyfriend, Jim thought to himself.

After a brief interview with Major Johnson Jim was assigned to an A Team in B Company, ODB 1120, as a team Assistant Detachment Commander. The team was led by Captain Raymond Arnold. Captain Arnold was a career infantry officer and Korean War veteran and an early member of Special Forces having gone through SF training in 1958 shortly after the Army stood up the Special Forces as a permanent component. Arnold had served two tours in Vietnam; one as an advisor in 1960 setting up a training program for the South Vietnamese Army and another in 1963 leading a training team and providing advisory assistance to the CIDG program. He had received a direct commission from Sergeant First-Class (E-7) to Captain during his last tour in Vietnam when he earned a Distinguished Service Cross for valor while leading the defense of his CIDG camp near the Cambodian border.

Captain Arnold was a believer in the Special Forces mission. He was a no-nonsense officer, very experienced, knowledgeable and proven in combat. He held high standards and expected everyone on his team to maintain the same. He was intensely loyal to his men and looked at Special Forces A-Teams as exactly that — a team — where everyone contributed their expertise to ensure the success of the assigned mission. He welcomed Jim as his second in command and Jim quickly came to realize that he had landed on a team where he could learn what it took to be a professional special operator.

ODB 1120 had eight members, two officers and six Non-commissioned Officers (NCOs) assigned. It was short two NCOs, a second communications sergeant and a second engineer NCO. Each of the team's specialist NCOs was a true expert in his field and all had at least one tour in Vietnam except Staff Sergeant Edwards, the communications NCO, and Jim. The Team Sergeant and operations chief, was Master Sergeant David Leroy, another veteran of Korea with two Vietnam tours and two purple hearts, one each from Korea and Vietnam, to show for his time in combat. He made his bones in SF as a weapons expert. While he seemed a gruff old soldier to outsiders, to his team he was more like a stern father who loved his children. He essentially ran the team, freeing up Captain Arnold and Jim to do mission planning and coordinate with higher headquarters. Even though it was short two members, the team was regarded as one of the top A-Teams in the 1st Special Forces Group.

When Jim arrived in Okinawa the 1SFG had a split mission, supporting the American effort in Vietnam directly and training up Navy and Marine units that were preparing to rotate to a tour in Vietnam. The duty was easy living and gave Jim a lot of free time to explore Okinawa and soak up some Japanese culture.

One evening, when Jim and a fellow lieutenant were off post at a Japanese restaurant enjoying a seafood dinner an incident occurred. As the two Americans were leaving the restaurant they saw a couple exit the restaurant across the street followed by another man who began yelling at the couple. The yelling man and the man with the woman argued at first and then the guy with the date kicked the other guy who fell to the ground. When he got up from the sidewalk he had a knife in his right hand and slashed at the kicker guy cutting his arm. The woman screamed at the first slash, but the guy with the knife continued his attack on the man who had kicked him down. The attacker slashed at his victim a few times ineffectively as the man held his wounded arm and retreated. The knifeman then turned towards the woman smacking her with the back of his hand knocking her down then again began to lunge and slash at her date. It all happened quickly.

As the fight unfolded, Jim and his companion ran across the street yelling at the attacker, who now turned his attention to them still brandishing his knife. While Jim's friend went to the injured man, picking up the wounded Japanese, moving him away from the fight, and attending to his wound, Jim confronted the attacker.

Jim towered over the little Japanese man who was in a rage and held up his knife in a menacing position prepared to cut Jim to pieces if he got the chance. But strangely Jim wasn't afraid of the little Japanese. As he stood before him Jim started to circle left around the man away from his knife hand all the while cautioning him to put down the knife. But the enraged little knifer wasn't taking any shit from a fucking American and in his fiercest Japanese he yelled at Jim to "get the fuck out of here" or he'd cut off his head. Jim didn't understand a word and continued circling the attacker's left side. As he did so a crowd started to gather and then a car drove by. When the little Japanese man looked away for an instant Jim reached out and grabbed a chair from a nearby outside table as he continued circling. He kept trying to talk to the wound-up little man as he circled, but to no avail. As he spoke Jim raised the chair over his head, now he was posing a threat to the knife man. When the knifeman lunged at him again Jim threw the chair at the guy. Who raised his knife hand to block the chair, Jim quickly moved in, grabbed his knife arm with his left hand and simultaneously punched the guy hard in the face with his right fist. It was a haymaker of a punch and the guy went down like a sack of flour. It was the hardest hit he had ever taken and one he would not soon forget. His two front teeth were dislodged and he was concussed as Jim's OCS ring had caught the guy dead in the front teeth. As he lay on the ground seeing stars he ceased being a threat, nor was he going anywhere anytime soon. Jim quickly picked up the knife, looked at the guy to be sure he was down, and then turning his attention to the girl who was now sitting up on the pavement still shaking over the slap. To his shocking surprise, it was Kiko from the S-1 Shop.

Jim helped her up and asked if she was hurt. Kiko said no, just shaken-up. She had a red welt forming on her cheek where the knife guy had slapped her. "What was that all about?" Jim asked, "That guy was seriously pissed off at something." "I know the guy and he wanted to date me, but I always said no. I don't like him. I haven't seen him in a while, but tonight as I was having dinner with my cousin he was at a table across from us. When he saw me, he started saying nasty things and causing a problem. My cousin told him to shut-up and we left the restaurant, but he followed us and continued to threaten us. My cousin was just trying to defend me when the guy attacked him. I'm sorry for causing a problem and I'm glad you and your friend were here to help us." Jim could now hear the sirens of approaching police cars. "Well, I'm glad I was here too and that you're not hurt. That guy could have really done some damage with that knife. I hope your cousin is OK. The police are coming and I guess they can handle it from here," Jim said as the cop cars pulled up with a screech.

Jim helped Kiko over to the police cars and she told the police what had happened, and how Jim and his buddy had come to her and her cousin's rescue. The cop took a few notes and asked Jim for his name and contact information, which he gave. The knife guy was just now waking up and the other police officers were cuffing him up as he uselessly struggled and kept running his bleeding mouth. Never a good idea when the police have you in handcuffs. When the guy wouldn't shut up one of the cops had had enough and cracked him across the forehead with his baton knocking him senseless again. Then two officers stuffed him in the back of the patrol car. After her statement to the police Kiko took her cousin to the hospital to get his slashed arm looked at. Jim and his buddy hailed a passing cab and headed back to base — discussing the incident on the way home. Jim told his buddy,

Tittsworth

"You know John, I've seen this movie before while I was in college. It never ends well."

Jim spent most of his time on Okinawa coordinating training for the Navy SEAL teams that sent their sixteen-man operational platoons to Okinawa for country training before they deployed to Vietnam. The training course was ten days split between classroom work and field/range training. Jim found the SEALs physically tough, but lacking in imagination and tactical smarts. They were, however, very professional and self-motivated. They were always prepared for training and trained hard earning the respect from all the SF operators they interacted with. They were also a hard-partying group.

In January of 1966 the SEAL Team that arrived on Okinawa for train-up included Lieutenant Junior Grade Edwin Thomas. He was the team's Executive Officer and an old friend of Jim's from the University of Nebraska. Eddie, as he was known to his friends, was from Denver, Colorado and had been a "preferred walk-on" safety with the Nebraska football team. He lived in the dorm room next to Jim his first year at school and they palled around a bit in Lincoln. Eddie lost interest in football when it became obvious he wouldn't play for Nebraska and never be more than a practice team player. Like Jim, after an injury in fall of his sophomore year Eddie lost interest in both football and school. Bored and uncertain what he wanted to do with his life, he decided to drop out and join the Navy and become a SEAL like his uncle. Like Jim he went through the Navy's officer training program and received a commission prior to attending Basic Underwater Demolition School (BUDS), the formal name of the Navy's SEAL course.

When Eddie's SEAL team showed up on Okinawa LTJG Edwin Thomas was responsible for coordinating their pre-deployment training. Jim was both surprised and happy to see his old friend. On several of the evenings he was on station Jim took Eddie off base for some real Japanese food and to catch up with where life had taken

58

them after they each left Nebraska. Jim was impressed with his old friend and thought he had become quite the professional.

The pre-deployment training on Okinawa was a gentleman's course with only five of the ten days spent in the field. Three of those days were a reconnaissance patrol where the team conducted a parachute insertion into a small drop zone from two Huey helicopters and moved cross-country to recon a designated target. It ended in a live fire exercise on one of Okinawa's ranges. Jim made himself the team evaluator for the three-day mission at the end of the course so he could see how a SEAL team operated in the field and also get in a jump.

Eddie was a sharp, tough and a highly fit officer, well respected by his team and his bosses. Much like the Army Special Forces, the Navy SEALs are unconventional warriors and while the teams are led by officers, like Special Forces A-Teams, they are run by the team NCOs. Although a little bit larger than a Special Forces A-team the configuration and duties are similar. The officers focus on planning and coordinating support like SF A-Team officers. The NCOs on SEAL teams run the teams day-to-day and are all specialized experts in designated areas. All Navy SEALs are both dive and parachute qualified. One of the things that attracted Eddie to the SEALs was the dive stories his uncle told. He even went the summer of his senior year in high school and earned his civilian diving certification. Eddie loved to dive — but he hated to parachute. He could just not bring himself to enjoy jumping out of a perfectly good airplane from 1000 feet with 80 pounds of gear strapped between his legs. Eddie made his jumps, but only for training missions and to meet the minimum qualification requirements.

As luck would have it Jim found out Eddie was a reluctant jumper from one of his NCOs. He had himself assigned to Eddie's aircraft as the Jumpmaster for the three-day field problem's parachute insertion. At the marshaling before the exercise, during the pre-jump parachute inspection, Jim made Eddie change parachutes. The exercise used old T-10 parachutes which are safe and serviceable but not very maneuverable — Jim told Eddie he didn't like his parachute and thought it had bad Ju-Ju and might not open. Already anxious, this really set Eddie on edge while the rest of his team just smiled and smirked. When the helicopter took off and headed to the drop zone Jim again teased an already pale-faced Eddie, telling him he didn't feel right about the jump, and if Eddie's parachute didn't open, and he augured-in, could Jim have this new stereo. Eddie didn't find any of this amusing — although his fellow SEALs enjoyed the ribbing.

The parachute for Eddie the SEAL did open, but he handled it poorly and in mid-air swung into one of his fellow SEALs, only avoiding entanglement when the other SEAL stretched himself out like a cross and bounced off Eddie's risers. The other jumpers could hear Eddie swear as he floated down. Even though it was a pleasant day when Eddie hit the ground he was drenched in sweat. Of course, Jim was there to ask if he needed a towel which brought a laugh from the rest of the SEALs, although Eddie didn't find it amusing.

The SEALs were sharp on the exercise and accomplished the mission in fine fashion. Jim was impressed with their discipline, ability to move under a load, and what great marksmen they were.

At the end of the ten-day training program Jim had a new-found respect for his Navy brethren. The night before the SEAL team departed for Vietnam Jim took Eddie out for a seafood dinner. During the meal Eddie told Jim they were being deployed to the IV Corps area in Vietnam and would be part of the Riverine Force that was being assembled to operate and patrol the Mekong Delta and its various water ways. Jim wished Eddie good luck. He didn't know that three months later his friend would be dead, killed by a sniper while on river patrol.

Shortly after Eddie's Seal Team left Okinawa Jim and John Portman, the Lieutenant he was with the night Kiko and her cousin were attacked, were called to the headquarters of the 1st SF Group. The occasion was to award them formal Letters of Commendation for the unselfish bravery and rescue of Ms. Matsuyama and her cousin. Jim and John were a little embarrassed by the whole fuss, they just did what they thought any self-respecting person would do when they saw someone in trouble. After the ceremony in the commander's conference room Kiko pulled Jim aside and thanked him again for coming to her rescue. Jim was taken by her beauty and humbled that she would take the time to thank him again personally. "I'm just glad we were there to help," Jim said, "and more importantly happy you weren't hurt." "No, you were brave and I and my cousin are in your debt," Kiko replied. "As a small repayment for your help my cousin and I would like to take you and your friend to dinner. We know a nice little place that serves the best seafood in Okinawa and we would be honored if you would join us as our guests." "Oh, that's not necessary," Jim replied. "No, we discussed it and would be honored if you would come. I think you both would enjoy it and I would like to know you better Mr. Jim," Kiko said, looking directly at Jim. "Well, it's hard to turn a beautiful lady down and I love seafood, but I would be the one honored and I am sure John - my buddy - would feel the same way. When were you thinking of going?" "If it works for you and Mr. John we'd like to do it next Saturday. Can I give you the address and you could meet us there?" My god this girl is beautiful, she looks like a Japanese movie star and she's asking me out to dinner, seems the stars are aligning, Jim thought to himself. The more he looked at her and her gentle smile with that soft voice, the more he was becoming infatuated with Ms. Matsuyama. "I think Saturday would be great, I'll stop by the S-1 Shop tomorrow and get the address and John and I will meet you there. What time should we meet?" "What time would you like? Will six o'clock be okay?" "Yes, that would be fine. I hope it's not a Fancy place, I don't have any dressy clothes and I don't want to look like the ugly American," Jim said with a smile only half joking. "Oh, don't worry, casual is fine. It's a little off the beaten track, but nice, very friendly and informal, and it has the best seafood on Okinawa. My family has known the owners for years. I'm sure you'll like it," Kiko replied, looking more and more radiating. "Great, I'm looking forward to it. I'll see you tomorrow for the address." "Good, I'll see you tomorrow then, and thank you again for rescuing us," the beautiful Ms. Kiko said, then turned and headed back to her office. Jim just stood there for a minute and watched as she ambled down the long hallway. That girl is something, Saturday should be fun, he said to himself then turned and headed to the team house.

For some reason Jim couldn't stop thinking about Kiko over the three days until Saturday. He couldn't figure it out? Was it her beauty that was so captivating or the way she looked at you when she spoke to you in that caress of a soft voice? He didn't know, but was anxious for Saturday to arrive so he could perhaps get to know her better. She said she wanted to get to know him. What did that mean? Was she interested in him? He didn't know, but hoped she was. She went to school in Arizona, he'd have to ask her about that, so she must have some experience with American males and she couldn't be too turned off by them. Hell, she worked in a Special Forces headquarters and was surrounded by the most red blooded and horniest Americans there were. Clearly, she wasn't some naïve, innocent young thing. Well, he would go by the S-1 Shop tomorrow and get the address of the restaurant and scope it out before Saturday. The weekend couldn't come soon enough.

When Saturday rolled around Jim and John took a taxi from base to the restaurant address Kiko had provided. They arrived just before 6 o'clock and when they walked in Kiko and her cousin were already there and waved them over to their table. The restaurant was a local Japanese place, small and with low tables on straw mats surrounded by pillows. Jim thought it looked like a place out of a Japanese movie. Clearly, it was a local's place and probably didn't get too many American guests.

When he approached the table Kiko and her cousin stood up and shook their hands giving a curt bow and asking them to sit. Jim sat on the side next to Kiko and John by the cousin. The cousin's name was Yoshi Matsuyama, a cousin from Kiko's father's side. He seemed like a pleasant guy and was manager of a food distribution company. He spoke with an Asian accent, but his English was good. After a little chit-chat Kiko asked if she could order dinner for Jim and John, she and her cousin would be having a traditional seafood dinner common to Okinawa. It would be served family style. Jim said sure, he'd be pleased if she ordered as neither he nor John could read the menu and were excited to try something different from the plain base food which was their daily staple and they were hungry.

When the waitress came over Kiko ordered dinner and Yoshi asked what the two SF officers would like to drink. Jim said a beer would be fine, John seconded Jim's order. Yoshi said, "Great" he'd have one too as would Kiko. Sapporo, a Japanese premium beer, was ordered for everyone and the waiter left to begin his work. When he was gone John asked Yoshi, "Should we have Saki with our dinner? What is the custom?" Yoshi smiled and said, "Well you can, but normally we wait until after dinner as it is thought to help with digestion — especially if it's warmed. But you know the local Saki is very good and you can drink it any time. Would you like some?" Thinking better of it, John replied, "Perhaps after dinner, I don't want to risk spoiling my meal."

The four continued to talk about a host of things, the war in Vietnam and where it might be going, the food and dinner customs in Japan. It was a casual, friendly stream of consciousness conversation, light and interesting. To Jim the most interesting topic was when he asked Kiko where she went to school in the US. She replied that she attended Arizona State for two years. She had done well in high school and wanted to go to the United States for college. She earned a small scholarship and worked at the university library to pay for school. Her plan was to study English and come back to Japan and be a teacher. She commented that she loved the "States" but after a few years she started to get homesick, she was very close to her parents. She noticed that there were quite a few Asian students at Arizona State, something she wasn't expecting. Jim asked if she had a boyfriend in the states. She smiled and said she kinda did, she hung out with a group of about 6-8 international students from the East like herself, and that she had an American boy she saw, but more as a friend than as a boyfriend. When her mother became ill she didn't go back for her junior year taking a break from school. Once her mother got better she took a job with the American military in Japan and eventually ended up in Okinawa. She never returned to finish school and didn't think she would go back now. Jim was impressed that she had the travel bug at such a young age. He reveled that he had only been out of Nebraska twice growing-up before he went to college and that was to go hunting in South Dakota.

When the meal came Jim commented that it smelled delicious and they wasted no time digging in. Every aspect of the meal was excellent. Jim and John particularly liked the shrimp and scallops that Kiko said was a local dish. Neither were fond of the seaweed salad, but they ate it so as not to offend their Japanese hosts.

Following the meal and more chit-chat about their backgrounds Yoshi and Kiko toasted Jim and John with a warm Saki, thanking them for their intervention and rescue. The two Americans were a little embarrassed, they didn't see their actions on Kiko and Yoshi's behalf as that big a deal, but it was a kind end to a pleasant evening.

When the four diners were outside the restaurant waiting for taxis to take them home, on the spur of the moment Jim asked Kiko if she would like to go hiking with him the following weekend around Ikei-Shima peninsula. Surprised at the request, Kiko agreed, giving Jim a big smile. She was starting to like the big American, he was such a gentleman. Jim was a little surprised that she accepted on the spot, Jim smiled and said he would come by her work with his plan and perhaps they could throw in a lunch. Kiko said that would be fine and she looked forward to it. Her acceptance put Jim in a great mood and he didn't even mind John's teasing him about getting "yellow fever" on the way back to their quarters on post.

The following Thursday Jim stopped by the S-1 Shop and told Kiko his plan. If she agreed, they could head out in the morning to Ikie and walk the trail that circled the peninsula. He'd done it before, and knew a good restaurant that overlooked the bay near the small village of Miyagi and perhaps they could stop there for lunch. Kiko said that would be fine and gave Jim another of her radiant smiles. Just looking at the beautiful Kiko Jim felt warm all over. Maybe there is a connection here, he thought. He seemed to be thinking about her a lot lately and whenever he was around her she seemed to brighten up. On Saturday he'd have time alone with her and see where things went, he thought, as he left the S-1 shop. Kiko was definitely someone he could spend some time with, her beauty was captivating.

When Saturday rolled around, Jim met Kiko at the S-1 Shop, and they took a taxi to the trail near Ikei, it was only a few miles away, but on the East side of the island. They were dropped off at a small park and picked up the trail that circled the peninsula. The trail was narrow on the sea side and had steep drop-offs in some areas, but neither had any problems negotiating the track. Kiko was quite fit and as they talked along the way Jim learned that she was a volleyball player and still played in a local recreation league, just another plus in Jim's opinion.

The hike was about five miles and took about two hours. They weren't in any hurry and stopped a few times along the way and threw rocks over the steep cliffs into the crashing sea. The weather was perfect and the leisurely hike pleasant allowing them to grow comfortable with each other. Just down from where they exited the trail was a small local restaurant and they took a table on the patio that overlooked the Pacific.

It was an idyllic warm day and clearly a spark was lit between them. Jim, captivated by Kiko's beauty, had to keep himself from just staring at her. Kiko, growing more and more fond and comfortable around Jim, liked that he was a perfect gentleman and treated her as an equal. He didn't seem like someone just interested in a local conquest. Working on the base Kiko has seen her share of knuckle-dragging Neanderthals who were just looking for a local roll in the hay. Jim didn't seem like that.

After a lite meal Jim ordered two glasses of a local Japanese wine trying to be cool and debonair, but neither liked the sour taste. When Jim made a face after his first sip Kiko laughed and said few people in Japan drink local wines and this one was particularly bad. Jim felt silly, but it was just another thing about him that Kiko liked. He didn't seem to take himself too seriously when he was with her. He was tall, strong and very fit. As an American officer he clearly had a good head on his shoulders. There was something about his deference to her, his listening to what she said and not trying to impress her with himself. The kind way he treated her drew her to him the longer she was around him. Kiko thought she understood Americans, she had lived among them in Arizona, worked with them here in Okinawa, but she sensed something different in big Jim Tittsworth. This guy definitely had possibilities.

Jim was savoring his day with Kiko as well. She was a great woman, mature for her age, and he really liked that she was fit and athletic and liked the outdoors. While her beauty attracted men like a moth to a flame, past the veneer was a bright, self-assured woman who was fun to be around. At this point in his life Jim had only been in love once and that had ended poorly when Sharon left Nebraska. Jim kinda felt the same way about Kiko as he had when he first started seeing Sharon. He'd just treat her with respect and see where the relationship went. He was sure many others, both American and Japanese, had tried to get in her good graces. He was in no hurry. If he was to have a relationship with her she would let him know and it would find its own way. No sense trying to make it happen too fast. He wanted to be sure Kiko was having similar feelings for him before he shared his feelings with her.

Over the next few weeks Jim and Kiko saw a lot of each other. Sometimes after work and every Saturday Jim was off. Kiko spent Sundays with her parents. The more they were around each other the closer they grew and Jim easily fell in love with the tall, beautiful Japanese.

Kiko felt the same about Jim. When he brought her flowers on her birthday, something no one had ever done before, she knew he was the one. That Saturday after another hike she invited him over to her apartment. Jim was the first man she had ever invited home. Jim for his part, ever the gentleman, had made it a point to keep his desire for Kiko in check. Up to that point he had never even kissed her or even tried to. He figured she would let him know when he should but he certainly wanted her.

After a simple early dinner of rice and sushi Kiko asked Jim if he wanted to stay. Jim was a little taken aback, he knew she guarded her virtue and wasn't sure what that exactly meant, but he of course said yes — he'd love to. With a smile he said but, on the condition, Kiko didn't try to make him drink any Japanese wine. Kiko laughed at him and said no she didn't want to torture him. During dinner they hadn't talked much, each wrapped up in their own thoughts wondering how the evening would go. Neither wanted their desire for each other to ruin things, but both knew what they were doing and thought it was past time to keep each other at arm's length. After dinner Jim helped with the dishes and when they were finished he put his arms around Kiko and gave her a soft kiss and said thank you. Jim's gesture broke the ice and Kiko kissed him back and took his hand and led him to the bedroom. They spent the rest of the night exploring each other and releasing the passion they had held back with great discipline over the past few weeks. It was a glorious night. They got up late the next day and Jim, knowing that she had to go to her parents' home, told her for the first time that he loved her and was grateful that she shared herself with him. She could rest assured that Jim would always be there for her and treat her with respect. "I know that you will," Kiko said, "that is why it was easy to fall in love with you too." "Well I'm the lucky one," Jim replied.

After they got dressed and had a breakfast of tea and sweets, Jim said he knew she was expected at her parents' house. He needed to get back to base too, he was the duty officer that evening. But he asked if he could see her later in the week and could they go out again Saturday, perhaps do another hike and explore more of the island. What a gentleman, Kiko thought to herself, always thinking of me. "Of course, you can! Jim, I'm the one who needs to thank you. First you saved my life and treated me like a princess and now you've captured my heart. I don't want to be with anyone else." "I was hoping you liked me," Jim said with a grin. "Then it's a date?" "Yep, it sure is Mr. Husker," Kiko replied, flashing her radiant smile. "Wow, you're turning into a real American girl. Can't wait to get you back to Nebraska." They both chuckled and after a long embrace Jim gathered his things while Kiko called a taxi.

On June 10, 1966, Jim was promoted to First Lieutenant. He'd been in the Army for just over two years and he was twenty-two years old. He was liking the Army, the physical nature of soldiering, the responsibility he was given, and the team he was on. He especially enjoyed the camaraderie of the Special Forces clan. It was a tight knit group of professionals, clearly to Jim the cream of the crop of the Army.

Life on Okinawa was also easy living, the duty wasn't complicated, although the war in Vietnam was growing more and more involved and was on everyone's mind. Jim was itchy to go to Vietnam and find out in person what the war was all about. He also wanted to test himself and see if he could cut it in combat, lead men in battle — fulfill his mission. The stories he heard from those who had served tours in Vietnam were both exciting and dreadful. The SF community had a low opinion of the Vietnamese Army in general and in particular its leadership. While most supported the war politically, those that had served there had some reservation that it could be won the way the US and South Vietnamese were fighting it. Jim figured it would be just a matter of time, short time, before he would receive orders for a tour there. Until then he'd continue with the training mission and try to see Kiko as much as he could.

A Taste of War

On June 15th a special tasking order came down from 1SFG headquarters to Bravo Company and the mission was assigned to ODB-1120. The tasking was to put together a six-man team to conduct Long Range Reconnaissance Patrols (LRRP) along the border of Vietnam and Cambodia. The ODB-1120 LRRP team would be attached to the 5SFG in Nha Trang. The team would operate in II Corps in the central highlands of Vietnam. It would be a temporary duty assignment for 30-45 days. Specifics of the mission would be divulged in Nha Trang once the team arrived on station.

When Captain Arnold received the order, he decided he would lead the mission and chose the six NCOs to go with him. The team had recently been pulsed up with two NCOs and was at full strength. One of the NCO's on the LRRP mission would be support and coordinate logistics for the team from Nha Trang or wherever they would launch from. He and five others would conduct the reconnaissance. Jim and the rest of the team would stay in Okinawa and continue supporting the 1st SF Groups' training mission. The LRRP mission would deploy to Vietnam on 1 July. Jim was a little disappointed as he was anxious to get to Vietnam, but was then OK with staying behind because he could spend more time with Kiko.

On Friday, 22 June, ODB-1120 was conducting a Hollywood jump, a parachute jump without any combat equipment, just to be sure the team met the minimum number of jumps to remain parachute qualified and earn their Jump Pay. They were jumping on the drop zone at the Northern Okinawa Training Area when Captain Arnold broke his leg. Upon landing a gust of wind grabbed Arnold's parachute keeping it inflated and drug him across the drop zone. As he struggled to release the canopy his leg became tangled beneath him and two bones in his lower left leg snapped. The injury was serious but not threatening. He would recover, but he would be out of commission for at least three months. The following Monday Jim received the assignment to lead the ODB-1120's Vietnam LRRP mission.

Jim welcomed the assignment, he would finally get to Vietnam and find out if he was a real warrior or just a wannabe. He was confident in his abilities and quickly got up to speed on things, especially the intel and the terrain he would be operating in. He also planned several meetings with his team to go over covert and emergency action procedures, communications and talk about how they would execute the mission on the ground. He also wanted to ensure everyone was aware of the operational contingency plans if things went south. The team spent several days rehearsing key drills. A critical aspect in the planning would be what equipment the small team would carry in addition to individual gear. It was a lot to coordinate, but the team was made up of professionals, several who had already served tours in Vietnam had the experience to know what needed done.

While Jim was excited to go, but sad he would be away from Kiko. His relationship with her had deepened and he would miss her. He couldn't tell her where he was going or what he would be doing, although she would probably guess that if he was away from Okinawa on temporary duty (TDY) it would be in Vietnam. For the week he had left in Okinawa he planned on seeing Kiko as much as he could. The team would go in isolation on the 29th and stay there until it deployed.

Two nights before he went into isolation Jim stayed at Kiko's apartment. He didn't talk to her about where he was going or what he would be doing, only saying he would be gone maybe a few months and that as soon as possible he would write to her and even call her if he could get to a phone. She had worked in the 1SFG long enough to know the reality of things. She understood Jim was a soldier and when duty calls it had to take first priority even over the ones you loved.

While Jim was at Kiko's apartment, between bouts of lovemaking, they pledged themselves to each other. While he didn't tell her, it was Jim's intention to ask Kiko to marry him when he got back from Vietnam. No sense staying apart when they were meant to be together.

He knew she would be safe on Okinawa while he was away. While he knew he would miss her he'd just enjoy the warmth of her charms for now and file them away to recall while he was gone.

On 29 June 1966, Jim and his team went into isolation and made final preparations for deployment. Equipment was drawn and packed, intel reports and maps scoured as well as operational updates from the Special Forces headquarters in Vietnam reviewed. The team was about as ready as they could be when they shipped out at 2000 hours on July 1st for Nha Trang on a C-141 Starlifter.

The flight was a little over five hours and they arrived in Nha Trang after midnight. An NCO from the 1SFG's forward detachment met them on the tarmac and showed them to their billets. They would spend a week in Nha Trang for updated mission and intel briefs and to get the lay of the land. They would also develop and coordinate their insertion and extraction plans in Nha Trang and develop specific mission contingency plans based on the current operational situation in their target area. There was a lot to get done. After a short rest the team met for breakfast and Jim assigned the various tasks. He and his team sergeant, SFC Pete Jeffers, would meet with the 5th SF Group's commander in Vietnam, LTC Arnold "Arnie" Anderson, to get an operational and intel update and hear his concept of the operation.

LTC Anderson was a well-respected, veteran Special Forces officer. As an orphaned teenager Anderson immigrated to the United States via England from Sweden in the later days of WWII. He joined the US Army in 1948 to hasten his path to citizenship. He served with the 1st Cavalry Division in Korea quickly rising to Sergeant after his heroic actions during the battle of Hill 303 in August of 1950 where he was wounded twice and earned a Distinguished Service Cross to go along with his two Purple Hearts. Following the war Anderson went to OCS at Fort Riley, Kansas and after a year as a Military Police officer volunteered for the newly formed Special Forces in 1954. After his initial SF training, because of his native language skills, he was assigned to the 10th Special Forces in Bad Tolz, Germany. Later, in

1961, he led a mobile training team (MTT) to Laos as part of Project White Star, one of the Army's first forays into the Vietnam war. Since February 1966 he had been 5th SFG's commander and 1SFG's man in Vietnam.

Anderson and 5th Group's headquarters were located in Nha Trang, also the headquarters of the Vietnamese Special Forces and the location of their Special Forces and Commando training center.

The mission of Jim's team was to conduct reconnaissance in a 5x10 kilometer box west and north of the small village of Duc An in the South western corner of II Corps on the border of Vietnam and Cambodia. The team would be inserted by helicopter just before dusk and move to a hide position. They were to observe the target area for ten days, identifying and recording routes, roads, trails and access points being used by the North Vietnamese Army (NVA) to enter South Vietnam from Cambodia and any infrastructure/base areas where NVA and Viet Cong units might stage their operations into the South. The clandestine mission was to report enemy sightings, for possible attack if air assets were available, but otherwise remain undetected. Other than when the NVA showed themselves they would report back to headquarters only at schedule times. Contact with the enemy was to be avoided and the team was to remain on the Vietnamese side of the border. Anderson informed Jim that there were four other missions ongoing similar to his in other locations. The concept was to identify as many routes, any new base areas and any movement emanating from the Ho Chi Minh Trail. The info was to be used for developing a concerted bombing campaign that was to be followed up with a multidivisional Vietnamese ground operation. The hope was that with more precise ground information the follow-up operations could significantly degrade the North Vietnamese forces and destroy their base areas to such an extent that any serious offensive operations in the South would have to be curtailed. The trick, according to Anderson, was for Jim to get his team into his operational area undetected, find good hide sites where he could observe the target zone and identify any North Vietnamese activity and any infrastructure, then to exfiltrate without being discovered. NVA targets of opportunity would be engaged as assets were available, if they were warranted.

Jim and his team sergeant listened to LTC Anderson's briefing and at the end had a few questions. Mostly about the communications plan and the team's access to air support should they get discovered or in trouble. The team had both FM and VHF radios, but needed to know who they should be calling and the frequencies they should use. Anderson informed them that the detachment's communications section would be coordinating that with his designated commo sergeant — and that II Corp had full time American Fast FACs on station 24-hours a day and unless something very unusual happened they would have access to air support at all times within a twenty-minute window.

Following the patrol Jim's team would return to Nha Trang, debrief and recover, and then conduct additional LRRP patrols until their TDY was up. No one was surprised about the mission and the team felt both well qualified and prepared to carry it out. The unknown factor was the North Vietnamese. While the intel folks knew generally where the NVA moved along the Ho Chi Minh trail, they really only had a guesstimate of their specific locations, exact base areas, their units and what they were up to. It was hoped the LRRPs would help answer some of those questions for II Corps forthcoming operation.

Over the next two days Jim and his team sergeant linked up with the aviation operations officer and the group Intel NCO and picked out the landing zones for both insertion and extraction as well as a few contingency locations in case things went to hell in a handbasket. The team insertion would occur late afternoon on 6 July. One aircraft, a Huey B-Model, escorted by two gunships, would fly the six-man team to the operational area. It would make four landings, but the team would only exit at one. The purpose of multiple touch downs was to confuse anyone who might hear or see the chopper as to what it was doing and where the real insertion point was. Jim was satisfied with the plan and it was briefed to the team. All the gear, about 50 pounds per man, was packed and staged before noon on the 6th. Each piece of gear and all the weapons were taped to ensure there were no rattles or noises when the team was moving. The team wanted to travel silently and minimize any chance of inadvertent exposure to the enemy. After a lite meal the men all laid down for a rest before the 1600 assembly at the flight line. Once airborne it would take about an hour to fly to Ban Me Thuot where the helicopters would refuel and then head off to the border and begin the insertion process.

Enroute to the first landing zone (LZ), a fake position, Jim had his communications sergeant make contact with the II Corps Fast FAC, call sign Arizona HellCat (AHC). He didn't want to get on the ground and have to fool around with the radios, he wanted to move quickly and quietly from the LZ to the first day's designated hide position. Arizona HellCat was on station and the commo checked out before the first decoy insertion began. The real insertion point was the third of the four landings and when the Huey hit the ground at the true insertion LZ Jim's team unassed the bird in four-seconds, dashed into the tree line on the North side of the landing zone and disappeared into the trees. By that time the helicopter was well on its way to the last fake LZ.

On the ground Jim's LRRP Team moved quickly a few yards into the tree line and made a hasty perimeter. They waited in complete silence for a few minutes listening for any signs of movement or human activity. When they heard nothing but the chopper blades in the distance slapping the air as it flew away and a few monkeys howling, using hand and arm signals they formed into a single file and headed for their first night hide position. Jim was third in the line of march.

The area was typical Asian highlands terrain. It was heavily forested with an abundance of tall hardwood trees, some as tall as 100 feet. There were intermittent open areas where scrubby bushes interspersed tall Savanna grasses. There were dry rocky washes between the rolling hills some of which were up to 400 feet high and steep. There were also some areas of jungle, with intertwined vines and bushes mostly near the beginning of tree lines on the sides of hills where direct sunlight could reach the ground allowing undergrowth to flourish. Much of the open ground was just tall Savanna grass interspersed with wide, low bushes. As the team picked its way west it stopped periodically to listen. All they heard were the sounds of nature as the birds and monkeys were finding their night roosts.

The area Jim was to patrol was deemed to be uninhabited. There were a few known temporary Montagnard camps used when tribes were moving between their various hunting and farming areas, but these were few and far between and not permanent. The trail system was mostly animal trails along the sides of hills and by streams, many of which were overgrown. There were few roads in the area on the South Vietnamese side of the border. The ones that were there were unmaintained logger roads only used during the dry season when the loggers came to the border to harvest hardwood trees. If Jim's team executed their plan correctly they could accomplish their mission and get out and no one would know they were even there.

It was just dusk when the team inserted and Jim figured there was about 30 minutes of fading light before it got dark. And it would get dark as hell with no moon and the tall trees blocking any ambient light. He had picked out a hide location about 3000 meters from the LZ and he figured with stops, if they didn't run into anyone, the team could make it in about an hour. One problem was the team had to navigate by compass in the fading light and that was always difficult even under the best of circumstances. Jim was hopeful the team would get to the hide site without any navigation problems.

The hide site itself was out of the way at the bottom of a tall forested hill that on Aerial maps was 400 meters from the nearest trail. It was heavily forested and overgrown according to the intel photos and should be a place no one would just stumble upon. It would also provide an elevated location to put up a directional wire antenna that would ensure solid communication between the observation team, Arizona HellCat, and Nha Trang. It was about 2000 meters from the first planned observation post, a small forested hill right on the Cambodian border. The observation team wouldn't have far to go to reach it and it should provide long fields of view north, west, and south. Jim was hopeful it would also provide the team a good look into Cambodia. The dirt road they wanted to watch was a heavily used section of the Ho Chi Minh Trail.

After reaching the hide site without any issues the team reported in and hunkered down for the night. The plan was to send a three-man team to the observation site at dawn where they could observe the road and stay concealed for the next three days. The team would report any sightings to Jim at the hide site in code and those would be reported back to Nha Trang at 0800 and 1800 each day unless there were significant targets of opportunity in which case Arizona HellCat would be contacted and he would determine if he had the assets to attack the target. The fifth day, upon the return of the observation team to the hide site, the entire team would move at dusk to the second hide site further north. From there a second three-man observation team would be sent out repeating the drill observing a different part of the Ho Chi Minh Trail. If things went right the team would observe the new target area from two different locations recording what they saw. On the tenth day the team would move to an extraction point and be pick-up by helicopter and flown back to Nha Trang.

On day-two the observation team moved to the initial observation point (OP1) arriving without any problems. However, their view of the main target road was poor and the team leader suggested his team move to a hill 1000 meters north so they could see more of the road unobscured. Jim approved and that evening the observation team moved. Over the next two days the team didn't observe any activity on the road and neither saw nor heard any signs of human activity. They moved back to Jim's location on the fifth day as planned without a hitch.

On the sixth day at dawn, the team moved to hide site 2, three kilometers north of the first hide site. Again, the team hunkered down in a heavily concealed location on the side of a tall hill. The next day at dawn Jim led two others to the second observation point (OP2), 2000 meters northwest of the second hide at the northernmost end of the team's operational zone. OP2 had a good view of the road as it came down from the North on the Cambodian side of the border for about four kilometers to where it turned east behind a large hill. They could also see a few kilometers into Cambodia.

The first day in OP2 was uneventful and Jim and his two-man team saw nothing. But early on the morning of the second day a single, covered five-ton truck with a small cargo trailer made its way down the road. Through the binoculars Jim could see there were three men in uniforms in the cab. The truck didn't seem to be in a hurry and stopped on the road just out of view from Jim's location. Thirty minutes later it continued south and Jim watched as the truck and trailer moved down the road until they were out of sight. Clearly it was an enemy vehicle but Jim was unsure what it was doing — was it clearing the road for others? Carrying supplies? Its mission was just unknown. At the 1800 SITREP with Nha Trang Jim reported what they had seen.

Just after dawn the next day, the OP2 team heard vehicle noise on the road coming from the North even before they could observe anything. Staying concealed, but focused on the Northern part of the road, just after 0800 a convoy of eight covered trucks, three with trailers, moved slowly south down the road. They stopped in full view of OP2 and what Jim estimated was probably a company size unit of uniformed men hopped out of the back of the vehicles when they stopped and took a break on the East side of the road. They were clearly NVA. Jim decided to contact Arizona HellCat and see if there were assets available to engage the convoy.

After a few calls AHC came on the net and Jim informed him of the target and its location. AHC rogered the call and said he was south of Jim, but had a flight of two, F-4 Phantoms about 10 minutes away. He would call to clear the target with the II Corps air controller and if he gave a "go" they would engage the trucks. He estimated it would take 15 minutes to get approval and coordinate with his fast movers and asked

Jim to keep him informed if the convoy started moving and to scour the area to see if he could identify any anti-aircraft guns or anything else that his pilots should know about. Jim rogered the request and he and his team began slowly sweeping the road and terrain on both sides — north to south — with their binoculars looking for any AA guns or other NVA positions. They didn't see anything except the eight trucks pulled off on the east of the road. The trucks were spaced about 25 meters apart and there were a number of troops milling around. One of Jim's sergeants thought the convoy had probably stopped for breakfast and a piss as they didn't seem to be taking any tactical precautions.

Five minutes later, AHC came back up on frequency and asked Jim for his precise location and the hide site's location to ensure he didn't mistakenly drop any ordnance on his team. Jim complied and gave him both the OP2 location and the coordinates of the hide site. AHC said his fast movers would be on station in five minutes. He would make the first pass at altitude south to north to pick up a visual on the road and trucks. On a second pass he would come north to south and try to mark the center of the convoy with a smoke rocket identifying the target for the fast movers. Once the smoke was on the ground it would be followed thirty-seconds later by the first F4's bombing run. AHC told Jim one F-4 had six Mark-81, 250-pound high explosive bombs, and the other four canisters of napalm. If the bombs landed anywhere near their target it would be destroyed and the folks that weren't hit would probably be walking around for the next few weeks talking to themselves.

AHC planned to use the napalm after the initial bomb run to paint the road with fire and destroy anything on or along it. Hopefully the first bombing run would block the road and keep the trucks from moving forward so the target center of mass would remain stagnant. AHC would adjust the rest of the bombs to ensure all the trucks were destroyed and if he had anything left he'd hit likely locations where the NVA might try to hide. Jim rogered the plan of attack and told AHC he would give him a read on the marker rocket and pointed out a few terrain features that would be helpful to AHC picking up the road as he came back around. AHC rogered and informed Jim he was about 25 miles out to the South following along the border at 15,000 feet and 400 miles per hour. Jim told one of his sergeants to look south to try and pick up AHC and he and the other sergeant would keep an eye on the parked trucks.

Ten-seconds later the sergeant looking for AHC told Jim he had AHC high on the southern horizon coming north quickly. Shortly thereafter the team could hear the roar of his engines as he zoomed on by heading north. AHC called in that he had the road in sight and saw a line of trucks facing south, parked on the East side just before the road turned east. Was that the target? Jim rogered and said the target was cleared to engage. AHC rogered and began his turn south to make his marking pass. As AHC was maneuvering to the North Jim informed him that the trucks didn't move after he flew by, they either didn't see him or didn't think they were observed. It was a huge mistake.

A few minutes later, AHC came screaming out of the northeast morning sun and fired a smoke rocket that landed just off the road to the east of the truck parked second in line. This sent the NVA into a panic and the drivers ran for their trucks as the soldiers on break ran for the hills on the East side of the road. They all knew what was about to happen and wanted to get as far away from the marking round as they could. But it was too late. Just as the first truck was pulling back on the road fifty meters in front of him the road exploded with a deafening CA-RACK, CA-RACK as the first F-4 delivered its initial two bombs. The explosions shattered the trees within a 50-meter radius and dug a 10-foot crater in the middle of the road ten yards in front of the lead vehicle making the road impassable and flinging the first truck off the road to the West like a discarded toy. The road was now blocked to the South and the truck drivers who were in their vehicles undamaged by the first bombing run jumped out of their trucks and started to run, leaving the trucks on the road and clearly exposed.

The second F-4 following 15 seconds after the first, also coming in from the northeast, unleashed two of his canisters of napalm washing the last six trucks in the convoy with flaming jelly. Jim and his team watched the engagement in awe. Jim thought to himself how glad he was that the NVA didn't have air support.

After the first bombing runs Jim called AHC and told him the NVA troops were running towards a ravine about 80 meters off the east side of the road. If he could, he should put some ordinance in the ravine at about the center of the burning convoy. AHC rogered the call and the next run of the first F-4 dropped two Mark-81s just behind the sixth truck about 100 meters east right where the NVA soldiers were trying to take cover — direct hit. No one was running now. The F4s made two more runs before the slaughter ended. It was total devastation. All eight trucks were totally destroyed and the road seriously cratered and would require a significant effort to repair. Only one of the trailers survived, but it was thrown over 50 meters off the road where it miraculously landed on its wheels. Who knew how many NVA were killed or wounded, but the loss had to be significant. The attack was all over in twenty minutes and AHC and his F4s signed off and headed back to their base in Thailand to reload.

Jim stayed in the observation site until dusk the following day and watched as a few survivors tried to assist the wounded and picked through the burning wreckage while trying to move some of the bodies of their comrades and place them by the side of the road for recovery later. When the light started to fade the second day Jim's observation team headed for the hide site to join the rest of the team. Their movement was uninterrupted and they made it to the hide site just as one of the sergeants was calling in the daily situation report.

At dawn the next morning, Jim called Nha Trang and coordinated the team's extraction. They would move to a prearranged LZ about five kilometers east and wait for the chopper to come get them. The pickup was scheduled for 1500 that afternoon. If the team was not opposed it could easily make the movement ahead of time and be there waiting when the chopper arrived. Jim assumed the NVA would still be busy trying to recover what was salvageable from the convoy attack and doubted they would be patrolling to the east. Still the team would move cautiously and use as much concealment as the terrain could provide. The pick-up location was a small clearing big enough for about three choppers on the western side of a large hill that was easily identifiable. Jim figured the team could make the movement in about two hours if there weren't any problems along the way.

The team started out for the extraction LZ at 1100 hours moving in file, keeping off the trails and practicing the "move and listen" drill they employed when they're inserted. They had gone about three kilometers, when the point man saw the lead element of an NVA patrol coming their way.

The NVA seemed to be coming from the direction of the extraction LZ but hadn't noticed the LRRPs. They too were moving in file, but didn't seem particularly attentive. They were moving towards the location of the previous day's truck attack and clearly not expecting any ARVN or American units to be in the area this close to the border.

Jim's team was moving deliberately and in silence using hand and arm signals to communicate. Suddenly after moving about 1000 meters the point man saw some NVA ahead and gave the signal to freeze and take cover — a hand placed over the face and pointing toward the direction of the enemy. The team could only see the first few men before it ducked into a dry creek bed to hide. The NVA were above the creek on a game trail that paralleled it running east and west. They stopped about 25 meters in front of Jim's team, quite unaware the Americans were there.

When the NVA unit stopped they bunched up, sat down on the side of the trail, pulled out their canteens and started talking. It was clearly a rest break and they showed poor tactical discipline. The LRRPs sat frozen against the bank of the stream holding their breath and praying they wouldn't be seen.

After a minute, Jim pointed to the hand grenades taped to his web gear and indicated he wanted the two men in front to prepare to throw their grenades. Both quietly took a grenade off their gear and made ready to throw. They would sit tight until they were discovered or Jim gave the signal. The hope was the NVA would finish their break and move on without discovering the team as it hid in the creek bed.

The team had practiced immediate reaction drills in Okinawa before they deployed so they all knew what to do. Immediate action drills come into play when a moving element comes into unexpected contact with the enemy. In this situation, if they were discovered the two leading men would throw grenades and lay down a base of rifle fire while the remaining four guys would quickly retreat 25 to 50 meters and take up covered firing positions and on command lay down a base of fire to cover the retreat of the first two men. It's called overwatch and allows a unit to hopscotch backwards or forward. The key to such a maneuver was to keep up a steady volume of fire so the enemy had to keep their heads down and couldn't shoot back or maneuver. This tactic would be repeated until the team broke contact and could run away.

The LRRP team sat in the creek bed for about 15 minutes listening to the NVA men shuck and jive, eat, and lose concentration about where they were. Then out of nowhere one of the NVA made his way down into the creek bed and began to drop his pants in order to relieve himself. As he started to squat down, he looked up and saw the team's point man no more than 15 feet in front of him hugged up against the creek bank. Shocked, he let out a yell which was instantly met by a burst of fire from the point man that just about cut him in half. He was dead when he hit the ground. The game was on.

When the point man fired, Jim and the two guys up front threw their grenades up onto the trail and the last three guys took off running to find a protected position from which they could provide covering fire to support the retreat of their comrades. Before Jim started his retreat, he threw a smoke grenade down the creek bed in front of his position and then took off running back towards his other men. The two guys up front opened with a final burst of fire towards the NVA, hoping to at least cause them to keep their heads down, then they too stood up and ran down the creek bed as fast as they could concealed by Jim's fizzling smoke grenade.

The scream and grenades caught the NVA completely by surprise. At the scream and automatic fire several of the NVA stood up and looked towards the creek where the gun fire seemed to be coming from. As a result, when the grenades went off several were wounded by the grenades which only added to their confusion. It didn't help that the NVA lieutenant in charge of the platoon was among the first wounded and severely so.

Like most battles the initial contact usually takes place fast and the side that gets the first and most rounds on target has a distinct advantage. When Jim and the two guys with him got to the first retreat position he took a quick assessment and then they continued to move back to find the next position where they took up covered positions from which they would provide covering fire if needed.

It took the NVA a while to get organized and they were as confused as to what they were facing. Since the Americans were retreating the NVA assumed it was a small force and they decided to pursue them. But without their officer they were slow to the task and disorganized. It took them a while to start moving and then slowly. By then Jim and his team were a quarter mile away and high-tailing it south.

When Jim thought they were out of reach he stopped the team to assess the situation and looked at the map. He had to make a choice: should they try and make the planned extraction LZ or should they call and coordinate for one of the alternate pick-up sites? It didn't seem like the NVA were in hot pursuit, but he had to assume they were coming. If he kept the team moving west then turned south around the hill behind them they could make it back over to the eastern side of the hill and get to the primary extraction LZ that way. It was a little longer but they could still get there well before the scheduled pick time.

Jim conferred with the team and they agreed they should try for the primary LZ. Getting out as soon as possible seemed like their smartest option. Jim agreed and the team moved out to the south then would turn and circle the hill east towards the original extraction LZ. Before the team moved-out Jim had one of his sergeants rig a claymore bobby trap on the trail next to the creek and another down in the creek bed itself just in case the bad guys chose to chase the team.

The claymore mine had been introduced into the American Army in 1960. It was a very portable antipersonnel mine that only weighed about four pounds, but had a killing radius of more than 60 meters, depending on the terrain. When detonated it blasted out 700 steel pellets at over 3000 feet per second, blowing away anything in its path. It could be set up on a tripwire as an automatic ambush or command detonated using a hand-held clacker. It was an especially lethal defensive weapon and exceptional when used in ambushes when properly positioned. It had become a staple of American infantry in Vietnam.

Once the claymores were set the team moved out. Jim had his commo sergeant contact Nha Trang and let them know they had had contact with an unknown NVA element, thought to be a platoon, and they were moving south to get away, but they still intended to be at the pick-up LZ on time. If they couldn't make the scheduled pick time or they were engaged with the NVA they would let HQ know. The team kept moving as fast as tactically possible and as silently as they could.

The NVA element the LRRPs had run into was a platoon from 1st Company, 2nd Regiment of 95B Division of the North Vietnamese Army. It had been dispatched to the site of the truck convoy attack to assist with the recovery/salvage operation and to help repair the cratered road. The 2nd Regiment had been clandestinely bivouacked northwest of Pleiku conducting disruption operations in II Corps. The platoon was a veteran group, but now without its leader and in some disarray.

The NVA platoon sergeant took command and divided what was left of the platoon into three sections. One would care for the three dead and eight wounded and move them west to the Ho Chi Minh trail where they could be cared for and evacuated. He would lead a second team, the largest with seven soldiers, and pursue the element they had come into contact with. The third group of five men would backtrack and circle the hill from the north to the east then head back south to cut off and ambush the enemy in the event they were still trying to move east on the south side of the hill. The platoon sergeant would lead the pursuit section. The two sections would link up on the east side of the hill where the creek and trail came together. Once together, if they didn't find the enemy that attacked them they would head back west to Cambodia. When he was sure his subordinates understood their missions the NVA platoon sergeant sent them off.

The squad heading back east moved out on the trail as it had the longest way to go, but their movement from here on would be slow and tactically sound.

For the next two hours Jim's team moved south, then east, around the hill. When they were about 800 meters from the pick-up LZ Jim stopped the team and put everyone in hide positions. They still had 40 minutes before the scheduled extraction and he wanted to rest a bit before they made their last push to the edge of the LZ.

After the short rest the team picked up and started moving to the LZ. The NVA squad that had circled the hill by going south had stayed too close to the hill and made no contact with the LRRP team. But for some strange reason the squad leader turned his men around when he was within 500 meters of the LRRPs, but unaware of their presence, and doubled back to the east side of the hill.

When Jim's team reached the LZ, they moved to the northeast corner, and set up a hasty perimeter in the tree line. They were about 10 minutes early. Jim had his commo sergeant call the aircraft, and let them know they were in position for extraction. The helicopter pilot answered the call and said he was about twelve minutes out and would be landing from the east. And asked for a strobe light indicator to pinpoint the team's location so he could set the chopper down in front of them to hasten the extraction. The commo sergeant acknowledged the message and told Jim the chopper was close and would land facing west and was a few minutes out. They needed to be ready with a strobe light to guide him in. Jim agreed and took his strobe light out of his pack and wrapped his boonie-hat around it creating a tunnel for the strobe, so it could only be seen from one direction. When they heard the helicopter then made visual contact Jim would go out in the LZ and flash the strobe in the chopper's direction. The team would move to the tree line and be ready to sprint to the aircraft as it came in for landing, three on each side as soon as the aircraft touched down. It seemed like the situation had settled down. Jim would be glad when the team was on the aircraft and headed back to Nha Trang.

Six minutes later the lookout spotted the helicopter coming towards the LZ from the east. The commo sergeant made radio contact again and said the team would flash a strobe in his direction in two minutes, he should put the aircraft down in front of the strobe and the team would load three on each side of the aircraft when he landed. The pilot rogered the call and said, "Coming on final!" Jim could see the aircraft dropping in altitude and ran out into the open area, knelt down, and flashed the strobe at the helicopter. The pilot easily picked it up and aimed the aircraft at the strobe. Two-hundred meters out he feathered his speed and dipped the Huey's nose to level off to set it down. When he touched down, the team ran out of the tree line to the chopper, three guys ran around the front of the aircraft and loaded on the south side. Jim and the two others moved to load on the north side.

The NVA squad was moving about 400 meters from the LZ when it heard the helicopter. The squad leader assumed that it was coming to rescue the unit they had clashed with earlier and had his men run toward the open area to their east hoping they could see the helicopter and take it under fire. It would be a fine day for him and his squad if they could knock down an American helicopter, especially one that was rescuing the unit that had ambushed his platoon. When the first NVA reached the west end of the open area the chopper was just landing and was about 300 meters away. They opened fire immediately.

Jim's team had just reached the helicopter when shots rang out from the tree line in front of the aircraft. The tall grass hindered the NVA's aim, but a few rounds struck the aircraft's front plexiglass. Jim and one of his sergeants immediately returned fire as did the right and left side door gunners who opened up with their M60 machine guns. After unloading a magazine on automatic Jim jumped onto the helicopter skid while both door gunners continued to whale away at the forward tree line. But just as SFC Jeffers got on the chopper he was hit in the back and knocked out of the aircraft as the pilot was pulling pitch to take off. Jim instinctively jumped off the skid to get him, but the helicopter pilot, concerned about the ground fire, flew off making a sweeping left turn to escape the NVA's fire.

When Jim reached his sergeant, he could see he was wounded, the bullet tagging him under the right arm. It was a through and through hit. The bullet entered at a flat angle below the arm on his right side breaking a rib and ricocheting straight out his front right side. It knocked the wind out of him, but didn't hit anything critical, it was essentially a deep flesh wound. He had been lucky.

On the ground Jeffers lay on his back and tried to catch his breath. He didn't seem to be bleeding much. Jim asked him how he was, could he move? He said he was hurting, but didn't think he was hurt too bad, he thought he could fight and probably move, but not too fast. Jim laid him on his back and put pressure on his side where he was starting to bleed and quickly put a field dressing on the exit wound, telling Jeffers to hold it there. If Jeffers could move Jim wanted to get going.

The extraction helicopter was gone and it was now just Jim and his wounded sergeant and some NVA on the LZ. Jim had his rifle and rucksack, and was unhurt. Jeffers had his weapon and rucksack as well so at least they could fight, but Jim's immediate concern was Jeffers. While Jim tended to his sergeant the two B-Model gunships that were accompanying the extraction Huey started to rake the west end of the LZ where the NVA had been firing from with rockets and mini-gun fire. Hopefully they would give Jim and the wounded Jeffers some time to move and keep the NVA stationary with their heads down.

Jim knew they had to move off the LZ immediately or both of them would remain a target even though the tall grass gave them some concealment. He had to assume that the NVA had seen them fall off the helicopter and as soon as the gunships broke off they would be coming after them. He didn't have a radio so he couldn't communicate with anyone, he had to get off the LZ and find some cover. With Jim holding him up, the wounded Jeffers limped to the closest tree line where they were at least out of the sight of the NVA. They kept moving while the gunships continued to pound the NVA positions.

Jim wanted to put as much distance between him and the bad guys as possible while Jeffers was still up to it. Once in the tree line Jim and Jeffers turned right and continued on towards the far end of the LZ. Once there Jim laid the wounded sergeant down and stepped out into the open area to see if he could get the attention of the gunships. To his surprise he could see the extraction slick circling east of the LZ out of range of the NVA's small arms. Apparently, it was not seriously harmed from the hits it had taken on the LZ. While the gunships continued to do their thing, Jim stood out in the open and frantically waved his arms trying to catch the attention of one of the aircraft. One of the gunships did see him and radioed the extraction Huey. Two minutes later as the guns laid down covering fire on the NVA end of the LZ, the extraction Huey came screaming back to the LZ toward Jim as he frantically waved his arms. When the aircraft approached the LZ, Jim went back to the tree line, grabbed Jeffers, braced him up, and led him to where the helicopter was setting down. When the aircraft touched the ground Jim quickly pushed Jeffers in and jumped in behind him as the other team members pulled them both to the middle of the aircraft and closed the aircraft doors as the pilot made a hasty retreat to the east. The aircraft hadn't been on the ground for more than ten-seconds. Once airborne and away from the LZ Jim let out a deep breath and said to no one in particular, "Well, we cheated death again!" as one of the other team members applied another dressing to sergeant Jeffer's wound.

When the extraction Huey got to Buon Ma Thuot the aircraft landed at the hospital helipad and was met by a team of medics. They took the wounded sergeant to the emergency room and tended to him. His wound, while serious, was not critical and after patching him up he would be returned to Nha Trang in a few days. Jim stayed with the wounded man. The rest of the team remained on the chopper and returned to Nha Trang after the Huey refueled. Two days later Jim and SFC Jeffers, who was quickly recovering, flew back to Nha Trang. After getting cleaned up Jim went to debrief LTC Anderson.

When he went into Anderson's office, the LTC praised him for not only the success of his mission, but for his courage in rescuing his wounded sergeant. "Your men will remember what you did Jim. You established yourself as a real combat leader and earned not only their respect, but their loyalty. It was well done Jim, well done," Anderson told him with a bit of pride. "Thank you, sir," Jim replied, "but I think any of the guys would have done the same. I guess it was just my turn first." "Well, glad it all ended up okay — could have been a lot worse," Anderson said. "I'm putting you in for an award for your heroic actions at the recommendation of your team." "Not necessary, Sir," Jim replied. "All the guys did a good job when we ran into that NVA platoon or none of us would be here. I'll be recommending they all get recognized." "I can agree to that and I'll have the S-1 get the paperwork together, we'll need your narrative." "No problem Sir, be a pleasure to write it up," was Jim's reply.

After Jim briefed Anderson on what the team had observed of the Ho Chi Minh trail and what he thought of the area they were in, Anderson told Jim that the intel team at II Corps was using the information the LRRPs had gathered to plan several B52 - ARC Light - strikes on that section of the trail to destroy the road and any containment areas. Further, the destroyed NVA truck convoy would significantly hinder the NVA operations in II Corps. It was a mission well done.

Anderson told Jim that his team would get a week's recovery and then he would assign him another LRRP mission a little further north. Intel had detected increased NVA activity southwest of Pleiku near the border and II Corps needed some American eyes on the ground to determine what was really going on. Jim said that would be fine, the team would be ready to go when tasked. The briefing finished, Anderson took Jim over to the mess hall for some lunch.

During the down time between missions Jim accompanied LTC Anderson to B-24 one of the Special Forces' older camps just south of Kontum. It was home base to a Mobile Strike Force — a Mike Force. It was a battalion in size with three operational companies and a weapons company along with several support attachments. B-24 supported II Corps north of Pleiku. The Mike Forces were relatively new as operational units, only adopted in the summer of '65 as an outgrowth of the "Eagle Flight" detachment — a quick reaction unit of indigenous fighters from the central highlands. The primary mission of the Mike Forces was to be a powerful, highly trained, quick reaction force that could respond to attacks on rural CIDG villages. However, with their success over time Mike Force missions were expanded to include traditional combat operations, search and destroy sweeps, reconnaissance in force, and rescue missions.

B-24 as a Special Forces camp had been around since the early '60s and the Mike Force in residence since last fall. The camp and Mike Force battalion was commanded by LTC James Tower, professional soldier and confirmed bachelor. He was an old hand Special Forces officer with three tours in Vietnam to his credit. Additionally, he had served as an infantry officer in the Korean War. There were few more experienced Special Forces officers in Vietnam.

The purpose of the visit to B-24 was to get an update on the Mike Force and LTC Tower's operational status. It didn't hurt that Tower and Anderson had served together in III Corps in '63 as A-Team commanders conducting training at the start of the CIDG program. When they arrived, Tower greeted them warmly and led them to the team house.

The briefing was informal and only LTC Tower and his operations officer were in attendance. Tower explained that his companies were mostly composed of Hmongs with only a few Montagnards and that he had over four hundred men in his battalion. Further, most of the soldier's families lived with the men on the B-24 compound. The camp total population was about 800 with only a handful of Vietnamese, all of whom were liaisons to Corps and the province. The operational tempo of B-24 was high and he routinely had one of his three companies in the field at all times, mostly sweeping along the border and following up intel reports of NVA and VC activity. They had been pretty successful in the several battles they fought the past few months. The NVA seemed to avoid the Mike Force when they could.

Tower sang the praises of the Hmong warriors who made up the vast majority of his battalion's manpower. He was less impressed with the Vietnamese side of the equation. Technically the Mike Forces reported up the Vietnamese chain of command and worked for II Corps, but the local provincial government and regular ARVN units, and even the Vietnamese SF units, looked down on the tribal soldiers and support from them was meager at best. It was essentially an American operation. Jim was impressed with LTC Tower and what he had to say about his soldiers. He had heard from others back in Okinawa that the Hmong and Montagnard soldiers were very loyal to the Americans and excellent in the field. You couldn't have too many good soldiers in war, Jim thought to himself.

After a tour of the camp, the four officers had lunch in the team house. Toward the end of the meal while they were discussing the accuracy of the intel reports that II Corp was providing, not very accurate according to LTC Tower, Anderson asked him if his men had observed any black soldiers with the NVA. Tower said no, that they had not directly seen any, but he had seen a few reports from II Corps that said a black man was seen leading some NVA units on a few occasions. He wasn't sure that was accurate, a lot of things get distorted when you're in a fight. "Ya, I agree. Probably just another myth, but since you have real eyes on the ground I thought I'd ask," Anderson said.

After the meal Anderson thanked Tower for the hospitality and update and told him that if there was anything he could do for him just to call. "Count on it," was Tower's reply. Then Anderson and Jim headed to the helipad for their ride back to Nha Trang. On the way back, Anderson told Jim of the stories about how LTC Tower had earned his Distinguished Service Crosses, one in Korea when his unit was overrun and he was the only officer who had survived. He led the remaining 35 men of his company in a fighting retreat back to friendly lines. He had personally killed several Chinese, one with a bayonet and had been wounded twice himself. His second DSC was earned in Vietnam in '63 on his second tour. He went to the rescue of four chopper crewmen who had been shot down near Tay Ninh. Tower was on a visual recon mission with his four man advisory group and had his pilot drop them off at the crash site. They fought off several VC attacks for three hours until help arrived. Although Tower had been wounded again it was because of his bravery and leadership that everyone made it out. Wow, Jim thought, the guy is a real warrior!

Five days later Jim's team was tasked with another reconnaissance mission. This time in an area southwest of Pleiku along the northern Ia Drang Valley, where it entered Cambodia. Less than a year before Jim arrived in Vietnam the 1st Cavalry had fought the American's first battle of the war against regular NVA troops there. The battle lasted four days and the US sustained over 500 casualties while the NVA was estimated to have lost over 3500 soldiers. Yet the Ia Drang Valley still remained a major infiltration route for the NVA into South Vietnam. Periodic forays into the area usually resulted in contact with the enemy. So now II Corps wanted an on the ground, clandestine, look at the area by Americans to see how much activity was really going on and assess whether the NVA was building any new infrastructure in the valley. The LRRP mission would last eight days and Jim's team would move into the target area by foot after being airlifted near Duc Co, a large village on QL-19 that had a Special Forces compound and was close to the Cambodian border.

Jim replaced the wounded SFC Jeffers with one of the team's sergeants coordinating its support. Jeffers would take his place at headquarters while he recuperated. This would keep the operational team at six. The team spent the days before deploying studying the map and reconnaissance photos of the area where they would be operating and preparing their gear. Then in the late afternoon of 8 August the team was transported by helicopter to the Duc Co SF compound on QL-19 east of the village. Duc Co was the last inhabited village in the area, just a few kilometers from the border. Once off the aircraft the team quickly moved off the air strip and faded into the low rolling hills to the south of the road. They would move silently and tactically for most of the evening to get close to the Ia Drang River and hide.

The terrain in the Ia Drang Valley was different from what they experienced on their last mission. The hills were low and rolling with the groves of trees farther apart and not as tall. There were also more open areas clogged with low bushes, Savana and Elephant grass, with water in a few of the creeks that laced the area running mostly east - west. There were also intermittent farm fields and rice ponds with terraces. The area along the border south of Duc Co near the Ia Drang River was dominated by the 700-meter Chu Pong Massif, ultimately the team's destination.

The first night the team moved slowly and without interruption and took up a hide site just to the north of the Ia Drang River. The hide site was well treed and bushy and provided excellent cover and concealment. The team would stay there three days sending out a three-man recon team each day to observation positions west, and then south along the unmarked border with Cambodia where they would hide and observe the area for any activity.

The first few days were uneventful, although there were signs of human activity in the area. The Montagnard camps looked used and there were trash piles that suggested soldiers had been there. But the team didn't see any NVA, local fighters or vehicles.

On day four the entire team crossed the Ia Drang River and moved south to the base of Chu Pong Massif. The mountain sits on the Cambodian border and at 700 meters high towers over the Ia Drang Valley to its north and all the area that surrounds it. Chu Pong would provide Jim's team with a commanding view of the Ia Drang River Valley and well into Cambodia. Chu Prong, which means "Uncle Prong" in Vietnamese, was a previously known headquarters for the NVA division that fought the 1st Cavalry Division during the 1965 Battle of the Ia Drang Valley.

Jim held the team below the mastiff until dusk, then they made their way up to the northwest outcropping and constructed three camouflaged observation positions that looked north, south, and west from Chu Pong. On the mastiff the team prepared a hide site on the lower north side in an overgrown area where the mountain reached the low ground.

The team would stay at Chu Prong for the last four days of the mission. From the heights of Chu Pong the team could observe any activity for miles around. It easily could see the various trails and two dirt roads that meandered south of the Ia Drang River all the way into Cambodia as well as the numerous trails that crisscrossed the area.

It wasn't until the sixth day of the mission that the team saw any movement in the area. On that day the team observed what appeared to be three logging trucks and a civilian jeep on the dirt road north of the village of Plei Me that winds along the south side of the Ia Drang and crosses into Cambodia before turning north. Plei Me was the only inhabited village west of QL-14 and south of Duc Co. It's about 8 miles east of Chu Pong. The team followed the convoy until it disappeared north into the rain forest on the Cambodian side of the border. The logging trucks were loaded, but not with logs, but boxes. The next day just after dawn the trucks with their lights on made their way back from Cambodia south down the road then headed east the way they originally came. Only this time some were filled with long logs and there were two additional covered trucks with them — five vehicles in all.

When the vehicles stopped just before the border for what appeared to be a rest break sixteen uniformed NVA got out of the covered trucks and milled around by the side of the road. Jim surmised that the loggers had delivered supplies to the NVA in exchange for hardwood logs and were now providing cover for their infiltration. When the trucks were a few kilometers northeast of Chu Pong, they stopped again and the troops dismounted. The covered trucks then turned around and headed back to Cambodia. The three loaded logging trucks and jeep continued on north towards QL-14, the hardball road that leads to Pleiku. The NVA soldiers dispersed and headed northeast in two eight-man groups. Jim reported the sighting to Nha Trang who said they would pass the info along to II Corps.

Later that day the team picked up several more trucks and three jeeps heading south on the logging road on the Cambodian side of the border. But this time they didn't turn into Vietnam on the road north of Chu Pong as the last convoy had, they continued south on the border road. They stopped about three kilometers south of Chu Prong where they unloaded additional troops that Jim estimated to be a company size unit. The NVA appeared to be heading southeast.

Jim wondered if the NVA had designs on Plei Me again, the isolated SF outpost to the east of Chu Pong that had been besieged in November of '65 at the beginning of the Battle of the Ia Drang. A successful attack on Plei Me would open up a clear infiltration route into II Corps. But an attack wouldn't be easy. The compound was now the home base of a Mike Force battalion who were much more capable than the regional militia that previously occupied the camp.

The team reported the truck convoys to Nha Trang, but they couldn't be engaged with air assets. This seemed odd to Jim, perhaps it was because the team was scheduled to egress the next day. Jim's team stayed hunkered down in the hide site that night but could hear constant noise from vehicles moving on the Ho Chi Minh trail on the Cambodian side of the border. Clearly something was up. At the 0600 report Jim told Nha Trang what the team had observed and heard. Nha Trang told him to just continue the mission as planned.

The following morning the team didn't observe any activity either on the friendly side of the border or on the Cambodian side. After a good visual reconnaissance of the area north of Chu Prong, Jim and the team left the hide site moving north to the Ia Drang River.

They moved tactically and everyone was on heightened alert, they knew there were some bad guys out there, just not sure where. They had about a 10-kilometer trek to get to the pickup LZ, which was just off QL-19 about three kilometers east of Duc Co. They crossed the shallow Ia Drang and kept moving north to try to steer clear of where they last saw the first NVA dismount their trucks. They then headed to the east of Duc Co where they were to be picked up at 1600 hours.

The team movement was slow and tactical and uneventful. They made it to the pickup LZ just before 1400 and took up a hidden position just to the north of the small field that was the LZ inside a tree line. About forty-five minutes later from their hide site the team spotted an eight-man NVA patrol walking in their direction outside the tree line on the southwest side of the LZ, about 1000 meters away. They were obviously unaware Jim's team was there. The NVA were walking in file in the open. Jim assumed it was part of the NVA group they had observed the day before patrolling the area. Through his binoculars he could see the fourth person in the group was talking on a radio that was on the back of the man in front of him as he walked. Jim decided a hasty ambush was his team's best course of action.

The team was in good concealed positions in the tree line, had cover, and a clear view of the NVA walking towards them. Jim quietly whispered to two of his men to stealthily move to a new position so that they could protect the team's right flank and still clearly see the approaching NVA. They quietly moved and now Jim's six-man team had three covered positions facing the approaching NVA and each man had good fields of fire. Jim would initiate the ambush when he opened fire. He would aim at the fourth guy who was talking on the radio assuming he was the leader.

As they approached the NVA stopped for a few minutes, still with no idea Jim's team was there. Jim thought maybe they would turn and move away in a different direction, but they didn't. When they started to move again they were unbelievably careless in their movement, walking in the open at the edge of the tree line with four of the eight guys bunched up behind the lead guy. The fourth man was still talking on the radio. The NVA point man was looking forward, but frequently turned to his right to look across to the far side of the open field as he walked. They must have felt safe as no one was paying much attention as they moved.

Jim's team had practiced hasty ambushes back in Okinawa as part of their immediate action drills so each man knew what to do. They all aimed at specific soldiers to shoot first and also identified who they would shoot second. In an ambush it is important that the initial fusillade hit as many opponents as possible to both reduce the number of enemy that could fight and minimize any return fire. In small ambushes against small groups the initiators were almost always the victors. So, it was to be with Jim's team.

Six minutes later Jim's initial shots hit the fourth man in the line of march in the chest when he was about 30 meters away and he went down in a lump. The rest of the team opened up an instant later and their fire was equally effective, taking out the next five guys in the line of march. The remaining two men hit the ground and tried to return fire, but they had no idea where to aim and they were quickly killed. In the space of two minutes all eight of the NVA soldiers were either dead or severely wounded. While three guys provided cover, Jim and two others approached the fallen NVA and determined that four were dead and two severely wounded in the head and would probably not survive. Two others had serious incapacitating wounds but might live if they could get proper medical attention.

Jim now had a problem. The ambush had likely alerted everybody in the vicinity that something was going on — and Jim didn't know where the other eight NVA from the original sixteen men they had observed the day before were. Now he had two severely wounded prisoners that he had to take care of if he wanted to capture them. The team still had about 30 minutes before pick-up. He decided he had to move the team and prisoners to an alternate LZ for the extraction, he couldn't take the chance that the other NVA were in the area and might come to see what was going on and look for their comrades. He had to move the team and soon.

Jim had his two of his men do a quick search of the dead NVA and two others attend to the wounds of the NVA that were still alive. The two with head wounds succumbed to their wounds in short order and another died while being attended to. The other wounded man was bandaged up and prepared for travel. One of the sergeants made a field stretcher out of ponchos and limbs cut from a nearby tree and put the wounded NVA on it. Jim and another sergeant moved the bodies of the dead into a pile where they could be found near the tree line. A sergeant booby trapped one of the bodies with two NVA grenades, to detonate if someone moved the stacked bodies.

Jim instructed his commo sergeant to try and make contact with Nha Trang and report the incident and then to try and raise the aircraft that would be picking them up. He hoped it might be close enough to contact, he wanted to let them know the situation and that he would move from the pre-arranged LZ. His plan was to move to the QL-19 hardball road about eight kilometers east of Duc Co and use the road as the new pickup location. It was close, about 1000 meters away from his present location and should be easy for the pilots to find. The team would come out to the road when they had the aircraft in view. Jim thought he could get to the road in about twenty minutes if he didn't run into anybody else.

The team quickly destroyed the NVA weapons before leaving by bending the barrels of the rifles and smashing the receiver groups. Jim took the dead leader's map and pistol. The commo sergeant couldn't raise the aircraft, but would continue to try as the team moved. Jim took the point with the commo sergeant next followed by two men with the homemade stretcher and the last two men providing rear security. The team moved out smartly, but cautiously.

Jim kept a sharp lookout as he moved and went as quickly as the team could with the wounded NVA on a stretcher. He was taking the shortest route to QL-19. Once at the road he planned to move east towards Pleiku for a few hundred meters to a good hide site. Once there he would set up a perimeter on the north side of the road and wait. When the chopper got to the team it would only take a few seconds to load the aircraft when it landed on the paved road.

Just before the team reached the QL-19 the extraction helicopter and its two escorting gunships contacted the team. Jim was about 100 meters from QL-19 when they called. The helicopter was alerted to the alternate pickup plan and was good with it. They were just nearing the junction of QL-19 and QL-14 and the pilot estimated he would be on station in eight minutes. Jim told the aircraft he would split the team and three men would load from the north side of the road and three with a stretcher from the south side. When he saw the aircraft coming down QL-19 from the east he would move to the road and wave to indicate the team's location. Jim recommended the pilot land heading east. The pilot rogered Jim's plan and turned down QL-19 to follow the hardball road.

Jim had the team split and moved three guys to the north side of the road, he and the two with the wounded NVA stayed on the south side. When he saw the three choppers in the distance Jim jumped up on the road and started to wave at the leading Huey. The pilot immediately saw him, flew past, and turned around in a big circle heading east as he dropped down. The helicopter landed on the road just in front of where Jim was standing. On touch down Jim's team immediately scrambled out to the chopper and jumped in, with the two stretcher bearers putting the wounded man on the chopper floor. The crew chief and a door gunner pulled him into the middle of the aircraft and then the men climbed in. Jim followed as last man. Fifteen-seconds after touching down, the Huey pilot pulled pitch, got altitude, turned left and headed for Pleiku and Holloway Field. It was another successful mission.

At Holloway Field the chopper landed at the hospital pad and the wounded NVA was transferred to the field hospital to be treated and then interrogated by II Corps Intel when he was stable. After dropping off the wounded NVA soldier the aircraft moved to refuel and then took Jim and the team to Nha Trang where they arrived early in the evening. Jim had the team stashed their gear in the team house and assemble in the mess hall for chow and a quick debrief. It was the end to a fruitful mission, no one was injured, and vital intel that was actionable was collected. The entire team was satisfied.

The next morning, Jim and his team sergeant briefed LTC Anderson, the group intel officer and his NCO on the mission. Following the brief LTC Anderson congratulated Jim on his team's good work and said he would be putting Jim and his team in for additional awards for their actions in ambushing the NVA squad and the success of their reconnaissance. Jim thanked the LTC and agreed to meet him for lunch. In the meantime he wanted to coordinate the movement of his team back to Okinawa with the group operations shop. As he was leaving the briefing the major who was the group S-2 Intelligence officer pulled Jim aside. He asked Jim if during the mission he or any of his men had observed black guys with any of the NVA elements they observed. Jim replied that he had not. The intel officer said that for the last few months there had been several reports from the Vietnamese about a black man leading NVA units in the II Corps area, but there was no hard evidence and no Americans had ever observed a black guy with any NVA or Viet Cong unit. Jim said he had heard that and asked if he thought it was true and what significance it had. The intel major wasn't sure, but there were a few black American soldiers missing in action or perhaps it could be an African. Until they had some creditable information it was all speculation — maybe it was an NVA with a bad tan? But he doubted American black soldiers were leading NVA troops. He thought that perhaps the ARVN intel was sketchy and the reports mistaken, but he always made it a point to ask when units returned from a mission close to the border. Interesting Jim thought. "Sorry I can't help," he said to the intel major and turned to go to the operations center to organize a flight to Okinawa.

Later at lunch with LTC Anderson Jim got a rundown of what was going on across Vietnam and the course the war was taking. It was August 1966, and the US had been in Vietnam advising since 1958 and American ground combat troops had been in the country since the arrival of the 9th Marine Expeditionary Brigade in March of 1965. LTC Anderson said that he anticipated that there would be a continued buildup of regular American combat forces, perhaps several more divisions. He also said there had been talk of additional Special Forces elements and he expected a full Special Forces Group to be stood-up by the end of the year. He said there was a need to up the training of the Vietnamese Special Forces and train more of the Civilian Irregular Defense Group (CIDG) militias, the fully indigenous militia that operated in the remote areas of the country. LTC Anderson had little regard for the Army of the Republic of Vietnam (ARVN), thought they were too political and poorly led for a force having been fighting for over a decade. They didn't operate very well with the local militia and as a whole were not very combat seasoned, avoiding a fight when they could. In LTC Anderson's opinion they lacked the aggressiveness needed to win wars. Jim was somewhat astounded at LTC Anderson's low opinion of the ARVN, but thought his assessment of additional American troops being sent to Vietnam was probably accurate. Clearly something needed to be done if the war was to turn in a positive direction.

Jim thanked LTC Anderson for his support during his team's mission and told him of the arrangements he had made for his team to depart for Okinawa in two days. Anderson approved and told Jim if he ever got assigned to Vietnam on a permanent basis to look him up, he'd always have a job for him if he was still around. Jim thanked him again and following lunch went back to the team house to complete the preparation for the team's movement.

The return to Okinawa went smoothly and everyone was glad to be back home. They landed just after midnight on a Tuesday. Jim arranged for the team to have a week off without using any leave to rest and recharge. He would do the same after briefing his chain of command on the mission. He was eager to rekindle his relationship with Kiko. Since he couldn't tell her where he was going or what he would be doing they couldn't exchange mail, although she surmised he was in Vietnam. Only once during the two months he was gone was he able to contact her — by radio-phone, and that conversation was sterile and short as he called her at the S-1 shop.

When Jim went to the S-1 shop the day after he returned he was informed that Kiko wasn't there. She had quit her job about three weeks prior and gone to Tokyo. No one knew how to contact her, but she had left Jim a letter.

The letter was kind, but essentially another "Dear John" letter. In it Kiko told Jim she had missed him while he was gone and that he was a kind and considerate gentleman. But Kiko's mother had a serious recurrence of her previous cancer and Kiko was obligated to take her to Tokyo for treatment. She wasn't sure when or if she would return to

Okinawa and she didn't want to string Jim along with the expectation of a future relationship. Gee, what a nice way to tell me it's over, Jim thought. He was taken aback by the letter. He had deeply cared for Kiko, even loved her, and thought she loved him as well. Perhaps he didn't understand the requirements of family responsibility that the Japanese had instilled in them starting at birth. Considering how things ended with Sharon, Jim was a little more stoic with Kiko's goodbye. But still his heart was wounded again and he was sad. To ease the pain of rejection Jim threw himself into his work.

The brief temporary duty in Vietnam had earned Jim respect within the 1SFG. He was now a decorated combat veteran having received a Silver Star, the nation's third highest military award for his selfless rescue of SFC Jeffries, and a few other awards for his actions during his brief visit to the war zone. But Jim didn't feel like a hero, just a professional soldier who did his duty. He assumed most of the men he served with would have done the same things he did in similar situations. But he was glad that he had passed his test: he could lead men in battle and was now a member of the warrior brotherhood. It was something he was proud of and knew could never be taken away from him. The best part was it came with the respect of his peers which meant more to Jim than any medal hanging from his chest.

With his nose to the grindstone the next several months seemed to fly by for Jim as he focused on his team's Okinawa training mission. He also tried to get as many parachute jumps in as he could so he could qualify as a Master Jumper. Then in March of '67 Jim left ODB-1120 and was re-assigned to the 1SFG staff as an Assistant Operations Officer. His job was to coordinate the group's activities in Vietnam. The 1SFG over the last few years had periodically sent MTTs, Mobile Training Teams, to the war to support the buildup of CIDG units and for other special operations, like Jim's previous LRRP mission.

By mid-1967 the war in Vietnam was in full swing with over 400,000 US combat troops on the ground in Vietnam. The 5th Special Forces Group was now a separate command under the Military Assistance

Tittsworth

Command Vietnam (MACV) and had decided that all rotations to Vietnam would now be permanent change of station (PCS) assignments for one-year tours and any temporary duty assignments would be restricted to essential extraordinary missions. Jim had had his taste of war and assumed that his next assignment would probably be back to Vietnam. He figured he'd be in Okinawa until the end of the year. But he was wrong.

Mike Force Commander

Twenty-three-year-old James A. Tittsworth was promoted to captain on 15 June 1967 and was pleased with the advancement. Captain is one of the best ranks in the Army and gives an officer lots of flexibility and opportunity for a variety of positions of authority and responsibility. Further, Jim was saving most of his salary, the little pay jump would be welcome and perhaps get him to his savings goal a little faster. He wanted to pay cash for a Corvette when he returned to the States.

Jim was also now eligible to command an A-Team. He had decided that if he could stay in the Special Forces community he would make the Army a career. He liked the closeness of the Special Forces officers and NCOs and that most of the soldiers were very professional self-starters. It made things easy when people were experts in their fields and you didn't have to ride herd on someone just to get them to do their job. He also assumed when he finished his tour in Okinawa he would be assigned a tour in Vietnam. At least he hoped so.

Sure enough, in the first week of September 1967 Jim received orders for the 5th Special Forces Group in Nha Trang, Vietnam. He was happy to go, after all if he was going to be a warrior and there was a war on, he wanted to fight. Jim didn't really have any political feelings about the war in Vietnam, he just knew the Vietnamese needed help and he would be glad to provide his expertise. He actually thought that the Vietnamese really just wanted to be left alone, to lead their own lives without any outside interference, but perhaps at this point in time that was just a dream. He also hoped his combat experience would be beneficial when he got to 5SFG so he could get command of an A-Team. On 25 September, Jim hopped a flight from Okinawa to Tan Son Nhut in Saigon. He was headed back to war.

When Jim reported in to the S-1 shop at Nha Trang a day later he was told LTC Anderson, who was now the deputy commander of 5SFG, wanted to see him. When Jim went down the hall to Anderson's office the LTC welcomed him to 5th Group.

After some small talk about Okinawa and the war, Anderson asked Jim what kind of job he was looking for. Jim without hesitation said he wanted an A-Team. "I suspected as much," Anderson said, "but Dave Tower, who you met on your TDY trip, has a need for a Mike Force company commander at B-24 in Kontum and I thought you might be just the guy for the job. I don't have an A-team slot open right now. If you don't want the Mike Force job, I can put you on staff until an A-Team opens up, probably in a few months. What do you say?" It didn't take Jim long to say he'd take the Mike Force job. It was a command and he would be working for LTC Tower, someone he admired and knew he could learn from. "Great," was Anderson's reply. "Tower extended his tour and I suspect when he gets promoted next July or August he just might get 7th Group back at Fort Bragg. I think he'll be happy to get you out to B-24. I'll get the assignment done and you get organized and read into what's going on for the next few days. Plan on getting to B-24 by the end of the week. I'll let Tower know you're coming." "Roger that Sir. Thanks for the assignment, I'm grateful," was Jim's reply and the office call was over.

After three days of in-processing, drawing his gear, boning up on B-24's operational status and II Corps' intel reports, Jim caught an early morning helicopter ride to Kontum to join his new unit.

When Jim arrived at B-24 on 29 September 1967, he was taken to LTC Tower's office next to the tactical operations center (TOC). Tower welcomed him and told Jim he was glad to see him again, that he heard great things about him. Jim replied that he was glad to be there. Tower told Jim he was putting him in command of his Bravo (B) Company, that the previous commander had been wounded on an operation a few weeks back and evacuated. SFC Rogers had been running the company since then and doing a good job. However, Tower said he wanted to get an officer in the command slot, but would keep Rogers on as his number two until he rotated out. Rogers still had several months remaining in his tour and could help Jim get up to speed with B Company.

Tower gave Jim a good run down on things at B-24. He learned that ninety-five percent of the battalion was made up of Hmong tribesmen, the rest were local Montagnards. Both of the tribes were indigenous to the central highlands of Vietnam and proud peoples. They were slash and burn farmers by tradition and extremely loyal to their tribes and extended families. The Hmongs in the battalion had adopted many of the Americans and Towers expected they would adopt Jim if they found him competent and trustworthy.

Unfortunately, the opposite of that was the serious lack of trust between the tribes and the Vietnamese, both the military and the government — especially the local Kontum province government. They provided little support to the battalion, yet wanted operational control. LTC Tower thought the administration in Kontum was corrupt and said he wouldn't be surprised if they were also in cahoots with the NVA. II Corps was not much better in their support, always late with pay and trying to send platoons to other provinces for operations which destroyed the integrity of the units and upset the men. The battalion was at about 85% assigned strength with 610 men operational and 35 convalescing. Bravo Company had a current strength of 137, but was authorized 150. Four men were recovering from wounds and not deployable. Many of the soldier's families lived inside the compound and took care of their soldiers when they were in camp and especially if they were wounded. The camp medics and hospital treated the families as well as the soldiers.

Tower told Jim that the Hmongs were some of the finest soldiers he had ever seen. They were resourceful in battle, physically tough and courageous. Their chain of command demanded strict discipline from the troops that was drawn from their ethnic pride. They were true professional soldiers who fought like hellcats unleashed - unlike many of the Vietnamese units. Tower expected his American cadre to treat their soldiers with the respect one warrior would give to another. Jim replied that that wouldn't be a problem.

Tower also told Jim that he usually kept one company at the camp as security, one designated as the Quick Reaction Force (QRF) for the province, who trained when not called out, and one in the field patrolling when he had actionable intel. But lately, they hadn't had any good results from the information provided by II Corps. Each company stayed on mission for a month then rotated into the next mission. Bravo Company was currently the province QRF until the end of the month.

Jim asked LTC Tower what he thought the North Vietnamese Army (NVA) and Viet Cong (VC) were up to, were they in a lull before a major offensive or was the buildup of American forces causing the NVA to pull back and just look for easy targets of opportunity? Tower said he didn't know. The battalion hadn't had much direct contact with the enemy lately, the patrols seemed to get to way-station camps just after the NVA had already gone and had only run into small patrols, usually no larger than a platoon, and they didn't stay and fight. Tower said that most of the NVA infrastructure was on the Cambodian side of the border and that was currently off limits. "Until we can really get at their base areas in Cambodia and Laos I don't think we'll be making much progress in destroying their ability to bring the fight to the South," Tower said, giving his frustrated opinion on the direction of the war.

LTC Tower also said he was disappointed that II Corps couldn't put together a better picture of the battlefield. His hunch was the NVA and VC were just biding their time until they could build up enough combat power to do something big while lulling the Americans to sleep. Time would tell, he just wanted to be sure the battalion was not caught napping. After his in-brief the LTC took Jim down to B

Company's area and introduced him to SFC Rogers, Jim's number two and the Hmong leadership of B Company.

SFC Roosevelt Rogers was a veteran Special Forces NCO from Cheyenne, Wyoming. So of course, his nickname was "Roy" Rogers, call sign Roy-6. He was well respected by both the American cadre on B-24 and by the Hmong and Montagnards in the companies. He was on his first tour in Vietnam. He had been with Special Forces since 1962, and by trade was a weapons sergeant. Rogers had spent most of his time in 7th Special Forces Group at Fort Bragg. Because he spoke fluent Spanish he had been deployed to South America and farmed out to both the CIA and the Drug Enforcement Agency working counter drug operations. He was professional, but laid back, never got too excited or too depressed. He knew his business. One of his best traits was that he never tried to boss the Hmongs around, but worked with the company's NCO chain of command and tried to be an advisor and sounding board, after all most of the Hmong NCOs had been at war for at least a decade. Jim liked what he heard of Rogers and thought they would make a good team.

After introducing Jim to SFC Rogers, LTC Tower told Jim and Rogers that he would like them to come to the team house about five o'clock so he could introduce Jim to the other Americans in the battalion, especially the staff and other company commanders. Jim rogered and said he and SFC Rogers would be there.

After learning each other's backgrounds, Rogers brought Jim up to speed on what B Company had been up to. Currently they were the QRF and training for the next two weeks. Rogers ran down the B Company Hmong chain of command. He took the time to give his impression of each Hmong NCO's strengths and weaknesses and how he had observed them react in fire fights during the five months he had been in B Company. Rogers, like LTC Tower, was also impressed with the short Asian warriors and told Jim they were damn good, he would go into combat with them any day. Jim was glad to hear it and expressed his eagerness to meet his Hmong NCOs. After about

30 minutes SFC Rogers took Jim to the B Company orderly room/ command post (CP) and asked the NCO on duty if he would round up the chain of command down to squad leader and ask them to come to the mess hall to meet the new company commander. The sergeant replied, "Yes Sir," and left the command post smartly to round up his colleagues.

Rogers told Jim that most of the NCOs spoke passable English, but many of the soldiers only spoke Hmong, which Rogers said was impossible to understand. He pointed out that the different clans often had different dialects and some could barely understand each other. Most of the soldiers in B Company were from the Kue clan that resided in the central highlands of East Laos and Western Vietnam. While waiting for the NCOs Jim and SFC Rogers looked over the large II Corps map that hung on the wall of the CP. Jim pointed out where he had run the LRRP missions the previous year. Rogers showed Jim where the company had deployed the last few months and where they had last made contact with the NVA. He also showed Jim on the map where Captain Russell had been wounded by mortar fire. He pointed out the areas where he suspected the NVA were in Cambodia. He also told Jim B Company's enemy contacts over the last few months had been chance encounters and not more than skirmishes. While B Company had killed several NVA and captured four, the company had suffered only two KIA and about a dozen wounded, including Captain Russell, but most were not seriously injured. It was SFC Roger's opinion that the NVA was mostly avoiding contact with the Mike Forces, but he didn't know why.

When the Hmong NCOs arrived in the company CP they were all in clean uniforms and well groomed. Clearly someone had told them they would be meeting their new American company commander that day and they wanted to give a good first impression. The Hmong NCOs all stood in line at attention, and it worked, they all looked quite professional and Jim was duly impressed. Jim had done his homework on the indigenous tribes that made up the American led Mike Force units. He knew that the Hmongs were fierce fighters and an ethnic people that did not have a home country — they lived in the mountains all over Southwest Asia having migrated out of China sometime around the 16th Century. They had their own spoken language with several dialects, but no written language until one was made for them by Catholic missionaries in the early 1950s. Patriarchal, they were very family oriented, slash and burn farmers and hunters.

Few of the Hmong had ever seen a white man until the French started to colonize southeast Asia chasing rubber and hardwood in the 1930s. The Hmong were renowned for their toughness and loyalty and were favored by the Americans for those reasons. They detested communism which they thought was godless and not family oriented.

As an ethnic group most Hmong distrusted the Vietnamese and there was serious tension between the ARVN and the Hmong and they didn't work well together.

To begin the introductions SFC Rogers introduced Jim to First Sergeant (1SG) Vang Kue, the senior Hmong NCO in the company and one of the most senior Hmong at B-24. He was very well respected as the senior 1SG in the battalion and a leader in the Hmong community. 1SG Kue was 47 years old and had been working with the Americans in Vietnam for almost ten years, first in Operation White Star from 1957-1962 when the US sent Special Forces teams into Laos to train the Royal Laotian Army and the Hmong and Yao, on guerrilla warfare so they could fight the Pathet Lao communists. Then he served as a bodyguard for SF teams when they were on MTTs organizing and training the rural CIDG units. 1SG Kue was from a small village just across the border in Cambodia northeast of Buon Ma Thuot and a senior member of the Kue clan, one of the largest of the 18 clans that made up the Hmong, and from which he got his name. Most of the soldiers in B Company were Hmong Kue. The 1SG had been at B-24 and in B Company as the Hmong 1SG for the past three years and spoke quite good English.

Once SFC Rogers finished introducing 1SG Kue to Jim, Kue took the lead and introduced the rest of the company's Hmong NCOs. When he had met them all Jim put them at-ease and had them sit while he gave them an abbreviated version of where he was from and his background. When he told them he was a Husker from Nebraska who grew up on a farm and played football at the University of Nebraska they didn't comprehend what he was telling them. Even 1SG Kue didn't know where Nebraska was other than it was a place in the United States. Jim tried to explain, but his men still didn't comprehend, they didn't have much of a concept of things outside the small world of the central highlands and nothing outside SE Asia. They just nodded respectfully. Jim ended by telling the NCOs that if they wanted to know anything about him they should ask. This amused the Hmong and they asked several simple questions like: what was a Husker - was it an animal? Where was Nebraska, was it big? What did he farm? How many cows did he have? Was he married? All in all, it was a good first meeting and when Jim left with SFC Rogers he was happy and honored that he would be serving with Hmong warriors.

After his meeting with his NCOs Jim and SFC Rogers went to the B-24 team house as directed by LTC Tower to meet the other Americans in the battalion. The team house was a large sandbagged building that was essentially just a big room — it had sandbags up to window height and two layers above on the plywood and PSP (porous steel plank) roof. The team house served as a sort of informal briefing room/club/gathering place. There were several tables and chairs and a plywood bar at one end. It was staffed by an older Hmong sergeant named Pha Roc who everyone just called Sergeant (SGT) Rock. He had been severely wounded and was no longer capable of being in a line unit or deployed so the Americans had put him in charge of the team house. He took the position seriously and did an excellent job of taking care of it. He was also the go-to person if someone wanted to obtain something that was hard to find in the way of military gear or anything from the local area. The team house bar served Vietnamese beer, and on occasion other beers that various folks would bring back from Pleiku's post exchange. It also had simple snacks to go with the beer and upon request local "delicacies" SGT Rock would make or procure.

There were two large maps on the wall: one of Vietnam and the other of II Corps. The Hmongs didn't come into the team house unless invited and in the company of an American. They had their own team house that was almost identical in another part of the compound that Americans didn't enter unless invited by a Hmong.

At the team house LTC Tower introduced Jim to his American staff composed of seven officers and seven NCOs. All but one, the intel officer, were SF qualified and most were on their second Vietnam tour. The Alpha Company commander, Captain David Jordan, and his number two were missing as Alpha company was currently in the field. It was patrolling near the border with Cambodia southwest of the village of Plei Re in the western part of the province. Jordan was a senior Captain and had received a direct commission shortly after Korea where he was a platoon sergeant in the 1st Cavalry Division. He completed Special Forces training in 1956 and was on his second tour in Vietnam.

The Charlie company commander was Captain Burwood "Bucky" Bonner. Charlie Company was currently assigned the camp security mission. Captain Bonner was from the Virginia hill country and had joined the Army in 1960, commissioned via OCS like Jim. He completed the SF Officers' Course in '62 and made his first trip to SE Asia on a training mission to III Corps as an A Team commander and then volunteered for Operation White Star. Single like Jim, he was a gregarious guy who loved a good time, telling stories, and pretty much kept the Americans of B-24 entertained. He could get a little crazy when he had a few drinks, but his self-effacing humor was a facade for a warrior of the first order. Bonner was awarded a Silver Star during his initial tour, when his compound had been attacked and the compound wire breached. First, he rescued his wounded team sergeant and then led the counter attack to recapture the compound. He killed three Viet Cong sappers inside the wire, the last in hand-to-hand combat beating the VC to death with a piece of rebar after he had stabbed Bonner. Bonner was sharp and fearless, a brilliant small unit tactician, and seemed always to know what was important when "the shit hit the fan." He loved his troops and they loved and respected him. They referred to him as Captain Bucky and they especially liked it when he sang to them. His extended tour would end in a few months — he preferred Vietnam to the States — which would give him 34 months service in SE Asia. Bonner was the kind of guy who thrived in war, but in peace time seemed adrift.

After the introductions LTC Tower welcomed Jim and Jim giving a short speech about his background the team relaxed for a "happy hour." Bonner and the intel officer, Captain Roger Hewitt, sat with Jim and gave him an informal run down on what life was like at B-24 and in II Corps. Jim told them about this previous LRRP mission and time in Okinawa. At the end of their discussion Bonner called SGT Rock over and ordered more beers and some fried grasshoppers. "Might as well break you in right Jim. Them hoppers are just like pork rinds, go great with cold beer, you'll love 'em!" Bonner promised. A few minutes later SGT Rock returned with six bottles of Vietnamese "Ba Muoi Ba" — Beer 33 — and a plastic container of dark brown fried grasshoppers, a salt shaker, and a pile of paper napkins. Bonner dug right in, popped a few grasshoppers in his mouth and said to Jim with his mouth full, "They pull the wings off these buggers before they throw them in the boiling oil and they come out crisp. I like them as they come, but you may want to salt 'em down." Jim just looked at Bonner figuring he best try the new field "delicacy" or he'd be off on the wrong foot in B-24. He picked out a big hopper from the plastic bowl and popped it in his mouth and bit down. It was crunchy and tasteless, like a crispy French Fry boiled in old cooking oil. He guessed if you didn't know what they were and didn't look at them, you'd just think they might be overdone fries. But he still quickly took a swig of beer to wash the oily taste out of his mouth. Bonner just smiled at Jim and remarked, "Glad you liked 'em, SGT Rock can get slugs too, they're a little sweeter and juicier." Jim just grinned and said, "Thanks, maybe next time."

Hewitt just laughed and when Bonner told him to have some hoppers he passed and said, "No, trying to quit — they're against my religion," and he took a long slug of his beer.

The happy hour lasted until it was time for dinner and by then Bonner and a few of the other officers were feeling no pain having each consumed several of Vietnam's most popular beer. After a few renditions of "Mary Ann Barnes" the ribald Mike Force theme song, the few remaining team members left the team house for the chow hall.

Jim was a little taken aback with the drinking. It seemed a bit reckless as they were in a war zone and you never knew when you could come under attack. He pledged to himself that he would never have more than one beer at the same sitting for the rest of his tour.

The following day, 1SG Kue came to the B Company CP with two soldiers and told Jim he needed to speak with him. When Jim approached he introduced the men as privates Tuo and Ren and told Jim they would be assigned to him as his bodyguards and assistants. One of them would be with him at all times when he was off the B-24 compound. They would also be his Man-Friday and that if he needed anything they would get it for him. Jim was a little surprised at the assignment of bodyguards and that he would now have aides. This was unheard of in the American Army until an officer reached flag rank. But this was standard practice for Mike Force commanders and a assignment of significance for the men who occupied the position, often leading to promotion. 1SG Kue had held body guard positions for American officers during his distinguished career and considered it a critical position only to be assigned to top performing soldiers. Both Tuo and Ren were skilled and experienced soldiers, chosen by 1SG Kue personally for the job. Both had learned English to qualify for the position. Jim shook their hands and told them both he was happy to have them.

Over the next two weeks, Jim focused on getting to know his company and read into what was going on in II Corps. He spent a lot of time with his platoons at the rifle range. He believed that being a good shot was critical for an infantryman. It was absolutely true that in combat the man that hit his target with first came out the winner of the engagement 97% of the time. He wanted his company to be great shots, he wasn't a bad shot himself, and to reach that goal they had to shoot a lot.

Towards the end of the month, six days before B Company was to relinquish the QRF mission, the company was called out.

A CH-47 Chinook helicopter had crashed southwest of the Dak Blau close to the Cambodian border - enemy territory - while returning from a resupply run to Dak To in Northern Kontum province. There had been no word from the downed aircraft since a May-Day call from the pilot as the Chinook was going down. It was not known if there were any survivors, although another helicopter had flown over the crash site shortly after the Chinook went down so its location was known. II Corps wanted the QRF to respond to the crash, rescue any crew that might be alive and report on the status of the aircraft. Based on the security situation and Jim's assessment of the Chinook a determination would be made if the aircraft should be retrieved or if Jim should destroy it. Getting friendlies to the crash site ASAP was the first mission. B Company was ready for it.

Fifteen minutes after B Company was alerted, two of the company's rifle platoons were sitting on the compound runway geared up and ready to go. Four extra medics were with the platoons to help with any casualties. While the rescue team was waiting for the Hueys to pick them up and ferry them to the downed helicopter Jim and SFC Rogers picked out a suitable LZ close to the aircraft's location to insert the QRF. The rescue party would require two flights of four aircraft. A team of B-Model gunships would fly cover for the combat assault. Once on the ground the B Company rescue party would move tactically, but quickly, the 1000 meters to the crash site. The plan was for Jim to go in on the second chopper. Once at the crash site the team would secure it, and render any aid necessary to the crew. Rogers would stay behind at B-24 and be prepared to bring out the other platoons if necessary and coordinate any support the rescue force might need.

Forty minutes after the alert call came in six Hueys left B-24 carrying two platoons from B Company headed for the downed Chinook. The rescue contingent was on the ground and moving to the crash site less than an hour after being alerted. The rescue mission was Jim's first operation as the commander of a Mike Force company and he was a little apprehensive. He had briefed the platoon leaders on the rescue plan and gone over the plan on a map at the airstrip, now it was time to execute. 1SG Kue was with Jim as his number two and inserted on the second to the last aircraft.

The insertion was unopposed and the lead platoon headed towards the crash site as soon as it hit the ground and organized. The two gunships that escorted the Hueys loitered around the LZ and would stay on station as long as their fuel would allow to provide fire support if required since the crash site was outside artillery range. But it was an easy day and the movement to the Chinook was accomplished quickly and without any resistance.

When the 1st Platoon reached the crashed helicopter, its medics went to the wreckage to search for survivors and render aid. The rest of the platoon pushed on to form a defendable perimeter away from the aircraft. Upon arrival the 2nd Platoon sent two squads to patrol the area in front of the defensive position out to about 1000 meters. The plan provided defense in depth and allowed the team working the crash site to do so without worrying about a surprise attack. There were no signs the NVA had attempted to reach the downed aircraft.

The medics discovered two of the four-man crew were still alive; both pilots. The two crew members in the back were dead, one found outside the chopper, apparently, he had been thrown out as the Chinook spiraled down and the other crewman was smashed and entangled in the collapsed wreckage of the Chinook.

One of the pilots had two broken legs but was conscious, still strapped in his seat. The co-pilot was also in his seat and alive, but unconscious. He had no visible external injuries and the medics thought he was severely concussed. The aircraft had spiraled down close to a small clearing, but had ended up smashed into the trees. Luckily there had been no fire as a result of the crash, although there was a sharp smell of kerosene in the wreckage. Jim instructed the rescue party to get the wounded men out and away from the Chinook as soon as possible. The dead were also retrieved and moved away from the crash site.

The conscious pilot told Jim that one of the Chinook's engines had flamed out and the aircraft had then lost hydraulic control. They had tried to auto-rotate down but the Chinook started to spin just as it approached the ground and the front rotor blades struck some trees. He didn't remember anything after that. He didn't think the aircraft had been hit by ground fire.

As medics went to work on the two pilots and prepared them for evacuation, Jim called in a situation report: there were two survivors - both pilots and two dead crewmen. The aircraft was a mangled wreck with a leaking fuel tank. He would move the pilots to his insertion LZ and requested they be extracted from there. There had been no contact or sightings of hostiles. His plan was approved and Jim sent 1SG Kue and the remaining squad from 2nd Platoon back to the insertion LZ to secure it. Jim had one of the squads from 1st Platoon salvage anything that could be carried away, radios: emergency kits, tools, etc.

II Corps had instructed Jim that if the aircraft in his opinion couldn't be salvaged he should destroy it in place. Jim thought the Chinook was damaged beyond repair so he had explosives and thermal grenades placed at strategic places in and around the aircraft, when the last B Company element left the crash site he set off the thermal grenades. The ruptured fuel tanks burst into flames when the leaking kerosene reached the burning thermals igniting a fire that quickly engulfed the entire aircraft. When Jim headed for the LZ the entire Chinook was a flaming inferno and shortly thereafter began exploding as the charges detonated, pulverizing what was left of the mangled helicopter..

The extraction at the LZ went off without any complications and the slick (slang for a Huey transport helicopter) with the two injured pilots and medics headed straight for Pleiku and the hospital chopper pad while the other five Hueys headed to B-24. The bodies of the two dead crew members were with B Company, it was policy that you never transported dead and wounded soldiers on the same helicopter, except in very extreme circumstances. After B Company was dropped off the flight of Hueys and the bodies of the two dead crewmen also headed for Pleiku and Camp Holloway. It was another day's work. The whole operation had lasted a quick four hours.

At the end of the following week, October 1st, B Company assumed the patrolling mission for B-24. A few days prior II Corps had presented the battalion intelligence officer a report about a suspected NVA supply point north and west of the village of Plei Grap on the Cambodian border. The location was in far West Kontum province about 50 kilometers from B-24. The area had a history of NVA activity and there were several logging roads and numerous trails in an area that the NVA were using for infiltration. Subsequently, B Company was given the mission to conduct an air assault into the zone and patrol the area to determine if the intel report was accurate. If so, the B Company was to destroy any NVA supplies and infrastructure they found. The mission was to last five days depending on what B Company discovered. Alpha Company, now on QRF, would be in support.

Jim and the company leadership spent the next few days coordinating the support for their search and destroy mission and getting up to speed on the intelligence. They coordinated for helicopter lift and air cover to support the operation, since they would be out of friendly artillery range. Jim's plan was to insert the company northeast of Plei Grap, the last western village in Kontum province eight kilometers from the border, take a circuitous route to the target area, and then sweep south along the border to a pick up LZ five kilometers southwest of Plei Grap for the return to B-24. The entire company would participate except a small element led by SFC Rogers that would stay behind at B-24 to coordinate any necessary support.

Four days after the tasking Bravo Company launched their combat assault at 0730 to an open field three kilometers northwest of Plei Grap. The LZ could only accommodate four Hueys at once so the initial assault was with four aircraft depositing 32 soldiers. The remaining four aircraft had to circle away from the LZ until the first flight landed and departed. They would then insert the last 32 men of the first lift. It would take two lifts of eight aircraft to get B Company and its gear on the ground. However, luck was on the B Company's side and the insertion was unopposed — although without a doubt anyone within a ten-mile radius knew some type of operation was taking place.

Once the first lift was on the ground the leading platoon secured the LZ and sent out fireteam patrols to recon the surrounding area. No surprise is a good surprise when operating in enemy territory. It took almost four hours to get the entirety of B Company on the ground as the aircraft had to refuel before they could complete the second lift. Once everyone was deployed the company moved seven kilometers west to a designated night defensive position (NDP), two kilometers from the border. The first night passed quietly.

On day two, Jim moved the company further west almost to the border then turned south in two columns paralleling the border with the platoons about 400 meters apart to try and get a good look at as much of the area as possible. The trails they crossed looked used and there were tire tracks on the road that followed along the border which had obviously been trafficked recently, but nothing of significance was found or observed. That evening Jim put out two squad ambushes, but there was no contact.

Things changed on day-three. Just before noon the lead squad of 2nd Platoon ran into a small element of soldiers dressed in khakis with web gear and weapons. They were clearly regular NVA troops and standing by a truck that was well camouflaged off to one side of a main logging road. It was a chance encounter and both elements were surprised at seeing each other. After an initial exchange of gunfire the NVA took off running south. Clearly something was up, but what? A search of the truck found it loaded with ammunition, food and four radios.

B Company didn't chase the scampering NVA, but Jim sensed danger and brought the platoons closer together as a precaution. He had the men take what they could use from the truck and destroy everything else including the truck engine and wheels. They set it on fire when they left the area and as they continued south they could hear the ammo on the truck cooking-off. The fire burned for the rest of the day.

By 1600, there had been no more NVA sightings or encounters, but Jim moved the company to the east away from their direction of march and the logging road. He found a small hill that was wooded and chose to set up the NDP there. The standard policy for B-24 units in the field was to dig in every night. At a minimum each position had to scrape out a fighting position that was lower than the terrain, the deeper the better. They were to camouflage it as best they could. This afforded soldiers some protection from indirect fire — mortars — and cover to fight from in the case of an attack. 1SG Kue supervised the preparation of the NDP while Jim called in his daily 1700 situation report (SITREP). He also checked to ensure he still had good communication with II Corps night forward air controller (FAC), it was his old buddy from the LRRP mission, Arizona HellCat (AHC). Communications were good and Jim felt a sense of relief when Arizona HellCat told Jim he was circling over Dak To and could be over his location in five minutes if needed and he had several sets of fighters at his disposal. Jim went over some procedures with AHC and told him he hoped he wouldn't need him. HellCat rogered that.

Jim also had two squad size ambushes sent out just before dusk, one to the west along the north-south loggers' road and one south targeting a prominent trail about 300 meters from the NDP. Two man listening

121

posts would be placed north and east at least 200 meters out from the company perimeter.

When the ambush squads went out Jim followed the one to the West several meters so he could take his "daily constitutional." He didn't like to relieve himself inside the perimeter even though he knew that 1SG Kue would establish a designated latrine. Jim just didn't cotton the idea that he would be squatting down in front of his men, so he always made it a point to relieve himself outside the NDP just before it got dark, it was bad enough in his mind that his bodyguard always came with him.

When he went back to the NDP 1SG Kue was waiting and told him everything was on track, ambushes were out, LPs in position and individual defensive preparations almost complete. Jim knew things would go smoothly, his Hmong warriors were just that — professional warriors — and knew how to operate in the field. "Good, let's walk the line," Jim said to 1SG Kue and he got up and pointed towards 1st Platoon.

As he moved out he turned and said to his bodyguard for this mission, "Ren, please help Radioman," slang for the radio telephone operator or RTO, "set up the CP. I'll be with 1SG Kue and return shortly." "Yes, Sir," was Ren's reply. B Company had two RTOs, one primary on the company net who was responsible for ensuring continuous contact with the platoons and with the B-24 tactical operations center when needed. The second, a backup RTO, Jim used to stay on the fire support net (FSN) which included the link to the II Corps forward air controller, currently Arizona HellCat. Both the RTOs knew what they were doing, spoke excellent English and could quickly and accurately pass on any messages Jim wanted sent.

Jim and 1SFG Kue left the CP just as the sun set to walk around the perimeter double checking the line, the positioning of the machine-guns, and to speak with the platoon leaders about their defensive plan. It was methodical and detailed, but when the "shit hit the fan" was not the time to be wondering if things were in order. At each platoon sector

Jim asked about avenues of approach to the position, cleared fields of fire, and checked for range cards. He also asked about positioning of the claymore mines and trip flares and how the LP teams would get back inside the perimeter if things went to hell. The Hmong platoon leaders were seasoned veterans and everything was as it should be. The NDP was as ready as it could be if the NVA chose to assault it.

One of the things Jim did on his round was to be sure each platoon leader's map had the same correct information plotted on it that was on Jim's. This was important if air support was needed or if the command group was incapacitated and one of the platoon leaders had to assume command and continue the fight. Jim also wanted to double check exactly where everyone was on the map and that everyone knew the locations of everyone else and the pre-planned targets he plotted. He didn't want any guessing. As he suspected, everything at the platoons was as it should have been and he and 1SG Kue returned to the company CP confident in the platoons' readiness.

At the CP, Jim did one more map study and tried to determine where he wanted to patrol the next morning. He also wrote out the coordinates of a couple of potential bombing targets around the NDP, just to save some time if he had to call for air support. The company had two days left before they would be extracted and he didn't want to get lazy now. When he was done Jim showed the map and targets to 1SG Kue and he marked them on his map. "OK 1SG, I'm going to eat and try to get some shut eye," Jim told 1SG Kue. "Roger, Sir. I have a few things and I'll do the same," Kue responded. Ren had heated some water under a poncho and offered it to Jim to pour in his indigenous ration pack that he always carried in his left pants pocket. "Thanks, Ren, remind me to get you a job as a waiter when this war is over," Jim told him with a smile. "Thank you, Sir," was Ren's reply also with a big smile on his face.

It was the line platoons that kept the watch — three-man positions, one man always awake, fully armed, and observing forward. While they had seen some signs the NVA was up to something in the area —

finding the truck loaded with ammo and some troops around it was a little concerning — there had been no big supply cache or camp found. Jim thought they had done all they could and tomorrow they'd look again further south and see if they could find anything for II Corps to bomb after they were gone. Two more nights and we're out of here, he thought to himself as he spooned some fried rice and vegetables into his mouth. When he was finished eating he stretched out, took out his poncho liner and pulled it over himself and closed his eyes to see if he could grab some sleep. It was about 2200 hours.

At 0300 the next day the listening post (LP) on the East side of the NDP in 1st platoon's area called in saying they had significant movement to their south. They couldn't see anything, but it sounded like a large group of people moving, maybe 150 meters or more to their south, slowly heading north/northwest towards the perimeter. The LP was about 200 meters east of the NDP hiding behind a large mahogany tree. They had put out three claymore mine ambushes to their north, east, and south, each about 30 meters in front of their position. They had coordinated a clear path back to the NDP, so they could scamper to the perimeter if the situation became too threatening. The 1st platoon leader alerted the CP about the movement and Jim put B Company on full alert. Jim had Radioman call in the movement report to B-24.

Around 0320 as the movement continued and edged closer to B Company the 1st platoon leader called the LP back to the NDP. As they got up to leave their position the claymore to their south exploded, followed by the screaming and yelling of wounded men. The LP kept moving as quietly and quickly as possible toward a piece of reflective tape hung from a tree about 50 meters out from the perimeter. There, they called the 1st platoon leader and said they were ready to enter the NDP. The 1st platoon leader gave the go ahead and the LP lead man took down the reflective tape, turned on a red flashlight, the signal it was friendlies and pointed it towards the perimeter. The 1st platoon leader saw the red light and said to come in on the path planned. The two LP men dashed to the perimeter and reported to their lieutenant. As they were reporting the claymore set to the east of their LP position exploded. Whoever was out there was paying a price for approaching the NDP, but it was clear that they didn't know exactly where the NDP was.

At 0400 the ambush squad to the southwest sprang their trap engaging what seemed to be at least a platoon of NVA moving up the trail. They had set the ambush so the first claymore was on a tripwire past the ambush squad's position. This gave them a clearer view of who was there, and good fields of fire into the flanks of the unit ambushed, creating a longer "kill zone." Instead of engaging just the lead element of whoever came down the trail they could now engage the main body of the unit. To the immediate front of their four positions facing the trail, several more claymore mines were set up that were command detonated. When the first claymore blew, wiping out the lead element of the NVA the ambush squad held their fire and waited several minutes silently in their concealed positions.

Foolishly, when there was no follow-up shooting the NVA assumed they had just hit a booby trap. They made the mistake of bunching up on the trail trying to figure out what had happened while assisting their wounded comrades and tending to the dead. Three NVA had been killed in the initial explosion and four others wounded. Then, to maximum effect, the Hmong squad detonated the rest of their claymores and unleashed a broadside of M-16 fire into the NVA who were milling around on the trail still trying to sort things out. The NVA were shocked, caught by complete surprise and decimated. When the shooting and claymores ended, the twenty-six-man NVA platoon sustained eighteen casualties with their platoon leader and platoon sergeant among the 11 dead. The remaining NVA who could retreated quickly down the trail in confusion. The B Company Squad threw three smoke grenades and two regular grenades and retreated to an alternate position about 150 meters away and closer to the NDP. As they moved to the new position they placed more claymores behind them in case anyone tried to follow. At their alternate position they hunkered down. They wouldn't try to return to the NDP until daylight unless they were called in.

Everyone in the NDP heard the claymores from the LP and then the ambush engage, but remained deadly silent in their positions. Everyone was locked and loaded and waiting. The Hmongs were disciplined not to fire until they saw a target they could hit. They didn't talk, move, or make any noise as they didn't want to give away where they were until they could initiate the fight. Jim wasn't sure how big a force he was tangling with and hoped the NVA didn't know for sure where the B Company NDP perimeter was. It was now about 0440 and it would start getting light out in about 40 more minutes.

Unbeknownst to Jim and B Company, the NVA was only a company size unit of 106 men. The three troops that had been chased away from the truck earlier in the day reported that they had only been engaged by a squad of ARVN. They thought it was just a long-range recon patrol that had stumbled onto the truck. Based on this report the NVA company commander decided he would try to find the recon patrol and destroy it. He was in charge of security for this operational sector of Kontum province and a significant amount of traffic would be infiltrating from Cambodia over the next few weeks. He wanted to make sure his area was clear of any ARVN so the infiltration would take place undisturbed and hopefully unseen. He didn't know precisely where the enemy recon squad was, but he directed a night movement back to the logging road near the truck so he could sweep the area when it got light out. If he ran into the ARVN squad before then he would attack them.

The NVA commander's plan was to send his three platoons after the ARVN patrol — he didn't have much respect for the South Vietnamese Army. He didn't think they were good fighters or very tough, and would run away if seriously assaulted. He'd move his company north from his bivouac in two columns; one following the trail that led northwest to the border logging road and the broken-down truck. Another column would move in parallel about 500 meters east, also heading northwest. Although he didn't know the enemy's location he assumed based on his experience fighting the ARVN, and his knowledge of the area, they would be somewhere on high ground east of the logging road, if they hadn't already left the area. He wanted his company to move during the night so he would be ready to sweep the area in the morning. Moving at night was standard for the NVA to avoid marauding US night fighter aircraft that were always looking for targets of opportunity. Even if his company was discovered an air attack would be less effective at night. He'd figure things out on the fly if the company ran into the ARVN squad his men had seen earlier in the day.

If he did find the ARVN he would launch a hasty attack with one of his two platoons to overrun them. He'd keep his other two platoons in reserve to mop up if needed. He didn't expect it would take long to dispose of a small ARVN recon squad. A successful attack on the ARVN would be a feather in his cap. Unfortunately, he had just about everything regarding the situation wrong.

The NVA didn't know they wouldn't be fighting an isolated ARVN recon squad, but an experienced company of veteran Hmong warriors who were dug in and prepared for battle. Under any circumstances one on one it wouldn't even be a fair fight, NVA conscript soldiers were no match for Hmong warriors, especially if they were dug in and waiting. Further, the Hmong had American air support if they needed it. With such overwhelming firepower, the NVA were at a huge disadvantage, even more so when it got light out. If the NVA stayed around to engage B Company in daylight they would be fixed targets for American jets and helicopter gunships. The NVA company commander knew from past experience that would be the case, but he foolishly chose to press on. He was determined to wipe out that ARVN squad.

By 0450 Jim had ordered both B Company ambush squads back inside the NDP along with the eastern listening post. He didn't want to take a chance the NVA would stumble on to one of them. Once inside the perimeter they reverted to their platoon sectors strengthening the company defense. The northern LP stayed in place and would not be called in until daylight unless they heard movement in their sector.

Jim was concerned about who he was fighting and where they would be coming from. He didn't want any surprises. He surmised from the ambush on the trail to the Southwest and the report from the eastern LP the NVA were moving towards B Company from what seemed like possibly two directions. He also knew the NVA were wounded, confused, and probably didn't know yet exactly where the B Company position was or what its strength was. He was hopeful the company could still surprise the NVA coming his way if they attacked and confident the company was about as ready as it could be.

At 0505 the lead element of the NVA's eastern most column tripped two claymore ambushes in 1st platoon's sector to devastating effect. The disciplined Hmongs of 1st platoon held their fire after the explosions, not wanting to give their positions away until they had good targets to engage. The claymores had been set in a staggered array of three then five starting 100 meters in front of the platoon's positions along the most likely avenues of approach to the NDP. Twenty-five meters behind them several trip flares had been placed along with additional command detonated claymores and 25 meters from the perimeter a last line of trip flares and command detonated claymores was waiting. It was a smart defense in depth scheme. By 1st Platoon not firing immediately, when the first claymores exploded the NVA stayed confused — still not sure if they were approaching an ARVN position or just running into stay behind booby traps. Either way they were losing more men killed and wounded and those not hit were now frightened and confused. All the while Bravo Company stayed hunkered down, quiet and continued to search for individual targets to shoot when the word was given.

After a long pause' as the easternmost NVA unit attended to their dead and wounded and sorted themselves out, they started slowly moving again. Although this time tactically in on-line formation and more cautiously searching for any enemy positions as they advanced. They still didn't know exactly where the B Company positions were, they could only guess that there were probably ARVN in front of them somewhere. Although the sky was clear it was still too dark to see very far forward in the bushy terrain.

Then suddenly, about seventy-five meters from the B company perimeter, the lead soldier of the NVA formation tripped a ground flare. In literally a flash it illuminated an area 25 meters around him exposing and startling the NVA formation, even though some dropped to the ground, clear targets for 1st Platoon were exposed and instantly engaged. A deadly hail of bullets aimed at individual NVA soldiers struck every one of that could be seen. While the NVA took cover where they could find it, some firing their weapons wildly at a still unseen enemy. After the initial skirmish the NVA platoon wisely drew back, seriously wounded, to determine what to do next.

The jig was up and the NVA now knew generally where B Company was, but was still not sure of its size as only Jim's 1st platoon had engaged with them. The other platoons had just watched their fronts and waited. After the initial deadly fusillade, the NVA commander wisely pulled his men back to regroup. He had taken significant casualties from the LP's booby traps, the ambush, and now the initial contact with the "ARVN" in front of him — he had lost close to twenty percent of his company. He began to think he was fighting more than a squad.

As he regrouped his men he decided the ARVN had to be dealt with. He would move the majority of his company northwest and then turn them east to launch a flanking attack on the ARVN position. He'd keep a reinforced squad on the southeast side to fire on the ARVN position and get their attention and pin them down so when he launched his attack from the West he would take them by surprise. At least that was his plan. Satisfied that he had a winning strategy, he directed his platoon leader in the East to form a twelve men squad with two machine-guns and remain with them in their current location. They were to stay in front of the ARVN positions and to attack them by fire on his command. The rest of the platoon was to draw back 200 meters and move northwest to join and reinforce his 2nd and 3rd platoons. They would then move to an attack position just east of the north-south logging road. When everyone was in place they would launch an all-out assault, two platoons abreast, from the West to overrun the ARVN position. It was now 0535, before morning nautical twilight — BMNT in military terms — the time before sunrise where there was light enough to see, but not yet clear daylight. The NVA commander instructed his platoons to move quickly and be in place to launch the final assault NLT 0615. Sunrise was at 0625.

After the initial firefight 1SG Kue walked the line again and checked on the men. When he came back he gave Jim an update on the casualties, there were none. First platoon thought they had really done some damage to the NVA who attacked them, but couldn't be sure. They also weren't sure of the size of the force that assaulted them, they guessed it was a platoon. Automatically with the lull in the fighting the Hmong redistributed ammo and made sure each man had at least 160 M-16 rounds, eight full magazines. Machine gunners and their assistant gunners had 2000 rounds. The company had six machine guns, two with each platoon. Standard combat load was for each man to carry at least two anti-personnel grenades and one smoke grenade. Each squad also had three claymore mines and four trip flares. With six machine-guns at the ready the company was heavily armed and had all of its organic fire power.

The perimeter claymores and trip flares were reset. The perimeter was still sound and everyone was alert. The 1SG had told the platoon sergeants to recheck their position defenses and then get the men fed in position and to rest who they could after sunrise when the chance of an attack would be reduced. Kue knew his company and was confident it could defend itself. When he returned to the CP he passed the update and his assessment to Jim who felt the same way.

These guys are as good as I thought they were, he said to himself as he studied his map under a poncho. When he came out, he had Radioman tell the 3rd platoon leader to bring in his LP. Everyone knew where everyone was now so no sense leaving the LP out by themselves. He followed up by having Radioman call in a situation report into B-24.

Jim then called Arizona HellCat on the fire support net. He was happy that AHC picked up right away. He advised Jim he was headed home to Pleiku and turning things over to Gunslinger6, the II Corp day FAC, who would be on station, hopefully within the hour. Jim advised him that he was under attack and expected another assault at any time, he needed air support if he could get it. He gave AHC his position coordinates. AHC rogered the location information and said he would pass it onto Gunslinger6 and notify II Corps Air Operations Center. AHC told Jim he had used his night allocation of F-4s in Dak To that was also under attack, but more air would be available for Gunslinger6, he just didn't know when. He thought he might get some diverts from I Corps if Jim was in contact. He would also suggest Gunslinger6 ask for helicopter gunship support from Camp Holloway in Pleiku, but they wouldn't fly until after sun-up. Jim said he could use all the help he could get and asked AHC to tell Gunslinger6 to give him a call as soon as he was on station. AHC rogered the request and said Gunslinger6 would have a better picture of the assets he would have available and when he could get them on station once he was airborne. Jim said that would be fine and signed off.

Jim was confident Gunslinger6 would have what he needed to support him when he came back on the net. B Company just had to hold on until then and he was confident they could. It was starting to get light out and would be sunrise soon so he knew the NVA probably only had about one more shot at him, if they chose to attack again at all before their situation became untenable once the air support showed up. Jim's main concern was that he just didn't know the size of the force attacking B Company. But the company was at 100 percent strength, dug in, had plenty of ammo and his men were experienced fighters. He couldn't ask for more. A little air support would tilt the playing field in his favor even if he was up against any serious size NVA force. He guessed he'd know the answer shortly.

Visibility was improving steadily and the NVA commander knew he was taking a chance, but he wanted to destroy this damn ARVN unit that had so decimated his company. They needed to be taught a lesson. He had moved his command post to a position on the west side of the ARVN just off the logging road in a shallow ravine with a group of tall trees that provided him good cover and concealment. He would command the attack from there. He knew that the ARVN didn't have artillery support or they would have used it by now. Of course, he didn't have his mortars either, they had been sent north several days ago to consolidate with other weapons units that were supporting an attack on the fire bases around Dak To. He wondered if the ARVN were important enough to get air support? It didn't matter now, he was just waiting for his lead platoon leader to tell him he was in place and he would give the order to attack. It shouldn't take long to over-run the squad that had become such a problem.

At 0617 a large flock of Little Egrets, beautiful white water birds, flew low over the small bump of high ground B Company occupied on their way to Lake Ho Ya Ly just west of Kontum. 1SG Kue looked up and watched as the birds gracefully flew by in the growing light, squawking as they flapped their wings in formation. He smiled and nodded his head pointing to the birds. The other Hmong in the CP looked up and smiled at each other. Jim looked up as well and commented that they were beautiful birds and smiled too. 1SG Kue looked at Jim and told him those white birds were special birds, pure and lived near water. They brought people good luck. It was a sign they would have a good day. Jim grinned and said, "I sure hope you're right First Sergeant, I sure hope you're right."

Three minutes later the NVA launched their attack from the south and west. The attack began with the NVA element in the South opening up with their machine-guns at what they thought were B Company's positions on the south perimeter. The firing was mostly high and off-target as the machine guns were poorly positioned and firing slightly uphill.

The 1st Platoon dug in on the south side of the NDP mostly kept their heads down and ignored the NVA suppressing fire. In reply the 1st Platoon Leader had his grenadiers lob a few grenades from their M-79 grenade launchers in NVA's direction to let them know they had a fight on their hands. First platoon was ready if the NVA chose to assault from the south. But they didn't, they just intermittently fired in the direction of the B Company perimeter hoping to hit something. The effort was essentially a waste of ammunition.

On the west side the NVA also opened up with their machine guns and fired several RPGs at what they thought were B Company's positions. Again, they were wrong and their fire ineffective. The NVA really hadn't identified the B Company positions and their lobbing of the anti-tank rockets at the B Company hill was useless other than to make loud explosions when the RPGs hit trees. Because the NVA still hadn't specifically identified any of the B Company positions on the west side of B Company's perimeter they weren't sure exactly what/where they were attacking. The assault up the high ground to the East was just a guess.

The NVA attack was a major miscalculation. It was based on erroneous assumptions derived from the reports of just three frightened soldiers who had been carelessly guarding a disabled truck. They reported that they were attacked by an ARVN recon squad, when in fact they had been chased from the truck by the lead element of a company. And it was not just any company, but a Mike Force company of well trained, experienced, and disciplined Hmong. The NVA had no fire support from artillery or mortars to soften up the enemy positions they were trying to attack or to cover their advance. The assault was straight-up infantry versus infantry which always gives the advantage to the defenders. And in this case the defenders had almost fifty more troops than the two attacking NVA platoons when the assault began.

The NVA commander's misconceived decisions that night had already exposed his company to two devastating ambushes as they crept through the bushy terrain looking for the enemy. A dawn attack against an enemy of unknown size, in unidentified defensive positions, significantly reduced the NVA's combat power from the start. The whole NVA operation had the makings of a textbook disaster.

When the main attack began B Company was fully prepared and in positions that were dug-in and camouflaged. In the poor morning light, the NVA could still not easily pick out B Company's positions among the dense vegetation as they advanced. B Company's perimeter in the west, like the south, had employed a defense in depth scheme by seeding the approaches to the NDP at various distances with an array of automatically detonated claymore mines and closer in with more command detonated claymores. They also had cleared fields of fire along the most likely avenues of approach to the perimeter and selected likely attack positions for the M-79 gunners to target. When the B Company positions were attacked the defenders enjoyed a huge advantage and could easily and effectively target any NVA moving in front of their concealed positions as they tried to negotiate the defensive minefield. The NVA commander's decision to continue the attack after the initial botched assault from the south was a colossal blunder that would ultimately result in the destruction of his company.

When the lead platoon of the NVA assaulting force got close to where they thought the B Company perimeter was, they stood up and rushed forward on-line, in mass, firing wildly. They were quickly cut down by the automatic and command detonated claymores, and plunging machine-gun fire that decimated the front ranks of the charge. No NVA got closer than 30 meters to the perimeter. Yet the NVA still tried to advance, following up the initial assault with a second. It was likewise cut down in a slaughter by the accurate and concentrated fire from B Company's protected positions.

After the two repulsed charges the ability of the NVA to attack was literally dead — they had sustained overwhelming casualties and it was now well past sunrise and air support could be expected at any time. The NVA company commander, having fatally expended his men, finally ordered a retreat that would take what was left of his smashed and crippled unit to a base camp in Cambodia.

When the retrograde began there were only two living officers left in the NVA company. The last 24 hours had resulted in the total destruction of the NVA company with 81 total casualties out of a beginning strength of 106 men. Most of the casualties were lying dead on the battlefield, killed in action (KIA). It was a resoundingly complete victory for B Company. With the withdrawal of the attackers Jim started to believe the NVA were really retreating. He started to relax when Gunslinger6 came up on the fire support net.

Jim was happy to speak with Gunslinger6 and filled him in on his situation. He told Gunslinger6, he thought the NVA were now in retreat, that he was not currently in contact and didn't have an immediate need for air support, but if there were aircraft available he could use them to attack the retreating NVA who he believed were heading west on the logging trail. Gunslinger6 rogered and told Jim he'd preferred not to use the air assets on retreating NVA unless it was a major unit and the targets a sure thing. His priority was units in contact. Jim understood and told Gunslinger6 he'd call again if he needed help. He thought he had seriously punished the NVA who attacked B Company, no sense wasting air assets when they could be used for someone in contact. Gunslinger6 said he was heading off to Dak To as it seemed that fight was continuing for a third day. Jim should call if he needed him, he'd be on the net. Jim wished him good hunting and ended the call. It was only 0730 in the morning.

Bravo Company's professionalism showed throughout the search and destroy operation. They had crushed an NVA rifle company and absorbed only one dead and six other casualties, just two serious, doing it. As the sky brightened Jim called B-24 for a MEDIVAC to evacuate his wounded. They in turn contacted the standby medical chopper who launched immediately from Pleiku and headed to B Company's location. The Tactical Operations Center (TOC) told Jim to move the seriously injured and other wounded men that needed to be extracted to a secure LZ and send the coordinates, the TOC would pass them on. Jim should expect the MEDEVAC aircraft to contact him within the next 30 minutes on his company net. Jim rogered the transmission and turned to 1SG Kue and asked him to find a close LZ for both the wounded and one the company could use for extraction. 1SG Kue replied, "On it Sir." He then called for the 2nd platoon leader and platoon sergeant to come to the CP. They quickly arrived and after a short map recon 1SG Kue and the 2nd platoon leaders left the CP, picked up a squad from 2nd platoon and headed east to check out a possible extraction LZ they had identified on the map.

As 1SG Kue checked out the LZ Jim made a call to LTC Tower and requested B Company be extracted that afternoon rather than the following morning. LTC Tower approved his extraction request pending him getting the aircraft to pull the company out. He would have the S-3 air contact II Corps and request lift helicopters and a pick-up time. Jim said that after the MEDEVAC of his wounded he would move the company east to a suitable extraction LZ and call the TOC with the coordinates. Tower said that would be fine and that they would get back to him with the answer on the lift aircraft and pick-up time as soon as they knew it.

LTC Tower also said that he was proud of B Company and the way they performed. It was a superb display of infantry skills and a resounding victory. It was something he would commend the whole company for when they got back. Jim thanked him and said his troops had carried the day, they truly were warriors of the highest order. LTC Tower replied, "No question about that Jim, they are as good as they come." He also praised Jim for his calm leadership during the battle.

Jim just replied, "Thank you sir." Tower then gave the radio handset to the S-3 who had some questions for Jim.

1SG Kue had identified an open field about 1000 meters due east from the NDP that would make a suitable LZ for the MEDIVAC and could handle the company's extraction as well. A 2nd Platoon squad was already there and the rest of the 2nd Platoon was tasked with joining them and securing the LZ making it ready for the extraction. First platoon would move the wounded to the LZ and get them on the MEDIVAC bird when it came. They would also be the first platoon extracted when the slicks showed up. Third platoon would be next to leave and the company CP would stay and leave last with 2nd Platoon. Shortly after the plan was briefed, 2nd Platoon moved out to the LZ and 1st platoon readied the wounded for MEDIVAC and moved out. Third platoon and the CP waited as a rear guard and followed thirty minutes later.

The company move to the LZ was smooth and professional, 2nd Platoon had secured the LZ before the rest of B Company arrived. The MEDEVAC showed up shortly after the wounded arrived at the LZ and they were on their way to the hospital in Pleiku by 0900. They would all recover. The TOC called back and informed Jim that the company would be extracted around 1530 and the lead aircraft would call him when inbound. Jim thanked the S-3 and closed the conversation with, "Roger, out here."

Now B Company had only to wait for their ride home. In the down time the platoons fed and rested their men. The extraction lift called in as promised just before 1530 and landed at the LZ shortly thereafter and moved 1st Platoon to B-24 on the first lift. Forty-five minutes later they returned for 3rd platoon. Following 3rd Platoon's drop off the slicks had to be refueled. When replenished they returned to the LZ for 2nd Platoon and the command group. By 1800 everyone from

Tittsworth

B Company was safely at B-24 and the Hueys headed back to Camp Holloway.

B Company was given three days off to recover from the field and then would assume the B-24 security mission for the month of November. The threat of attack on B-24 was low and the security mission static guard duty at home base. It was a time B Company could relax and when not on duty and be with their families, most of whom lived inside B-24.

The day after B Company's return Jim briefed LTC Tower, the B-24 staff and an officer from II Corps S-2 intel about the mission and battle. Following the briefing Tower told Jim to let him know which of his men should be put in for specific combat awards for their actions in the battle. Jim said he'd get with 1SGT Kue and the platoon leaders and have the recommended list to him by the end of the week. Tower was good with Jim's timeline.

The next few months went by quickly and quietly for Jim and B Company. They were deployed only once while on December QRF when an aircraft went down west of Kontum. The pilots and crew were killed. B Company's mission was to secure the crash site and help recover the bodies. The operation went off without a hitch.

In January 1968, B Company assumed the patrol mission for B-24. January was a confusing month for operations. It was after the Christmas holidays, but included the Asian Lunar New Year of Tet. The Viet Cong and NVA were usually quiet during Tet and the ARVN normally gave maximal leave to their troops. Operations on both sides were usually minimal. But the start of 1968 was different.

On January 30 the NVA and Viet Cong launched a coordinated nation-wide attack on strategic Vietnamese cities and American military bases. The NVA and VC units took the initiative and had initial success wreaking havoc on many of their surprised targets. However, the Vietnamese population did not welcome the invaders as anticipated by the Communists, nor did any ARVN troops desert over to the

NVA side during the campaign. In fact, the ARVN and US responded aggressively and over the following two weeks literally destroyed the Viet Cong as a fighting force while punishing the regular NVA units, setting back their operational capabilities significantly. The Tet attacks, despite the opinion of much of the press, were a failure and proved that the NVA invasion of the south could not result in the north holding any ground and that the VC did not have the support of the South Vietnamese population.

When Tet erupted B-24 was on high alert. Intel reports had indicated something was up, but no one was sure exactly what or where. II Corps had issued warnings to all of its commands to be cautious and alert, although normal leave and rest was permitted. LTC Tower placed two of the three line companies, Bravo Company and Charlie Company, on the QRF mission as a precaution. A Company took over camp security.

As part of their strategic plan the NVA attacked Kontum early morning on 30 January with the main effort coming from the Northwest. Their objective was to capture the province capital. While the NVA had the element of surprise on their side and made some initial gains, the ARVN and American forces responded with a fierce defense and prevented the NVA from overrunning the city. The NVA did, however, manage to get into the build-up areas around the airfield and near the provincial headquarters in the northern outskirts of the city. But the Americans of the 1/22 Infantry from the 4th Infantry Division and elements of the ARVN 23rd Division fought fiercely causing the NVA to curtail their assault and take refuge in a small area on the northwestern part of the city.

Following the initial set-back on 30 January, the Americans launched a coordinated counterattack with the objective of ejecting the NVA from their small conclave on the northwestern edge of city. The fighting was brutal, lasting three days until the NVA units, after suffering heavy losses, attempted to withdraw west to two small hills outside the city. But this too resulted in disaster when they were surrounded and eventually destroyed to the last man.

The Battle for Kontum was an all hands-on deck effort. Every ARVN unit in Kontum along with all the American units, local defense forces (Regional Forces/Popular Forces), and special troops were thrown into the fight. B-24 was given two tasks: keeping the Chu Pao Pass, sometimes referred to as the "Rock Pile," on QL-14 south of Kontum, open and establishing a blocking position west of the city to prevent the NVA from being reinforced or escaping. Alpha Company was assigned to establish the blocking position west of the city. Bravo Company was given the task of keeping QL-14 open.

The Chu Pao pass is about 15 kilometers south of Kontum and is the only road that connects Kontum with Pleiku, the two Central Highlands provincial capitals. The pass was critical for resupplying Kontum by road. If it was blocked Kontum would only be accessible by air and resupply would become very difficult with the numerous battles underway. Kontum's airfield was under continuous indirect fire attack making its use for resupply sketchy at best.

The Chu Pao pass itself is a three kilometer stretch of road that winds between Chu Pao Mountain in the west and Chu Hreng Mountain in the east. It is a perfect place to cut QL-14 either by ambush or indirect fire. Chu Pao is the higher of the two mountains at nearly 700 meters. The section of Chu Pao that flanks the hi-way on the west is a 1000-meter-long peninsula sticking out to within 200 meters of the highway. The Americans referred to it as the rock pile because there were numerous outcropping of boulders on Chu Pao's eastern face.

The mountain itself rises moderately for the first 150 meters and then becomes very steep the last 200 meters to a crest after which the mountain flattens out before gradually rising again to its relatively flat summit further west. It has bushy vegetation and tall grass from the highway until the steep upgrade is reached, then it becomes rocky and open. After the western crest there is dense bushy vegetation with intermittent groves of medium broad-leaf trees dominating the landscape. The very top of the Chu Pao is about five kilometers to the west of QL-14. Only a few trails are on the eastern side of Chu Pao leading up to the crest, but on top there are a number of larger and more frequently used trails that run both east and west and north and south. It was a frequent filtration route for NVA and VC units into Kontum province.

Chu Hreng on the eastern side of the pass is the smaller of the two mountains at 575 meters, but initially much steeper, rising steeply 75 meters off the highway up to a crest 200 meters above the road. Like Chu Pao it has heavy vegetation on the pass side of the mountain and the steep West side is mostly unsuitable for military movement. Although Chu Hreng is close to inaccessible from QL-14, it could not be ignored because from the western crest of the mountain there are clear views north and south for the length of the pass and several kilometers south down QL-14 to the highway junction where the road turns west toward Pleiku. If Chu Pao pass was closed the 15,000 troops and 15,000 civilians still in Kontum could be in serious trouble.

On the 2nd of February, after movement by truck convoy 13 kilometers south of Kontum on QL-14 to just below the Rock Pile, Jim deployed B company on each side of the Chu Pao Pass. Jim placed 1st platoon on the East side of the road with the mission to move to the top of the pass on the eastern flank and sweep the crest and high ground and establish a defensive position beyond the crest. This would keep the NVA from occupying Chu Hreng or causing any mischief from the east. Second and Third platoons were to go up Chu Pao on the west side of the pass and set up a defensive perimeter on the high ground near the center of the pass. They would patrol to the west, the most likely avenue of approach to the pass in the coming days to ensure no NVA were in the area and to prevent any from occupying any positions on the western side that could interfere with movement on QL-14. B Company would remain in place ensuring the pass remained open until the assault on Kontum was defeated or unless ordered to move sooner. By nightfall on February 2nd, B Company was in its planned defensive position and no NVA activity had been observed. However, things changed quickly on the 3rd of February.

At 0630 on February 3rd an NVA mortar squad casually walking east down a trail on top of Chu Pao stumbled head-on into the 2nd Platoon's newly constructed defensive position. It was an unlikely ambush, but effective. The mortar squad never saw 2nd Platoon until it was too late. In the short-violent firefight five of the eight mortar-men were killed outright, two were wounded and a third man captured. Second platoon had no casualties.

When Jim had the prisoner interrogated he said he was part of Weapons Platoon, 4th Company, 95B Regiment. He was new to his company and had only been in the south about three weeks. Yesterday his squad was ordered to establish a mortar position behind the Western crest of Chu Pao. The rest of his company with additional mortars were to link up with his squad tomorrow and finish setting up firing positions where they could fire on QL-14. Their mission was to cut the pass and prevent north-south travel starting on 5 February or until told to withdraw. Based on what he heard from the captive, Jim decided that he would set up several ambushes along some of the trails that crisscrossed the top of Chu Pao. His intent was to catch the NVA early, unexpectedly, and try to reduce their numbers and combat capability. He'd get his squads deployed before sunset so they would be in place if the NVA tried to move at night or early the next morning.

Just as Jim was finishing briefing his plan to the platoon leaders, one of 3rd Platoon's sergeants came running up to the CP and reported that his listening post (LP) had discovered a landline with a Chinese field phone connected to it. It was hidden behind a small tree just off the main trail about 200 meters west of the B Company position in front of 3rd Platoon. The phone was on the ground and the line led to the west. What did Jim want them to do with it?

Jim thought for a moment and determined that only companies or larger units would lay landlines and only then if they thought they would be in the same place awhile. He now worried that he might be facing an NVA company or even a regiment. He called for 1st Platoon on Chu Hreng to come over and join the rest of the company on Chu Pao after they completed their sweep on the eastern side of the pass. He wanted them on the west side of the pass NLT 1500 to consolidate his combat power just in case he was right and he had to deal with something big on top of Chu Pao.

After a quick discussion with SFC Rogers, Jim also decided to move the company north a bit so they could set up a stronger defensive position. Jim would go with the ambush squad so he could see the phone and landline for himself and get a better feel for what was going on. SFC Rogers would move the company and establish a new CP/ NDP with 1SG Kue and get the rest of the company dug in on high ground and prepared to defend itself. After the company had killed the mortar squad Jim guessed the bad guys generally knew something was wrong and would come looking for their people. To confuse them a bit he wanted the company moved. He also wanted 1SG Kue to find a safe route for retreat down the mountain to QL-14 from the new position just in case they had to get off the mountain in a hurry. Lastly, he ordered 3rd Platoon to ambush the land-line after following it west a distance from the position where they found the telephone.

SFC Rogers did a quick map recon selecting a very defensible location about 1500 meters to the North and ordered the company to move there. Second Platoon would lead the way. The new position was on a low hill that sloped down on its western side and offered good cover and concealment in a grove of small trees. It was protected on the east side by a steep drop off from the crest of the mountain. He had the company to move there with all due haste. The move was fast and uneventful and by 1400 the new position was occupied and platoons were digging in and setting up an NDP.

At the new location SFC Rogers spoke with 1SG Kue about a path on the northeast side of the hill that seemed to lead down northward towards QL-14. He asked him to check it out and see if it might be a route of retreat if the company had to move-out quickly. 1SG Kue said he'd have a fire team from one of the platoons walk it to make sure it was suitable. Kue also said he had advised the platoons not to set their claymore ambushes and trip flares until Captain Tittsworth returned to the company. He also instructed the platoons on the south and west to use CS grenades on some of their far-out automatic ambushes. If they had to fight an NVA regiment he wanted to restrict the battlefield as much as possible. SFC Rogers agreed with the First Sergeant and Kue went off to look over the platoon NDP preparations. SFC Rogers then radioed Jim informing him the company was in the new position and gave him a quick update.

By 1445 1st Platoon had completed its sweep of the high ground on Chu Hreng and had moved over to Chu Pao joining the company's new defensive position. The entire company except 3rd Platoon's ambush squad was now on the west side of the pass preparing the new defensive position. After digging in and plotting defensive targets SFC Rogers told the platoons to feed and rest the men and prepare for a high alert night. He told the platoon leaders to follow standard procedure and put out LPs just before dusk, but again reiterating not to deploy the claymores and flares until the captain had returned reinforcing 1SG Kue's previous orders. It would start getting dark just after 1745 and Rogers assumed Captain Tittsworth would be back well before then and the LPs could be sent out while it was still light out.

At 1310, Jim and his contingent; Ren, his bodyguard, the 3rd platoon leader and his sergeant arrived at the 3rd Platoon's LP location where the landline had been discovered. Jim wanted to personally get a look at the phone and exactly where it was found. When he arrived at the landline site he saw that a squad from 3rd Platoon was already there and had pushed a little forward and set up defensive positions facing west. What professionals, Jim thought to himself. He was continually impressed with the level of detail the Hmong attended to when operating in the field.

Jim examined the telephone and black insulated wire that was running off to the west. It was obviously set up in anticipation of someone returning to that location. There wasn't a good view of the pass so it probably wasn't an artillery or mortar observation post. But it had to be an important location if it had a landline. Clearly the NVA who placed the phone had been in the area before and considered it safe or they wouldn't have left it there unattended. The mortar squad was killed beyond the telephone's location so Jim guessed the phone's location was going to be a headquarters of some type. The NVA obviously didn't expect anyone, let alone a Mike Force company, to find the phone. This would prove to be a lazy, expensive mistake.

Jim told the 3rd Platoon leader, he would use the field phone if it was operational to call whoever was on the other end and try to set a trap to ambush them. He assumed the NVA didn't know the line and phone had been compromised or expected it would be used to set a trap. The 3rd Platoon leader had designated the squad at the site to be the ambush squad. On order they would set up an ambush near the line further to the west. Jim, the platoon leader, Jim's body guard Ren, Jim's RTO, and one other soldier would stay with the field phone where it was found and join the ambush later after the trap was set. Jim told the ambush squad to advise him when they were in position and set up. He would then initiate the trap. The ambush squad leader rogered his orders and quickly moved out following the land-line west.

The plan was that once the ambush was executed, after the bodies were searched and any wounded tended to, everyone would hastily move back inside the B Company defensive position. If the ambush wasn't sprung everyone would stay in the ambush position until the next morning. Jim said he didn't want the ambush to evolve into a sustained firefight. It was a shoot and scoot mission. Jim had the 3rd Platoon leader coordinate directly with the B Company CP and then directly with the platoon leader manning the sector of the perimeter on the trail where they would enter the NDP. Jim wanted to be sure of the route back to B Company and identifying signals were clearly known by everyone so there would be no mistakes, especially if the ambush was set off at night, and the squad was hustling back in the dark.

About 1400 the ambush squad called the 3rd Platoon leader and said they were in position about 200 meters further west down the landline. They were in a concealed ambush site on the east side of the main Chu Pao trail just where it turned west. They had laid out an L shaped ambush and deployed five claymores. They were ready to go. The ambush site was about 1500 meters southwest of B Company's new defensive position so it shouldn't take long for Jim and the rest of the ambush squad to make it back to the NDP once the trap was sprung. After the trap was set Jim and his group would quickly move forward to join the ambush and provide rear security.

Following the ambush squad's call, Jim told the platoon leader to ring up the phone and if someone answered to just say, "Hello" and then hang up, acting like he was cut off and couldn't hear who was on the other end. They would then wait a minute or so and do it again, only the second time the platoon leader would say, "Hello, this is sergeant..." and then Jim would use his Randal knife to cut the wire, they would then all move out smartly and follow the landline to the ambush position. The idea was that if they reached someone on the call they wanted it to sound like there was something wrong with the line. The hope was that it would cause the NVA to send someone down the line to find out what the problem was and the ambush would be waiting for them.

Everything was ready and at Jim's command the 3rd Platoon leader made the first call. Someone picked up on the call after the second ring and said, "4th Company..." then the lieutenant hung up. He waited a minute and made a second call, and when it was answered again he said quickly, "This is sergeant ..." and Jim cut the line and it went dead. The trap had been set. Immediately Jim and his small group got up and followed the landline to the ambush site. After Jim and his crew arrived the squad leader went out and cut the landline again dragging both sections into the middle of the trail where it would be easy to see. It was now in the center of the ambush kill zone. Jim was happy with what he saw, the ambush was well prepared. Now all they had to do was wait.

At about 1440 hours Jim and the ambush squad could hear movement to their front, someone was approaching from the west walking down the land-line. But they were not sure what size of an element it was. Everyone was locked and loaded and tense. Several minutes later a squad of five NVA were observed following the land-line looking for a break. Their heads were down as they followed the line right into the middle of the kill zone. When they bunched up to examine the wire the Hmong detonated the claymores and opened fire quickly killing them all. The engagement only lasted about 15 seconds, but it was surely heard for a considerable distance from the ambush.

When the firing stopped Jim ran with the search team to search the NVA bodies. He took a marked map from a dead NVA sergeant who apparently was the squad's leader. The markings on the map appeared to show where specific units were. He also had a notebook with different call signs and frequencies, Jim took that as well. It was a gold mine of information. The search team took what they could use, destroyed the NVA's weapons, and stacked and booby-trapped the bodies in a pile just off the trail where they died.

The ambush struck Jim as an example of one of the cruelties of war. Unlike the Americans who would fight to recover their dead's bodies and return them home, in many situations the NVA didn't or couldn't and their dead were left where they fell to rot away. Their families would never know what happened to them, where or how they died. They were just gone forever. It was a war wound on families that never healed.

After the search of the NVA soldiers the ambush squad changed one of the command detonated claymores to an automatic ambush and repositioned it for maximum effect. Jim let B Company know they were enroute to NDP and the ambush squad moved out smartly maintaining tactical integrity. The movement was without incident and Jim and the ambush squad were safely back inside the B Company defensive perimeter a little before 1600. Now all of Bravo Company's elements were together and prepared for a fight.

The ambushed NVA were carrying a reel of commo wire, another field phone, and tools common to signal linemen. Jim surmised that they were some kind of communications squad. This indicated they were affiliated with at least a regimental sized unit and that scared Jim. While he had confidence in his company, it was still only one-fifth the size of an NVA regiment. He knew the "shit-was-hitting-the-fan" all over II Corps and the NVA and its Viet Cong affiliates were attacking every major city and military base in II Corps as part of the Tet Offensive. What Jim didn't know was how the American and ARVN counter-offensive was going either in II Corps or elsewhere in Vietnam.

B Company had only been in the field a few days, but it seemed like they had been out of touch for a week. Jim and the rest of the company were starved for information about the NVA offensive. So far B Company had only seen and engaged two small NVA squads, just one a regular combat unit, the mortars, and a support squad from a communications element. This told him something was up and a larger unit was in the area — or would be soon. It concerned him that if he had to take on a regiment or something larger while every other II Corp unit was also engaged B Company might not get the priority it needed for air support — he was well outside the range of friendly artillery — to defend itself against a larger foe. But the die was now cast and all he could do was set up a solid defensive position, report where he was and what was going on, and ensure he kept solid commo with his higher headquarters and the fire support net so he could ask for help if/when he needed it. When he called in his 5 PM SITREP he also had Radioman double check communications on the fire support net (FSN). Jim didn't want to wait for an attack to find out he had a problem calling for help. The radio communications with higher and the FSN were "5 by" solid and clear.

The NVA 95B Regiment had been given the mission to block QL-14 NLT 5 February, to prepare a new base area around Chu Pao, and to establish several supply caches around the mountain. The regimental commander gave this mission to his 3rd and 4th Companies and placed the deputy regimental commander in charge. The four other 95B companies were part of the NVA force attacking Kontum and were operating north of the Dak Blau River.

The new base area was to be occupied by 95B only if the Tet Offensive was unsuccessful in capturing Kontum. Currently 95B's companies on Chu Pao were on their own and not expecting any contact with the ARVN. When the ambush of the NVA commo squad erupted just about everyone on top of Chu Pao could hear it. When the NVA deputy regimental commander heard his headquarters couldn't raise the commo squad sent out to fix the landline he knew there was something seriously wrong. He decided to have 3rd Company sweep the area and check out what had happened to the commo squad and see if they could also find the missing mortar section no one had heard from since their morning call in. He would keep 4th Company with him in reserve as he looked for a suitable location to establish 95B's new base camp.

Just after 1700 B Company heard an explosion that indicated that someone had tripped a claymore. A few minutes later there was another explosion that could only mean someone had tried to move the dead commo squad bodies. It also meant the NVA were only about 1500 meters away. There was only about 60 minutes of daylight left, so if the NVA were going to try to find B Company they had to get a move on it.

The commander of 3rd Company, 95Bravo was a veteran NVA commander. He had fought the French, the South Vietnamese and now the Americans. He was in his 14th year as an officer in the NVA. He had good confidence in his experience and believed he knew how the ARVN and Americans fought and could defeat them. He also knew that daylight was running out and that whoever was ambushing the regiment's troops had to be somewhere on Chu Pao. He decided to sweep the high ground on top of Chu Pao in a looping movement from south to north with two platoons abreast. He'd use the crest of the mountain to protect his Eastern flank. With any luck he might catch the offending unit as they were moving and could conduct a hasty attack to wipe them out or at least drive them off the mountain.

He too knew there were numerous battles going on in II Corps and figured that the ARVN had probably called in all its main units to defend the cities and the Americans would be defending their bases. That meant it was probably a local Regional Forces/Popular Forces (RF/PF) militia patrolling Chu Pao and setting ambushes and they seldom operated in more than a platoon size. If he could find them and close with them, his veteran force would destroy them if they didn't run away. RF/PF units were low on the priority list when it came to getting US air support so he wasn't too worried about that and suspected they were also out of artillery range or he would have been fired on by now. No, if he could find them he would attack them and destroy them.

After a short briefing in which the NVA commander laid out his plan to his platoon leaders he directed third and fourth platoons to move out as soon as they could get organized. The 3rd platoon moved first and when it reached the eastern crest of Chu Pao, where it started to fall in a steep decline down to QL-14, the platoon turned north and stopped. Fourth Platoon waited just past the ambush site until 3rd Platoon had reached the crest of Chu Pao then it began moving east until its right-flank squad had contact with 3rd Platoon's left squad. Both platoons then went on line and began advancing cautiously north. The other two platoons followed in column as reserves. It was 1715.

It didn't take long until B Company's two LPs reported hearing movement to their south, estimated 300 meters out. They couldn't be sure the size of the force moving — they estimated a company advancing on a broad front. Since there was still some daylight Jim called both LPs in to join their platoons, he didn't want anyone left alone outside the perimeter to be killed or possibly captured. He then sent SFC Rogers to anchor the eastern side of the perimeter and 1SG Kue to the western side to shore up that end of the NDP. Jim would stay in the company CP in the center and. manage the expected fight from there. Then he immediately got on the fire support net and asked for air support.

When Jim called the B-24 Fire Support Officer (FSO) he was told the FACs were all tied up over Kontum as the city was still under attack from the northwest and now northeast. He asked about helicopter gunships. The FSO told him that may be possible, there were two enroute to Holloway Field to refuel and rearm, he anticipated that would take about an hour maybe 90 minutes as they still were north of Kontum. Jim said he'd take them as soon as he could get them, he anticipated he would be under assault by elements of 95B shortly. The FSO said he'd see if he could speed-up the gunships and if he got any fast movers he'd try to send them his way, but 1st 22nd Infantry, the American battalion defending Kontum, was in quite a fight just west of the city and they would get priority. Jim said he understood and would wait for the FSO to call him when he knew what support he could provide.

The lead elements of 3rd Company, 95B were in attack formation as they moved north along the crest of Chu Pao's eastern flank. They were moving slowly, but methodically because they didn't know where the anticipated RF/PF unit was. When they were about 150 meters from the B Company perimeter the point man for the company tripped a claymore and was blown away along with his slack-man, two other soldiers were wounded. There was a CS Grenade (tear gas) taped to the front of the claymore. When it exploded the CS gas was thrown forward and the NVA not hit by the claymore's pellets were caught in the gas cloud and began to cough and choke — incapacitating them and giving away their locations. The immediate area they were in was now a hazard to any NVA who tried to move through it. The NVA had not yet seen any of the B Company positions, but B Company now had eyes on them, experienced and disciplined, they held their fire.

The NVA's 3rd Company commander halted the company and drew it back as his lead platoon attended to its wounded. He assumed the RF/PF unit was up ahead, but still didn't know exactly how far since there was no direct engagement, just a mine ambush. After a quick review of the terrain on the map the 3rd Company commander surmised that the RF/PF were probably on a small hill to his front left, if they were still around. He'd assault that hill, but first try to soften them up a bit.

He called the weapons platoon, actually it was just two tubes of mortars, his other mortar squad was unaccounted for. The 95B regimental weapons company and the line company weapons assets (mortar and rocket squads) had been consolidated for the Tet Offensive. Most of 95B's company mortars were currently deployed north supporting the attack on Kontum. Only four mortar tubes had been left to support the blocking of QL-14 at the Chu Pao pass. After the earlier ambush one squad was missing. Now there were only two tubes available and these were attached to the 4th Company of 95B. Luckily 3rd Company was still within their support range.

The 3rd Company commander's call for fire was approved and shortly Bravo Company was subjected to a short barrage of incoming mortar rounds from two tubes of 82mm Chinese mortars. The fire lacked adjustment and most of the rounds fell long outside the B Company perimeter. However, a few rounds did land inside the company's position and four Hmong were wounded by the barrage, one seriously. Because B Company was dug in the mortar rounds were minimally effective, but they got everyone's full attention. Jim assumed the NVA now knew where the company was and he could expect a ground assault soon. It was just before sunset.

The commander of 95B's 3rd Company chose to attack as soon as the weapons platoon's mortars finished softening up his objective. He surmised he was fighting a squad — maybe a platoon — of local RF/PF militia. He didn't think they would put up much of a fight, especially after they were pounded with mortar fire. But he was dead wrong. He was fighting Hmong warriors, experienced Hmong warriors, who were dug in and expecting an attack. He couldn't have dreaded a more seasoned or formidable opponent.

When the mortars stopped the 3rd Company commander ordered his two lead platoons to firm their lines and assault the small hill just to the north of their location and destroy or capture anyone occupying it. If things got bogged down he would send in one of his remaining platoons to reinforce the attack and restore momentum. He didn't like the idea of attacking near sun set, but it was better than attacking at night. He launched his ground assault at 1740 about 20 minutes before sun down.

The initial assault was a disaster. The platoon on the right of the line was devastated by the claymore ambushes B Company had set. And when the remaining NVA stood to rush forward at the few Hmong positions they thought they had located, they were cut down with murderously accurate small arms fire. The NVA platoon on the left of the line didn't fare much better. They too got entangled in the claymores and were pilloried with small arms fire. Neither platoon advanced very far forward from their attack positions.

B Company easily repulsed the first wave of attackers with only two minor casualties. The NVA on the other hand had lost a third of the two platoons in the assault, 13 killed and over 15 wounded. Shockingly the 3rd Company commander now realized that he was not facing any rag-tag RF/PF troops, but probably a veteran ARVN company at least. As he drew his company back to regroup and tend to the wounded he decided to bring up his trail platoons and re-launch the assault. Surely the ARVN couldn't withstand another assault by fresh troops. This time he would focus the attack on the right side of the enemy position attacking from the west, he had more room there, and perhaps he could find a weak spot or even an exposed flank and roll up the position from there.

He ordered his 1st and 2nd Platoons to reload and prepare to attack again. He moved his third platoon to his left flank just behind the 1st Platoon. They would closely follow the 1st Platoon's assault, and then once the ARVN positions were identified, attack through 1st Platoon and over-run the enemy's right and then sweep east to clear the objective.

The 2nd Platoon would attack on the right, the ARVN left, in the same sector it had before. If it broke through it would consolidate on the crest of the hill before the drop-off. If not, it would engage the ARVN and keep them from moving to assist their left flank.

At 1815, Sunset, the 3rd Company, launched their second assault. It was no more successful than the first. The lead elements of the attack on the western side of B Company's perimeter were devastated by the claymores and still hindered by not knowing exactly where the Hmong positions were. It didn't help that the sun set was behind them and they couldn't see very far forward. B Company, on the other hand, had many of the advancing NVA silhouetted when they stood up to move and easily cut them down with well-aimed rifle fire. The NVA's 3rd Platoon was similarly cut down and stopped when they tried to pass through the lead platoon and the battle field became a jumbled mess with wounded everywhere and small pockets of NVA seeking cover from B Company's well aimed fire. The attack quickly bogged down with significant casualties and the attackers never got within 30 meters of the B Company perimeter before the attack faltered. After twenty minutes without advancing, and sustaining significant casualties, the 3rd Company commander ordered a withdrawal. The 3rd Company's effort had resulted in only more casualties with no ground gained. B Company suffered only three soldiers slightly wounded from the second assault.

It was now quickly darkening and 3rd Company was not in any condition to continue to attack. Fully two platoons were combat ineffective after sustaining over 50% casualties. The company only had one remaining platoon that had not been engaged. The company commander wasn't sure what he should do next and even less sure of how big a force he was fighting. He called the Deputy Regimental Commander and explained the situation. He was told to hold in place and the 4th Company would be moved forward and ordered to attack at first light. The Deputy Commander thought it was too risky to try a night assault. Third Company was ordered to recover, attend to its wounded and hold in place. The mortars would be used to soften up the ARVN position with some additional mortar fire as 4th Company moved forward and got into position.

The second assault on B Company had been as ineffective as the first attack. The company sustained only three casualties from the assault. SFC Rogers was one of them, hit in the arm by a deflected bullet. Wounded, but more pissed-off than anything, after he was seen by a company medic and bandaged up he was back in the fight. Jim was still uneasy with the situation, especially that he didn't know what size force he was fighting and it was now dark out and he hadn't heard from the FAC about any air support. When he called again they reiterated that all the air assets were being sent to Kontum and Pleiku and he was on his own for the time being.

After consulting with 1SG Kue and SFC Rogers he decided to move the company off Chu Pao that night and not chance facing a possible regimental assault in the morning. He also worried that the NVA would pound B Company all night with mortars and this time adjust the fire. If he could get the company down the mountain quickly to a new location by QL-14, he could escape the mortars and be positioned to get his wounded out in the morning. When he got air support he would pound Chu Pao with air strikes. This seemed like the wisest course of action. He felt like B Company had bloodied the NVA's nose so they would probably be reluctant to chase him until it was light out at which point he would have the advantage.

1SG Kue and SFC Rogers agreed with Jim that moving to QL-14 made sense. Jim called in this plan to B-24 and LTC Tower approved the move. Jim wanted to get going and told 1SG Kue to get the wounded rounded up and start them moving down the trail he had reconned earlier in the day ASAP. The company would move by platoon and 1SG Kue would take 2nd Platoon with the wounded and set up an NDP somewhere defensible to the north on the east side of QL-14. He would move out as soon as he got organized. SFC Rogers would take 3rd Platoon and the company HQs with him and follow 1SG Kue 15 minutes later. Jim would stay in the NDP with 1st Platoon as the rear guard and move down the mountain once everyone else reached QL-14. It was now close to 2000 hours and Jim wanted the mountain to be clear by 2130.

One of the best qualities of the Hmong was that they were disciplined. Fifteen minutes after Jim's order 1SG Kue had the wounded ready to move and he set off down the trail with the 2nd Platoon to QL-14. They had reconned the trail previously and so could now move quickly. Jim and SFC Rogers consolidated the rest of the company ensuring the NDP was defended. Rogers then organized the rest of the company except 1st Platoon and prepared them for movement. At 2045 he and his contingent moved out down the trail. Jim again consolidated the NDP positions and had several automatic ambushes set at strategic locations around the NDP as a gift to anyone who might try to follow the company as it withdrew. Precisely at 2130 he and 1st Platoon moved out of the NDP and down the trail towards QL-14 and the rest of the company. Twelve minutes later, the NVA started shelling the small hill B Company had evacuated with mortars. The mortar barrage would be intermittent on and off for the rest of the night. But since their target was an unoccupied hill the barrage and subsequent fire was a colossal waste of ammunition. No one was anywhere near where the rounds were falling.

By 2300 all of B Company was off Chu Pao and in their new NDP on the East side of QL-14 three kilometers closer to Kontum. The new location was called in to both B-24 and the FSN to ensure B Company's new location was not mistaken for an NVA position. The new NDP was secure and defensible and unlikely to be directly attacked. The rest of the night passed uneventfully.

The following day, 4 February, the NVA assault of Kontum was broken and the city cleared of NVA. The bad guys had withdrawn what was left of their main force to a hill complex west of town where they were ruthlessly attacked from the air and by elements of the American 1/22nd Infantry. Over the coming days the entire force was destroyed and the Tet Offensive in the highlands soundly defeated by the 7th of February.

The Chu Pao pass remained open during the entire attack on Kontum. B Company seriously hurt the two companies of 95B on Chu Pao when they attacked. The next day Jim coordinated several air strikes on Chu Pao to devastating effect. This was followed up by a B-52 strike on Chu Pao on the 8th of February, then a combat assault by a regiment of the 21st ARVN Division. What was left of the two battered 95B companies on Chu Pao quickly hightailed it to Cambodia. By the 9th of February 1968, 95B was no longer an effective fighting force in South Vietnam.

The Tet Offensive was declared officially over by 8 February. While the NVA and Viet Cong had initially wreaked havoc with their surprise attack across the country, the end results for them on the battlefield were disastrous. The Viet Cong were essentially crushed following the counter attacks by the South Vietnamese and Americans and would never again be a significant military force. The regular force NVA units were also decisively defeated on the battlefield with most of its deployed units suffering significant casualties and forced to withdraw to their safe havens in Laos and Cambodia where it would take years for them to reconstitute. The South had taken a punch, but responded effectively. However, from a media and political standpoint one would think the NVA and Viet Cong had been successful. The ground truth about the North's Tet Offensive was almost 180 degrees different from the media's portrayal of the offensive.

On the 7th of February B Company was convoyed back to B-24 by truck to recover from the operation in Chu Pao Pass. LTC Tower was pleased with the overall performance of the battalion. To ensure everyone understood what had gone down during the week of Tet he held a debriefing and after-action review on 12 February where each of the company commanders went over their unit operations during Tet and what they learned/could have done better. All-in-all the battalion had performed very well and suffered only minimal casualties. Two of the wounded were SFC Rogers and A Company's commander Captain Bonner, but neither were hurt badly.

Captain Bonner had been wounded during a battle on the 4th of February. That day Alpha Company was still in a blocking position along the Dak Blau River west of Kontum and had engaged an NVA unit trying to escape the city along the river. Bonner was struck by shrapnel from a mortar round that peppered his left leg. He was hurt and hobbled but had stayed in the fight. During the encounter A Company had punished the NVA element in a fierce firefight, killing a number of them and astonishingly capturing six NVA including the unit commander. Bonner was put in for another Silver Star, his third, for his actions during the battle. Following the fight Bonner was MEDEVACed to Pleiku for a few days to have the shrapnel removed from his leg. He returned to B-24 three days later.

When he got back to B-24 on 10 February he was now an official "short timer" scheduled to leave Vietnam in March when his tour of duty was up. Rather than going to Nha Trang to out process early he was staying at B-24 until the last-minute waiting to see who his replacement would be. On his way home, he was planning to go to Thailand.

At the team house a few days after the debriefing Jim and Bonner and SFC Rogers were relaxing over a few beers and rehashing Tet when LTC Tower came in and asked if he could join his fellow warriors. They were glad to have him and he sat down and joined the conversation. When Bonner started talking about his upcoming trip to Thailand on his way home he asked Jim if he had ever been there. Jim answered no, heard it was a great R&R destination, but he hadn't thought about it. He was thinking about Australia or perhaps Hawaii for his leave when it came up. LTC Tower chimed in that Jim's R&R could be taken any time since he'd been in the country for over six months. Bonner then suggested that Jim join him in Thailand for a week. He knew a few places and sites to see as well as the best clubs in town. He also offered that the Thai women were the best looking in Asia and the most talented. Everyone got a chuckle out of Bonner's comments, he was the only one at the table that had been to Thailand and he had a reputation as quite the ladies' man.

LTC Tower thought Bonner's suggestion was a good idea as he wasn't sure Bonner could stay out of trouble if he went back to Thailand alone. "Why don't you go with him Jim?" Tower said. "Rogers can run the company while you're gone and I believe B Company is scheduled to be on security detail in March. It's a good time to be gone." "That might work Sir, let me think about it," Jim replied. "Ya, Jim come to Thailand with me, I guarantee you'll have a good time," Bonner piped in with a big smile on his face. "Gentlemen, give me a minute to think about it, I'm not sure I can afford to go to Thailand with the esteemed Captain Bonner as I don't think I have the bail money that will be required!" That set the table to laughing and Bonner called out to Sergeant Rock for another round of "Ba Muoi Ba" for everyone.

A Warrior in Bangkok

Three weeks later, on 3 March, when Jim arrived at Don Muang air base north of Bangkok Bucky Bonner was there waiting for him. Bonner had left Vietnam a few days earlier having out-processed from 5th Group in Nha Trang and was on his 30 day leave enroute to his next assignment at Fort Bragg. He had come to Bangkok for a little vacation prior to heading back to the States where he would take the remainder of his leave before showing up at Fort Bragg for an assignment at the Army Special Warfare Center. Jim had coordinated this R&R to link up with Bonner in Bangkok, but he didn't expect he would be at the airbase to greet him.

Bonner was happy to see Jim and Jim was pleased as well. He thought he was lucky to have someone to show him around Bangkok and the surrounding area. There were several things he had picked out of a guide book he wanted to see and Bonner had been there a few times previously and knew his way around. During the taxi ride into Bangkok Jim marveled at the tidiness of the countryside. It looked a lot like Vietnam, but he guessed a lot less dangerous as Thailand was not at war with itself.

After a thirty-minute ride into town Jim arrived at the SQ Boutique Hotel, a place Bonner had recommended and reserved a room for Jim. He was staying there as well. The SQ was right in the heart of Bangkok within walking distance of the main club district and not far from the best restaurants and the Grand Palace district where Wat Pho and several of the renowned ancient palaces and temples were located.

Bangkok was like most major Asian cities in the 60's, a thriving, over-crowded, metropolis. It was along the Chao Phraya River, just north of the Bay of Thailand and a major commercial hub. The city had been established in the 1500s. Because of its strategic location it became the official capital of the various kingdoms that ruled Thailand from the mid-1700s when Thailand was known as Siam. It had an estimated population of about three million in 1960, as far as could be assessed. Bangkok was also the center point of the western modernization of the region and became the focal point of various political power struggles for Siam and then Thailand over the years.

Sadly, Thailand was allied with Japan during WWII and Bangkok was largely destroyed by Allied bombing during the campaign to liberate Indochina. Following the war Bangkok revived rapidly because of its location and flourished as a major trading center for Southwest Asia. Then with the increasing US involvement in Vietnam Bangkok became a major destination for troops on leave from the war zone and developed a thriving tourism industry, a major part of which was the sex trade.

On Jim's first night in Bangkok Bucky took him to the Peninsula Restaurant. It was a huge floating barge on the river that specialized in various Asian delicacies and a variety of seafood dishes. A Nebraska farm-boy, Jim wasn't sure what some of the offerings were, but after the sea urchin and squid rice with lobster and snow peas he was hooked. It was the fanciest meal Jim had ever had, perhaps the best, and astonishingly one of the cheapest. Sitting out on the veranda Jim thought to himself, to think ten days ago I was filthy dirty, eating plain rice out of a pouch I carried in my pocket and guys were trying to kill me. Damn life has a lot of ironies! He'd visit the Peninsula twice more before he left town.

After the fancy dinner Bucky took Jim to the Club Keynote. It was in the heart of the Nana Plaza District, one of the city's designated "free zones". While it advertised as a disco, it was really a well known bordello. Whoring was legal in Thailand as long as it was not on the streets and there is a cornucopia of clubs, massage parlors, dance halls and bars that cater to whatever taste you had for sexual company. With Bangkok close to Vietnam and the war in full swing there were plenty of single American GIs who were looking for some intimate female company to reduce their pent-up testosterone levels. Bangkok was just the place to cure that condition and the city's sex tourism was a growth industry.

The Club Keynote was a straight up whore house with a bar and a dance floor. It was in a medium sized three-story building. The place had a typical modern disco themed front entrance complete with a sign with flashing lights and a rotating disco ball. Speakers on the roof of the entrance blared the latest pop music. Inside on the first floor, the lighting was dim and there was a long bar on one side of a large room. Around the room were groups of overstuffed chairs in various configurations situated around a dance floor that had a small stage at one end. When Bucky and Jim walked up the steps to enter they were met by a large, well-groomed man dressed in a coat and tie. It seemed to Jim his purpose was to keep the drunks and undesirables out of the club. He asked the two Americans if he could be of service. Bucky, who had been to the Club Keynote several times before on his prior trips to Bangkok said that they would like a table to have a few drinks. The man graciously bowed and said in perfect English, "Certainly," and led them inside to a group of four overstuffed chairs with a small centered table near the middle of the room. The quaint location was across from the bar and with a good view of the small stage at the far end of the dance floor. Both men sat in the comfortable chairs and glanced towards the stage and bar trying to get a feel for the place as the music blared a tune by The Beatles. Lights were flashing over the dance floor and on the stage. With the music so loud, it was hard to hear when Bucky tried to say something to Jim. There was a reason the music was loud in these types of places — it made you get close to the person you wanted to talk to and so conversations couldn't be overheard.

Jim noticed immediately that the stools around the bar were full of young, scantily dressed girls who all were looking over at the two new arrivals sizing them up. Bucky and Jim looked like what they were: two young American GIs on a Rest & Relaxation vacation from Vietnam. The place wasn't crowded, but there were a number of other people, all men, sitting in the overstuffed chairs with half-naked women who had joined them. A DJ was at a small table beside the stage where a tall and slender young girl was dancing to the music.

Shortly after they sat down a woman, well made-up and attractive, but clearly not a teenager, came to the table and asked what they would like to drink. Bucky had warned Jim that he should keep his wallet in his front pocket and only drink beer. Also, he should ask for the price of everything he ordered so he wasn't hit with a surprise bill when he wanted to leave. This was especially true when one of the girls would come by and ask if he would buy her a drink. Bucky told Jim the story about the first time he had visited the club and bought a girl two drinks as he negotiated some time up-stairs. He was shocked when he got the bill for the drinks and it was $52. The girl's company was only $60!

Bucky asked the lady what they had and she rattled off a list that included just about every kind of alcohol. Jim asked how much the beers were and she said $5. Jim and Bucky both ordered San Miguel beers. After the beers were delivered two attractive girls from the bar sauntered over to where Jim and Bucky were seated and asked if they could sit down. The two horny Americans happily said "sure" and motioned to the empty chairs at the table. The small talk with the girls was pleasant and a bit of a worn-out routine: "Hi, are you American? Where you from? How long you in Bangkok? You Army man from Vietnam?" It always ended with, "You buy me drink? You want company?" Like a whore house veteran, although a straight-up rookie, and remembering what Bucky had advised, Jim responded to the drink request, "How much is a drink if I buy you one?" "Depends on drink," came the reply. "Well, what do you like?" Jim asked. "Bangkok Tea, very good," was the reply. "Ok, how much is a Bangkok Tea?" Jim asked. "Me thinks maybe $10," was the girl's reply. "OK, order one," Jim said. The girl raised her hand and the good-looking older waitress immediately came over to the table. "Get us a Bangkok Tea - how much is it?" said Jim wanting to double check the price. "It ten dollars," said the waitress. "OK, get one for the lady please," Jim commanded and the waitress turned and headed to the bar to retrieve the drink.

Because of the loud music Jim couldn't hear what Bucky was discussing with the girl beside him, but they were engaged in deep conversation and the girl was nodding and smiling as was Bucky. Jim had never been to a bordello before, hadn't even been laid in quite a while, and wasn't sure exactly how to proceed. Clearly, by the look of things Bucky was an experienced whore house veteran. Jim figured he'd just play along and when he felt the urge tell the girl he wanted to go upstairs — but he'd get a price first!

The girl sitting beside Jim was tall for a Thai woman, she stood about five foot seven. She was well built with long legs and perky breasts nicely proportionate to the rest of her body. She had smooth tan skin and almond eyes with a shiny smile and pretty face. Jim thought she couldn't be more than eighteen, but it was hard to tell with Asian women. Jim thought she had a little too much make-up on, especially the red lipstick, but she was quite attractive and her English was good, if halted. Jim decided to try to find out a little about her and wondered if he could pierce the personal veil most whores kept between what they told potential clients and their real life. He'd give it a try.

Jim turned to the girl next to him and said, "So what's your name?" "Mary," the girl replied. "Interesting name for a Thai girl," Jim replied, "What is your name in Thai?" "Mary, my English name," she said. "Dara, my name in Thai. It means flower." "That's a beautiful name, can I call you Dara? Is that OK?" Jim asked. "Sure, you can call me Dara - but at work Mary is better," came the reply. Jim guessed Dara didn't want to get too personal while she was working. "OK, I'll call you Mary then," Jim said. "Where are you from in Thailand, Mary?" Jim asked. "Me from north near Lampang, you know Thailand?" came the reply. "Oh no, this is my first time in Thailand, I don't know much about it. I don't know where Lampang is," Jim said. "It way north, very beautiful, but not so many people and not fun like Bangkok," Mary said smiling. "Wow, how did you get all the way down here to Bangkok? Did you come down just to work in the club?" "No, I go school, I want to be nurse. I just work Club sometimes, I need money. Very expensive live in Bangkok." "Interesting," Jim said and wondered if any of it was true. Whores needed a cover story, but it really didn't matter to Jim, he wasn't at the Club Keynote to find a wife, or even a girlfriend. Both he and the girl knew that they were just playing the game so everyone got comfortable before things got down to business. Jim wondered if he was expected to say something or the girl would offer to take him upstairs. He wasn't sure, he'd just play along and assumed things would work out the way they were supposed to.

As Jim was talking to Mary, Bucky and the girl with him stood up from the table. Bucky leaned over to Jim and said, "Partner this girl and I are going upstairs for a little horizontal mambo. Don't wait around for me — not sure how long I'll be gone. I'll catch you for sure at the SQ tomorrow. Make sure you take care of yourself." "Roger that," Jim replied, "You just make sure YOU take care of yourself." "Don't worry, Ms. Kathy and I are old friends!" Bucky said with a grin and he grabbed Ms. Kathy's hand and led her towards the stairs. Jim just smiled and shook his head.

"Your friend look happy. You want to go upstairs too?" Mary asked when Jim sat back down. Nothing like being direct, he thought. "Perhaps a little later, let's talk for a while." "Ok, what you want to talk about?" Mary replied a little miffed Jim didn't want to play, the night was getting on and if Jim wanted to waste time talking she might miss out on additional customers. But Jim was in no hurry, he knew he'd get laid and he wanted to get the full experience including the foreplay banner. He also wanted to know a little more about "Mary."

"Tell me Mary, how long have you been in Bangkok?" Jim started a new conversation. "I be here almost a year," Mary honestly replied. "How long have you been at Club Keynote? There are lots of clubs in Bangkok. Why here?" "I know girl friend from Lampang she used to work here say money good, men here nice." Interesting Jim thought, it might even be true. "How old are you?" Jim asked next. "I 22," Mary replied growing tired of the questions about her.

"How long you be in Bangkok?" Mary asked back. Two could play this game. "Just five days, I'll head back to Vietnam next week." "You like the fighting, the war, you not afraid?" was Mary's next question. "Well, I don't think about it. I just do what I'm told and try to take care of my men," was Jim's honest reply. "Where you live in America? I hope I go there someday. Maybe next year." Mary was on the offensive now. "I'm from Nebraska, in the middle of America. I'm a farm boy." "Oh, I come from a farm too. Farming not have much money in Thailand. Better farming in America." "I suppose you're right, we Americans are pretty good farmers. On my farm we grow wheat and soybeans and have some cows." "My farm has chickens and some pig and my mom grow squish. How you say in English, big green and yellow like carrots?" "You mean squash. We have some of that in the US, but not where I come from." Jim was starting to warm up to this girl. "So, Mary, tell me how you really got to Bangkok, I don't think it was for school," Jim asked, genuinely interested. It amazed him how so many cute young girls in Asia, anywhere really, went into prostitution. He always thought good looking young girls would have better options than whoring. "Well, I want to be nurse, but my family have no money so I sign to take job in Bangkok with a woman who say she have lots of good jobs in Bangkok. She says she can help me get in school to be nurse too. But once I get to Bangkok she does not has job and without money I can't get in school. I have no money so I need job. I know a friend who work at club and she say money good if you are at a good club and so I give it a try. It not so bad, but I save my money and will go to school when I have more money." "Well, I hope you do," was Jim's reply, thinking Mary's story might be true. For the next while Jim and Mary exchanged stories — dreams really — she mostly about wanting to travel and see the world. Jim telling her about the places he'd been in the States. After a while Jim kinda took a liking to Mary, after all she was good looking and interesting, and didn't yet seem hardened by the superficial glamor and plastic life of a prostitute.

After about 30 minutes, another San Miguel and Bangkok Ice Tea, they both had grown comfortable with each other. Jim asked politely, "Mary, how much does it cost if I go upstairs with you?" "You nice guy, I give you deal — $200 American you spend night, if we just go a little while it $80." "Wow girl, will you be nice to me?" "Yes, I be very, very nice," Mary replied with an evil smile. "Ok, let's go. Do you have a room?" "Yes," was Mary's reply and she stood up. Jim did the same and followed her. When she got to the stairway leading upstairs a lady at a small counter by the steps handed her a key and she motioned for Jim to follow.

On the second floor there were about 15 rooms off of a plain carpeted hallway. It could have been any motel on Highway 66 in the US. When they got to the room Mary opened the door and stood by it as Jim entered. She closed the door but didn't lock it. Then she turned to Jim and said, "You give $80 now." Jim said, "OK," and took out his wallet and counted out four $20 bills and handed them to Mary. She took the money and walked to the door and said, "You stay here, I be back," and left the room. Jim dropped down in one of the two chairs by the window and looked out at the flashing signs of the other clubs and restaurants along the street wondering if he had been had. Well, good lesson if I did, he thought to himself. He was single, at war, didn't have a girlfriend since Kiko dumped him, all he wanted was to relax, enjoy a little female company and get laid. What was wrong with that? He'd be back in the shit soon enough, he should enjoy himself while he could. As SFC Rogers said, "Whenever you can eat, drink, shit or fuck do it! You never know when it will be your last time." Perhaps he was right.

As Jim was looking out the window and pondering where he was in life Mary came back in the room with a tray and two drinks, a San Miguel and a glass of tea. She walked over to Jim and said, "I bring this for you. Everything OK?" "Yep, fine. Thanks for the beer, I was getting a little thirsty," was Jim's reply. "Ok, I glad you happy." She took Jim's hand, pulled him up and led him to the bed. "You lay here and relax," she commanded. Jim did as he was told and didn't say anything. He kicked off his shoes and laid down, with the San Miguel in his right hand. He still had his clothes on. Mary went to the end of the bed, took a drink from a glass of ice tea and turned around and looked at Jim. She had kind of a smile or maybe grin on her face, then she started to peel off her clothes; stepped out of her shoes, unbuttoned her shirt, slipped it off, unzipped her skirt and let it drop, and when she was in just her bra and panties came over to the side of the bed and pulled Jim up.

Then she started to take his clothes off; unbuttoned his shirt and took it off, placing it on the chair next to the bed. Then she unbuckled his pants and let them slide to the floor and Jim stepped out of them. They went on the chair too. Then she slid Jim's underwear off and he was fully exposed — except for his sapphire ring and the beer he was holding in his right hand — he was naked as a Jaybird. Mary then pushed him and Jim sat down on the side of the bed with a thump. Mary then took off her bra and slid off her panties and stretched out her arms and twirled around slowly giving Jim a look at her perfect olive-skinned body. She was truly beautiful and well proportioned. Jim just sat there somewhat amazed appreciating the oriental goddess that was standing naked in front of him. Mary said softly, "You like?" To which Jim replied, "Yes, you're very beautiful." Mary just smiled and knelt down in front of him and began caressing him, first on the shoulders and then his chest and working her way down. Jim set down the beer on the nightstand and just leaned back and watched the skilled Mary work. For the next hour Jim learned firsthand what he heard others rave about with Asian lovers. Mary took him to the height of ecstasy and when their tryst was over he was exhausted. Totally satisfied, Jim lay on the bed with Mary next to him. He was a little surprised she didn't just jump up and put her clothes on and start to leave. It seemed to Jim she had enjoyed pleasuring him as much as he enjoyed being pleasured.

After a few minutes Jim turned up on his side and looked at Mary and said, "Wow, thank you. That was wonderful, I needed that. I haven't been with a woman in quite a while and my goodness you are a real woman. Ms. Mary, you're a wonderful lover and beautiful too. I'm lucky I met you — even under these circumstances." Then he smiled and leaned forward and gave her a soft kiss on the cheek. Mary, a little embarrassed now, said, "Thank you, you a kind man." "No, I mean that. Look, I know this is business for you, but I more than enjoyed it. I like talking to you and enjoy your company, everything." "Oh, you too nice, I happy you enjoyed being with me." Jim caressed her face once more, said thank you again, and turned and got out of bed and started putting his clothes on. Mary laid there for a minute with her own thoughts then got up and did the same.

When they were both dressed Mary came over to Jim and said, "You're a nice man sir. Will I see you again?" Jim wasn't sure if she was just trying to arrange another session — he clearly was interested in that — or wanted to see him outside of the club. He'd be in Bangkok five more days. "Perhaps," he replied. "Maybe I could take you to a nice dinner and not see you at the club." "Ok, well this is hard, my boss he no like that we see people from the club on our own, but maybe." "Well, if you figure it out I'm here for a few more days and I would be happy to take you out for the evening. It wouldn't be work — but a date, you know, just like friends. How would I get ahold of you if I wanted to reach you?" "I'm work at the club three nights a week, mostly Thursday to Saturday. Maybe I can see you other days?" "Well, maybe. You could even be my guide around Bangkok. I don't really know my way around, someone who knows Bangkok, speaks the language, and could show me around would be great." Jim wasn't sure what Bonner's plans were, but he was planning on doing his own thing, and if that included Bucky or not that was okay too. "Here's the deal. I'm at the SQ Hotel, you know the place?" Jim said. "Yes, I know it," was Mary's reply. "Well, if you want to be my guide and have a date outside work, let me know. I will be going back to Vietnam in five days." "OK, I know," was Mary's reply.

Following a last hug Mary led Jim downstairs to the club entrance and said goodbye. Jim shook her hand and gave her a wink as the big guy in the suit watched, then he turned and walked out of the Club Keynote. When he got back to the SQ Hotel he went straight up to his room and had the best night's sleep he'd gotten since he left Okinawa.

The next day Jim got up late, around 10 o'clock, and took his time moseying downstairs to get breakfast. He stopped at the gift shop and picked up an English newspaper and went into the dining room and ordered Eggs Benedict with an extra side of toast and orange juice. It was a typically American meal and, farm boy that he was, he loved real eggs for breakfast. He was relaxed, hadn't been this rested and clear minded since before he headed to Vietnam. When he finished his breakfast, he decided he would lounge around the pool for a few hours and try to figure out the different sights he needed to see.

On the way back to his room to change Jim ran into Bucky who was just coming down for breakfast or maybe early lunch as it was after eleven o'clock. He looked terrible. "Buckshot! How you doing partner?" Jim said with a big smile and a look of wonder at the shuffling captain with droopy, blood-shot eyes. "Man looks like you had a rough night, glad you survived!"

Jim couldn't wait to hear the story. Last time he saw Bucky he was headed upstairs with his cute little consort. "Oh man, I feel like shit. Drank way too much last night and now I just want to die," the ill looking Bucky replied to Jim's inquiry. "Bucky, I thought you were an experienced playboy that could handle long tough nights. Seems I was mistaken," Jim said in mock shock. "Man, that little chick took me for a ride in more ways than one last night. I dropped over $200 at that club and can't even remember getting laid or coming home," the pale, red-eyed Bucky confessed. "Now I have a splitting headache and my stomach is upset and I'm nearly broke. I hope I had fun!" "Well, partner, me thinks you need to take a few days off and regain your strength. Lots to do before we blow town." Jim was rubbing it in now. "Ya, I'm not sure you're living up to the warrior code, I may have to report you when I get back to Nha Trang." "Fuck you," was Bucky's reply, he was in no mood to take a ribbing after his disastrous night. Jim just smiled and said, "Dude, I'm headed to the pool to work on my tan. If you ever find your head and promise not to throw-up, come see me. I'm making my plan for what I want to see while I'm here." "If I live I might come see you," Bucky replied, "but don't count on it," and he continued to shuffle on to the restaurant.

After changing into a pair of gym shorts and a t-shirt Jim headed to the pool. Once there he chose a nice chaise lounge chair with a small table and sat down. There weren't many other people in the pool area. After finishing the paper, he took a cooling dip in the water. It was quite refreshing. He got back in the chase lounge, laid back and just relaxed letting the warm sun dry him off. Time to enjoy the warm sunny day, he thought, I don't need to do anything but chill. As he lay there he had a sweet view of a couple of well-built airline stewardesses playing around in the pool. It added to the pleasant surroundings. No worries here, he thought, I've got five more days of this and to see some of the sights around Bangkok and forget about the war. I'm going to make the most of them.

After a few minutes Jim picked up and thumbed through the tourist guide that lay on the table by the chase lounge. There were several places that looked interesting and he made a note to try and visit them. He also certainly wanted to go back to the Peninsula Restaurant again. For today he thought he'd just walk down to the Grand Palace and check it out and also maybe the Wat Pho temple complex that was also nearby. They were both well known attractions and seemed interesting. He didn't want to come to Thailand and not see the famous tourist places. Forty minutes later he put on his t-shirt, picked up his paper and started to walk back into the hotel. When he got to the lobby Ms. Mary walked in.

Mary looked great even though she was wearing the typical Thai outfit; a simple loose shirt and the common long pajamas pants most Asian women wore. She had on a big floppy hat and wide sunglasses. When she noticed Jim, she walked over to him and said, "Hello sir, do you remember me?" Jim was a little taken back. "Sure, you're the beautiful Ms. Mary."

Then it hit Jim, last night he had never told Mary his name, just where he was staying, hence the greeting "sir." "I glad you not forget me. You say you want a guide for Bangkok so I think I can do it and I come to SQ to find you and see if you really mean it." "Well, I did mean it, but is this business or do you want us to have a date?" Much as he thought of Mary, following Bucky's advice, he wanted to know up front if there was a charge for Ms. Mary's guide service. "No, I not working now, this be a date if that OK with you," Mary was a little apprehensive now. "That would be great, but if it's a date then you need to call me Jim and I need to call you Dara. That work for you?" Jim replied. Somewhat relieved, Dara said, "Yes, you can call me Dara if we have a date and I will call you Jim." "Well, Dara I need to change my clothes, so why don't you come up to my room or if that is a problem please wait here and I'll change and come right back down. I know the places I'd like to go today." "It's OK, I come to your room," Dara said and Jim pointed to the stairs and led her up to his room.

Once in the room Jim pointed to the chair next to the bed and said, "Please sit down while I change, it will only be a minute." Dara didn't reply but went to the chair and sat down. She wasn't quite sure if Jim was really just going to change his clothes or if he would want to have an encore to last night's love making. The thought did cross Jim's mind, but he figured there would be plenty of time for that later. Now he just wanted to change and go on a real date with a good-looking girl to some interesting places. Ten minutes after they entered Jim's room they were exiting the hotel and headed for the Grand Palace.

As they walked Jim asked Dara how she got out of work to escort him around. She said she just told her boss she needed a few days off to meet up with her mother who was coming to Bangkok. "Good story," Jim said as they walked towards the Grand Palace.

It was only a short walk to the Grand Palace which is really a complex of several buildings that have been the "official" seat of the Thailand's government since 1782 - even before it was Siam. Once inside the palace complex Jim and Dara spent two hours touring the palace, temples, and grounds. Dara was an excellent guide and knew the history of the palace as well as some local stories about the place. The more Jim was around Dara the more he liked her. As they sat waiting for an ice tea in the palace gardens Jim ran through his mind how he ended up with Dara. Fate, he guessed. Dara was no ignorant street whore, but sophisticated and intelligent. And he didn't look at her as a prostitute, although that was what she was. He thought she could probably be a nurse if she had the opportunity to go to school. He guessed she really wasn't much different from a lot of poor rural girls that get to the big city one way or another, don't have much, and use the only assets they had to get along. Reality, but kinda sad, the world is a tough place. The longer Jim was around Dara the more he liked her.

After the Grand Place, they had a lite lunch on their way to Wat Pho, the world-famous royal temple that houses the Reclining Buddha. It is still a house of worship and the largest temple complex in Thailand. Dara explained the temple's significance to the Thai people and the basic tenets of Buddhism. Jim was not a religious person, but he respected people that were. He thought it especially hard in this modern age for people to believe in any religion and even more so to live their lives following any specific religious dogma. He never gave religion much thought, but the more he learned about Buddhism, the more it made sense to him. Wat Pho was a magnificent place and he was awed by the size of the temple complex and the unique architecture of the shrines and temples. The visit was even more rewarding with Dara along acting as a guide.

The visit to the Grand Palace and Wat Pho took the greater part of the day. Jim suggested they go back to SQ and refresh before they headed out to dinner. Dara agreed and the pair headed back to SQ Hotel arriving about 1630. Once in the room one thing led to another and the two casual tourists ended up in bed. The afternoon lovemaking was gentle and satisfying and Jim started to think that Dara giving herself to him willingly was something special and not a transactional demonstration of her professional abilities. In any event, both parties were satisfied and they took a short nap after the love making. When they awoke it was early evening and Jim suggested they go to the Peninsula Restaurant for dinner. Dara agreed and they dressed and headed out both satisfied and refreshed and wondering where their "date" was leading them.

Dinner was casual and uneventful and the food again spectacular. The conversation remained easy and they questioned each other about their lives up until they met. Jim was somewhat surprised that a beautiful woman as sharp as Dara ended up working as a prostitute, even though she worked in what was considered a "high class" place. She seemed to have much more to give than just her body. Perhaps you just do what you need to in a third world country to get ahead, he thought. If Vietnam taught him anything it was that the world is a tough place and not a lot of people had the advantages of Americans. Clearly, it seemed that life in Lampang would only have at best limited possibilities. At least Dara wasn't in a war zone so she had a chance to improve from the life she was born into.

Dara was a realist and knew life could be both cruel and rewarding — depending on how you approached it. She had fallen for the common trap of poor rural girls believing someone else had her best interests in mind when she signed-up to leave Lampang and come to Bangkok for a promised job that was really nonexistent. Once in Bangkok without skills and no money, and less than good prospects for getting into school or a good paying job, she succumbed to an offer to work at a club where at least she could make some quick money. She just tuned out when she was working, guarding her real self. She didn't like whoring, especially with the stigma attached to you if people found out what you really did. But it could offer a quick means to a different and better life. So, she did what was required to give herself a chance. She was still young, and pretty, and smart, and might have options once she got on her feet, but she didn't plan on continuing in the club for long. Living as a whore for the last seven months steeled her to men.

But, now she had met a big American who seemed different from the other men she had run into in Bangkok. He was kind and treated her with respect, even though he knew what she did. He was more like a lover than just viewing her as a transactional piece of ass. The more she was around Jim the more she thought she could possibly go for a man like him. But she was under no illusions. He was a soldier escaping a gruesome war no one really understood and would be gone in a few days. She knew she had no real future with him despite how well he treated her. Really Jim was just a respite from her real life for a few days, much like she was a respite from his. She was determined to enjoy the change and his company while she could.

Following dinner and a drink at the restaurant's outside bar Jim suggested that they head back to the hotel. Dara was quiet at the request and Jim asked if something was wrong. "Jim I can't stay with you tonight, I must go home," Dara said, looking sad and directly at him. Well, bad news doesn't get better with age, Jim thought. "What's wrong, did I do something? Are you upset with me?" Jim was confused. He thought they had spent a great day together, like a real date, visited interesting paces, made love, had a great dinner and relaxed — now was the night over? Why? Dara understood Jim was probably confused — they had just spent a wonderful day together and he had every right to think she was going to stay with him, but she couldn't. She said, "Jim you are a most kind man I ever knew. Today was one of the best days of my life, but I can't be with you tonight. I must go home. But not because I don't want to be with you. If you want I will come and be for a date tomorrow and we can see more Bangkok and have fun. Please don't be mad. I sorry, I should have told you this morning. Please don't think bad of me." "Dara, I don't think bad of you, you're a wonderful girl - I just don't understand, but if you can't stay with me — you can't stay with me." "You too nice man Jim, can I see you tomorrow? Take you to markets, be with you then?" Dara asked hoping Jim would agree. "Sure, be glad to have another date tomorrow. But I have to ask, you're not going back to work at the club tonight, are you?" "No, Jim, I no work at club anymore while you here. I hope you don't think bad about me. I sorry." "It's OK, you do what you have to do and perhaps we can meet tomorrow and have another date," Jim replied, not understanding what was going on, but at least she was truthful and not trying to lead him on. He could deal with it, after all he would be back in Vietnam in a few days. "Should I walk you home?" he asked. "No, I take a taxi it too far. But I come to you tomorrow. I like our dates. What time you want see me?" She asked. "Well, how about 11AM and we can go to lunch and I'll pick out a few places I'd like to see and you can guide me there. Will that work?" "Yes, thank you. You good man Jim, I be at SQ at 11AM tomorrow," Dara replied, quite relieved that Jim wasn't upset and had not just sent her away. After finishing their drinks, the day was over and Jim walked Dara to the restaurant's front entrance and hailed a Tuk-Tuk, the three wheeled taxis common throughout Asia. Dara told the driver where she needed to go. Before she got in Jim gave her a peck on the cheek and hug and said, "Hope to see you tomorrow." Dara smiled and said, "Thank you Jim, see you tomorrow." Jim gave the guy a 100 Baht note and the whining Tuk-Tuk took-off in a cloud of blue smoke. Jim watched it for a minute and wondered if Dara would really come by tomorrow at eleven. He hoped so, he enjoyed her company. He then turned and started walking back to the SQ Hotel. I wonder how

Bucky's day went, Jim thought. He hadn't seen Captain Bonner since he was heading to the restaurant to try and get rid of his hangover.

The next day Jim followed the same routine: slept late, bought an English language newspaper on the way to breakfast, had a great omelet with orange juice, and went to the pool to finish the paper. He was in his room at 10:50 when there was a knock at the door. When he opened it there was Dara looking radiant in a long silk Chakkar and blouse, the dress of modest Thai women. She was even more beautiful than he remembered. "May I come in?" She asked. "Of course, you look wonderful, happy you came. I wasn't sure you would make it," Jim said honestly. "No, I come because I want to see you, I very much like our date," she said with a smile. "Me too," Jim replied as Dara came into the room and sat down at the table by the window. "Jim, I sorry about last night. I tell you why I cannot stay. My brother very sick. He was in Laos Army and become very sick and come to Bangkok to be in hospital for over three months. My family has to take care of him at night and last night my turn to be with him. I didn't want to tell you because he was in Laos Army and I afraid you would be mad and not see me. But now I need tell you. I don't have to take care of him again for a while so I can stay with you if you want," Dara said, trying to explain why she left him alone last night. "It's Okay Dara, I understand. He's lucky you're around to care for him." Dara continued, "His wife and children mostly stay with him, but I do also sometimes. It like family duty. I hope you understand." "I do, don't worry about it. You're here and we can have another great day together. Dara, you don't have to sleep with me if you don't want to or it bothers you. You're a good woman and I respect you. You should do whatever you feel is right when you're with me. It's Ok." "Thank you, Jim, you are a kind man and I like being with you and I like sleep with you too. And our date!" She said with a smile. "Well, let me put on a shirt and show you where I'd like to go today," Jim said as he grabbed his shirt off the chair and put it on.

Ten minutes later they were headed out the door of the hotel for the famous Damnoen Saduak Floating Market. The market was within walking distance and a wondrous place. Hundreds of stalls and small boats on the Chao Phraya River and its banks hawking everything from clothes to pots and pans to jewelry to produce. To see the market, you cruise around in a small private long-tail boat visiting the various vendors in their own small boats filled with goods. After spending a few hours floating around the market Jim and Dara had lunch at a small cafe on the eastern bank of the river and watched as the boats and barges went by. Afterwards they sauntered over to the MaeKlong Railway Market. It was another unique Thai market where many vendors place their goods on and by the train tracks only to have to move them out of the way every time a train comes through.

Both markets are extraordinary attractions and Jim found them interesting. Dara explained that most of the people who buy things at the markets are tourists. Jim just bought one thing, but sampled a menagerie of fruits and vegetables many of which he had never seen before. It was another pleasant day when they arrived back at the SQ Hotel just after five.

They were both tired and like the previous day they ended up in bed where they made love and fell asleep. They didn't wake up until after seven. Dara suggested they not go to a restaurant, but eat at a street vendor and take in a kickboxing match or go to one of the big hotel bars and have a nightcap. She reminded Jim she would be staying with him if he wanted her to. It sounded like a plan to Jim and he opted for the street vendor dinner and the rooftop bar at the Mandarin Hotel, one of the best hotels in Bangkok. When they got back to the SQ just before midnight they were both exhausted. The love making was sweet and tender and they fell asleep in each other's arms.

The next two days were much the same but seemed to pass in a blur: late breakfast, relax at the pool, and then off to sight-see. They took a bus tour to Ayutthaya the World Heritage Site one day and then on Jim's last day in Bangkok just lounged around the pool at the hotel.

That night they went back to the Peninsula Restaurant for dinner and drinks outside.

For Jim it was a super week and a chance to recharge his batteries for his last few months in Vietnam. He enjoyed Bangkok, the city, the people and just being able to get away from Vietnam and not think about the war. He had also grown quite fond of Dara. The time with her was everything he could have asked for and he considered his meeting her, despite the circumstances, a blessing. Regardless of what she did for a living Jim found her to be a quality person; beautiful, smart and generous. However, he didn't try to fool himself and think that they might have a future together. No, she was in Thailand and he was in Vietnam. It was great while it lasted, but they both knew that it was just a temporary escape from their real lives. When Jim left the SQ Hotel for Vietnam they would go their separate ways.

Dara too accepted the fact that Jim would leave her. He was honest and didn't try to deceive her with promises of a future together or that he would come back to Thailand and find her. No, it was what it was, an interlude for two different lives that gave them a taste of what life might be like if circumstances were different — but they weren't. They both were realists and just enjoyed their time together by living in the moment.

In the room before they headed downstairs where Jim would catch a taxi to the air base and an Air America flight back to Nha Trang, they exchanged small gifts. It wasn't planned, but they each had wanted to give the other something to remember them by. Jim gave Dara a hand-carved brass pin of a peacock with a ruby eye that he had bought at the market a few days before. He told her he had very much enjoyed their days together and thanked her for making his trip to Bangkok such a great escape from the war. When she wore the pin, she should think of him.

He also gave her $500, for being his tour guide. Dara was surprised at the gift and somewhat shocked at the money, and told him she was grateful, that Jim was a good man and whoever ended up with him would be a lucky woman. "I don't know about that," he replied.

Dara then gave Jim a gold necklace with a carved jade elephant pendant. She told Jim he was the finest man she had ever met and she'd grown to love him, but knew he was a soldier and must leave. And while she was sad, she would cherish the time they had spent together and hoped he wouldn't forget her. "Jade will bring you good luck and when you touch the elephant you can think of me, an elephant never forgets," she said. "Dara, I can never forget you even if I tried," he told her. "Thank you for staying with me, loving me, and making my stay in Bangkok wonderful. You are a special girl and I think the future will be bright for you."

After a last warm embrace with a soft kiss Jim picked up his A-bag and they went downstairs to the taxi stand. Dara stood on the steps of the hotel as Jim arranged a taxi and loaded his bag. She was sad, but she didn't cry. When Jim opened the door to get in he turned and faced her and said, "Dara I do love you, don't forget that, take care of yourself and be safe!" He then turned, got into the cab, and closed the door. Dara stood on the steps and replied, "me too." As much as she tried to hold them back tears began to run down her cheeks. When the door closed the taxi drove off to the air base and Jim was headed back to war and out of her life.

After running into the hungover Bucky that second morning in Bangkok Jim only saw him once more, the next morning as he was checking out of the SQ. Bucky told Jim he was headed up country to see some of the ancient ruins and temples and then was going to a beach resort near Chon Buri south of Bangkok on the Gulf of Thailand. He knew some British SAS guys who would be there and he wanted to see them before he headed home. He said he intended to stay in Thailand until 15 March and then go back to Nha Trang, finish any out processing, then head to Saigon to catch a flight home. Jim warned him to be safe, but this was Bucky's third trip to Thailand so Jim figured Bucky could take care of himself. He just said goodbye and told Bucky he'd look him up when he got back to Fort Bragg. Bucky said he looked forward to that and gave Jim a big hug and said, "Jimmy you big warrior, don't you ever fucking die!" The "don't you ever fucking die" was a kind of Special Forces term of endearment that only warriors who served together would say to each other. Bucky grabbed his bag and headed out the door.

Return to War

Eight hours after he got in the taxi at the SQ Hotel Jim checked into the transit quarters at Nha Trang. He'd be there until he could catch a hop to B-24, hopefully the next day. His trip to Thailand had been a wonderful experience, largely because he had run into Dara and the city itself was so amazing with its blend of ancient culture and Asian hustle and bustle. Now that he was back in Vietnam, although well rested, he was anxious to get back to B Company and updated on what had gone on the week he was gone. Not much he hoped.

From the papers it seemed the Viet Cong and NVA's Tet Offensive had been a strategic failure. Clearly, the country-wide assault on the South did not provide the NVA the results they were looking for. Jim thought the enemy losses must have been huge just because the papers seldom said anything positive about the US efforts in the war. Even after crushing the NVA and Viet Cong forces during Tet the press seemed to report the allied victory as a loss just because the NVA and Viet Cong had launched the surprise attack. The press was no friend of the war or the Army.

The evening Jim got to Nha Trang, after dinner at the mess hall, he went to the SF Club. When he walked in Colonel Anderson was there and when he saw Jim motioned him to come over and sit at his table and have a drink. Anderson had been promoted to full colonel (COL) and took over as commander of 5th Group. He greeted Jim warmly and asked how he was doing and how things were at B-24. Jim said good last he heard, but that he was just returning from R&R and didn't have the latest on what was going on. COL Anderson said LTC Tower would be coming to Nha Trang the next day for a formal "After Action" briefing on Tet by folks from MAC-V in Saigon. Jim was invited to the briefing if he wanted to get an update. He could return to B-24 with LTC Tower when he flew back. Jim thanked the colonel and said he'd like to attend and he would try to contact LTC Tower first thing in the morning and let him know he was in Nha Trang and if he wanted him to do anything while he was there. "Good idea," COL Anderson said.

COL Anderson ordered himself another gin and tonic and asked Jim what he'd like. "An American beer if it's cold, sir," Jim replied. COL Anderson ordered the drinks and while they waited told Jim he would be remaining in command of 5th Group until September, then he would be rotating back to the Pentagon where he would be assigned to the Army's Directorate of Operations and be responsible for coordinating the International missions for all the Army's Special Operations units. Jim congratulated the colonel on his promotion and assignment. "Bet you'll be glad to be home," Jim told him. "Ya kinda, it will be almost two years here in one capacity or another. I've enjoyed it and think we've made a contribution, but I doubt we'll see long term success if we don't get the politicians on board with the war effort. Mostly they're a bunch of flakes and only care about themselves." "Sir, I'm with you on that," Jim replied. "Well, don't you rotate out about then too?" Anderson asked Jim." "Yes, sir, my DEROS will be in September too if I don't get a drop. I'm not sure where they'll send me. I'd like to stay in a group. 10th Group in Europe if I can get a slot." "Well, Jim, I'll need a smart SF officer on my staff in Washington. Would you be interested in joining me?" The colonel asked. "Gee sir, I appreciate the offer, but I'm a little junior to be in the Pentagon and I think I need to avoid Washington until I get some more experience with the teams and groups." "Right answer Jim, but I thought I'd ask. You can't have too many good people around you, especially in Washington. If you change your mind let me know and I can make it happen." "Thank you, sir, I'll keep that in mind."

COL Anderson also told Jim that LTC Tower would be rotating back home shortly and he would be replaced by LTC E.K. Jones from Fort Bragg. COL Anderson said he knew Jones well and that he was a fine officer. He had good experience with two previous tours in Vietnam: one as an A-team leader on an advisory mission in '64, and in '66 as an advisor to the Vietnamese SF Group. He was currently the operations officer for the Special Warfare Center at Fort Bragg. He thought Jim would like him as he was a consummate professional. Jim replied that he was sure he would.

The rest of the evening Jim listened to Anderson talk about the war and how he thought America was fighting with one arm tied behind its back. He didn't have confidence in the American politicians back home or that the Vietnamization plan that was recently announced would be successful. Too much corruption in the South Vietnamese army he thought and he didn't think the ARVN had the will to fight. He was concerned about what would happen to all the South Vietnamese and especially the tribes that had worked with the American SF teams. He didn't have any answers, but loyalty was a big thing with him. Jim liked COL Anderson and thought he was a straight shooter. He himself had really not given the politics of the war too much thought, he was too busy just trying to accomplish his assigned missions and take care of his people.

The next day Jim rang up B-24 at the operations center and asked to speak with LTC Tower. When he got LTC Tower on the line he let him know he was in Nha Trang and headed to Kontum and asked if he could hitch a ride back to B-24 with him when he returned. Tower said sure, glad he was back and hoped he was rested and ready to get back to work, "Yes sir, I am," Jim replied. Jim asked if there was anything Tower wanted him to do while he was in Nha Trang - supplies, info, check on things? LTC Tower said no B-24 was good to go, but that he was interested in hearing what the MACV guys had to say about Tet. Jim told him he had been invited to the briefing by COL Anderson and was planning to attend. Tower replied, "Good! I'll see you in a few hours." "Roger, out," Jim replied and hung up the phone.

The briefing was scheduled for 1300 hours so Jim had some time to kill. He wanted to go to the PX and get some personal items and drop by the admin office and post a letter to his mom and dad. He wouldn't check out of his room until around noon and then he'd take his A-Bag to flight ops and make sure they knew he'd be returning to Kontum with LTC Tower. He'd store his bag at flight ops and try to meet LTC

Tower's aircraft when it landed and then head to the headquarters with his boss. Jim wasn't sure when they would be heading back to Kontum, but he assumed shortly after the briefing and LTC Tower's meeting with COL Anderson.

The MACV briefing team consisted of three officers: a LTC assistant Ops officer, an Air Force LTC, and a Major intel officer. The objective of the briefing was to inform the different commands about what had taken place over the past six weeks of fighting. The NVA and their Viet Cong subordinates had launched a country wide attack on South Vietnam on January 31, the Vietnamese Lunar New Year known as Tet. The North's plan was to attack all of the major military installations in South Vietnam and destroy or capture them and great swaths of territory. They also aimed to kill as many Americans as possible, degrade the South's Army (ARVN) and assassinate the political leaders of the towns and cities in the South. The North anticipated some units in the South Vietnamese military would desert and join them and the population would support the North's offensive. They thought their military success would end the war by placing the Americans, and especially the South Vietnamese political structure in an untenable position and cause the South to sue for peace. While the initial attacks largely surprised both the US forces and the ARVN, after some initial setbacks the South crushed the offensive and the South Vietnamese population and military showed no signs of supporting the North's invasion or favoring a communist government.

It was the third week in March and the initial assaults from the NVA's Tet Offensive had been soundly defeated at great cost to the North Vietnamese and especially the Viet Cong units in the South. Except for the battle for the Citadel in Hue the offensive was all but over. In Hue the Marines were still heavily engaged in Hue's old citadel and would be for another week. The Battle for Hue would be the second costliest battle of the war — prolonged by the reluctance of the American and ARVN senior leaders to let the Marines use their firepower to root out the NVA regiment that had dug-in inside the old fort. The infantry on infantry fighting in Hue would last until early April, but the outcome was always assured.

When LTC Tower arrived in Nha Trang he greeted Jim warmly and told him he was glad he was back and hoped he enjoyed his time in Bangkok. Jim assured him that he had, it was an interesting place and that it was a good break. He felt rested and renewed and was ready to get back to work. He also said he had linked up with Captain Bonner in Bangkok for a few days and that when he left Bonner was headed for a resort south of Bangkok on the Gulf of Thailand. He seemed to be enjoying himself as well. LTC Tower smiled and said, "Ya, Bucky enjoys himself wherever he goes, I just hope he stays out of trouble." Jim just laughed and said, "You're right about that, I hope for the same!" Then LTC Tower and Jim headed to the 5th Group headquarters.

At 5th Group LTC Tower met informally with COL Anderson and the other Special Forces commanders who had come in for the briefing. After several minutes of kibitzing the commanders and some key staff moved into the briefing room for the Tet Update Briefing. The briefing was formal and professional. The briefing team went over the timeline of the Tet Offensive to date: where the NVA and Viet Cong had attacked and what units on both sides were involved. They also reported how the ARVN and American units had responded, pointing out the successes and the shortcomings in a lessons learned format. The briefing covered the past six weeks of fighting and recognized that there were still a few engagements on going, but the only significant battle remaining was the mop-up operations around Hue.

The MAC-V Team estimated the Tet Offensive aftermath could continue at a low level for a few more weeks, but that all in all the attack had been a significant failure for the North from a military standpoint. They didn't get the support from the South Vietnamese civilian population they expected nor from the ARVN. The team reported the preliminary casualty figures for both sides for Tet. As of the date of the briefing, the initial assaults and US and ARVN counterattacks had resulted in an estimated 50,000 NVA and Viet Cong casualties with another 6000 captured. The American and ARVN losses were 2100 KIA (American about 900) and 8000 WIA (3000 American). It was estimated that civilian casualties were in the 7500 killed and 18,000 wounded range, but there were no hard numbers for civilians.

It was MACV's position that the Tet Offensive had been catastrophic for the North and especially the Viet Cong. Their losses had been so dramatic that they would likely not be capable of launching a significant offensive in the south for the foreseeable future. A return to mostly guerrilla and sabotage tactics were the expected recourse, but it should be anticipated that sporadic small level attacks would continue in the south. The NVA was capable of launching attacks on outlying bases and lightly defended villages close to their sanctuaries in Cambodia and Laos, but major cities and bases were not expected to be attacked as the NVA just didn't have the forces or logistics for large and sustained battles. Intelligence confirmed that most NVA forces had already withdrawn to their safe base areas in Laos and Cambodia to recover and re-arm.

The intel Major also reported that there had been some reports by the Vietnamese of foreign advisors with the NVA units. These had not been verified nor had any American units reported seeing any foreign nationals with NVA or Viet Cong units. However, since the 5th Group worked mostly with indigenous tribes and special operations units away from major cities in the border areas, they should be aware of what had been reported. The major said that if any of the 5th Group units saw a foreign national leading or even with an NVA or VC unit, they should report it immediately.

One of the major concerns MACV had from the fighting over the last month was how the press was covering the Tet Offensive. So far, the coverage had been deemed mostly negative. MACV thought this would put additional pressure on both the American and Vietnamese political leadership that would not be helpful to the military effort going forward.

Following their presentation, the Briefing Team fielded questions. There weren't many, but COL Anderson asked if MACV was launching or developing a bombing campaign to attack the NVA safe areas in Cambodia and Laos. The answer was that such a plan was in the works, but it had to be cleared with the politicians back home before it could be implemented since the targets were outside Vietnam.

The other significant question was about the training and leadership of the South Vietnamese Army. Most of the Special Forces commanders had a low opinion of ARVN leadership, their unit combat readiness and will to fight. The briefing team had no direct information on that, but believed that Washington was looking hard at putting significant pressure on the South Vietnamese to increase the size of its military and to take over more of the direct combat operations in the south. Nothing formal had been proposed, but that was the direction MACV advocated. The briefing team believed there was something in the works at the Pentagon, but had no specific information. The briefing had lasted 90 minutes and at the end COL Anderson thanked the Briefing Team for the presentation and the session was over.

After the briefing LTC Tower met with COL Anderson to discuss the handover of the battalion to LTC E.K. Jones. The anticipated date was for 20 July, but could change if Tower got a drop or was asked to come home earlier. Following his meeting with COL Anderson, LTC Tower and Jim headed to the airfield to fly back to Kontum. They landed at B-24 just before 1900 hours.

The following day Jim spent time with SFC Rogers and 1SG Kue who updated him on the company's status. All had been quiet while he was gone, no NVA/VC activity in the province since the attack on Kontum had been crushed and the NVA chased west following heavy losses. There hadn't even been any rocket or mortar attacks on the city or surrounding villages. Everyone thought the NVA had taken a lick'n and was in Cambodia somewhere reconstituting. Jim told Rogers and Kue about the Tet briefing in Nha Trang, he wasn't sure the NVA would be staying still for the next few months, but he agreed that they could probably expect more gorilla type activities, ambushes, and perhaps attacks by fire. Now was not the time to let down their guard.

1SG Kue also informed Jim that they had received eight new recruits that week. This put the company strength to 141 with the wounded in the head count. 1SG Kue wasn't sure if and when the wounded would return fit for duty. He thought of the nine wounded six would recover and come back. He wasn't so sure about the other three. Jim reiterated that for the last few weeks of guard duty he wanted the men to get max rest and leave. He also wanted to rotate the platoons through the rifle range again when not manning the perimeter. He noted that the engagement on Cho Pao proved that the company's accurate shooting gave it a significant advantage. Both SFC Rogers and 1SG Kue agreed. Kue said he'd get the platoons to the range and ensure the new recruits got extra time on their guns.

After Jim's in-brief he and his command group walked the B-24 perimeter positions manned by B Company and Jim spoke with the soldiers in each bunker. He wanted them to know he was back and show he appreciated their efforts and professionalism. He was glad B Company had more time on security duty so the men, assuming no incidents, could continue the easy living and rest and he could get himself back up to speed.

At the beginning of April B Company took over the patrolling mission for B-24. While there had not been much contact with NVA forces across the province since early March when the NVA was finally chased back across the border to Cambodia, II Corps wanted to keep up the patrolling out near the border to prevent the NVA from establishing any new infiltration support stations or supply caches. Another area of concern was the pass at Chu Pao where B Company had had the run-in with the NVA company in February. Since the Chu Pao Pass was close and B-24 had experience in the area II Corps assigned a patrolling mission to the battalion to sweep the top of Chu Pao east to west to see if there were any new signs of NVA activity or supply caches in the area.

During Tet, after B Company had withdrawn from Chu Pao, II Corp had placed two different Arc Light (B-52) strikes on the mountain where B Company had fought and followed it up with a battalion combat assault from the 21st ARVN. There had been a few small skirmishes, but nothing major. Now it was time to go back up the mountain and do some additional battle damage assessment (BDA) and see if the NVA had returned. Jim didn't like the mission, he thought it would be best if an ARVN unit did it, but if he had the support he felt he needed he thought B Company could handle it.

On April 12 B Company moved from B-24 again by truck to the base of Chu Pao. Jim chose to move up the mountain the same way he had come down in February. He knew that once he got over the steep incline the area was mostly flat on top. He just didn't want to be surprised while the company was moving uphill. Since he was again out of artillery range he brought three tubes of 81 mm mortars with him to set up just off QL-14 so that he would have some indirect fire support if he needed it. Once the company was assembled on the east side of QL-14 at the mouth of the pass he had 1st Platoon lead to the trailhead and on to the crest on the north side of Chu Pao. The mortar section was already in place and ready to support the company's movement with indirect fire if needed.

The movement up Chu Pao came off without incident. Once 1st Platoon reached the top of Chu Pao Jim had them secure the area where they had fought the NVA last time. They reported no evidence of enemy so far. Jim then quickly moved the rest of the company up the mountain.

In February the NVA suffered a bloody nose in its last battle with B Company on Chu Pao. The NVA 95B's desire to set up a regimental base area on the western side of Chu Pao was abandoned after that fight. It was only prudent for them to retreat into Cambodia where they would be relatively safe and could reconstitute. This was good for B Company, which after three days combing Chu Pao and finding only old positions and trash they returned to B-24 with no contact and most importantly no casualties.

The rest of the month of April passed with little activity in Kontum Province. The NVA seemed to be biding their time and trying to rebuild their forces for some future operations. The fourth month of the year they restricted their war making to mainly indirect fire attacks on outlying fire bases and rocket attacks on Kontum, all of which were minimally effective. B Company ran two more patrols to the west and north of Kontum that month with the same results — no contact.

The Last Patrol

On the 1st of May, B Company became the QRF for the province and Jim laid out a training schedule that consisted mostly of weapons training. He was hopeful, operationally, it wouldn't be a busy month and he could get in a lot of training and even some down time. For the first half of May B Company never left Kontum.

Ironically on 10 May the US and North Vietnamese representatives met in Paris to begin "Peace Talks" even though fighting continued unabated in Vietnam. The very week of 3-10 May 1968 was the deadliest for American soldiers in the war when 562 lost their lives. Despite the positive publicity of the Paris meetings, that same day the NVA launched Phase II of their Tet Offensive, sometimes called the May Offensive. In some ways these attacks were more surprising than the initial Tet Offensive battles in late January and early February because the NVA/VC forces had suffered such debilitating losses in those first attacks. The Americans and South Vietnamese commands did not believe they were capable of another large-scale offensive so soon. But they were wrong.

On the 18th of May, Polei Kleng, an SF camp about 25 kilometers west of Kontum, began receiving sustained mortar fire. Polei Kleng was the home base of Special Forces A-241 who advised the local CIDG company of Montagnards. There was also a company of ARVN Rangers co-located in the camp.

Polei Kleng had been established in 1966 in a strategic location not far from the tri-border area of Cambodia, Laos and Vietnam. Its primary mission then was to keep tabs on the infiltration routes coming into South Vietnam, but that evolved as the Vietnamese took over more and more of the fighting and the Americans SF outpost started to focus on training and supporting the local RF/PF militias. The Vietnamese Rangers picked up the border surveillance mission.

Polei Kleng's specialty then became long range reconnaissance patrols (LRRPs) to identifying cross border targets for American air power. The effectiveness of Polei Kleng's operations became a thorn in the side of the NVA's infiltration efforts.

After the disaster of the Tet Offensive in February a decision was made by the NVA to take the camp out before they launched their next major offensive. The May attack on Polei Kleng was the start of that effort and a way to occupy forces from the south so they could not respond to attacks on other more critical targets.

After 15 hours of intermittent shelling a ground assault was launched at dawn May 19th against the well defended camp from the north. The initial attack was easily repelled with minimal casualties, while inflicting heavy losses on the assaulting NVA units. Another attack was made near dusk from the west in an attempt to overrun the camp which, although also ultimately unsuccessful, got to the camp's wire perimeter before it was beaten back. The assaulting force was identified as the 24th Regiment of the NVA's 1st Division who had been operating from the North's B3 Front combat zone since the past September. Anticipating the remnants of the defeated regiment withdrawing towards the safety of Cambodia, II Corps chose to try and intercept the NVA retreat by launching two Mike Force companies to the border to block their escape and try to destroy what was left of the wounded NVA regiment.

On the evening of 19 May B-24 received a mission to deploy two companies to the Plei Re and Plei Grap area west of Plei Kleng near the Cambodian border and establish blocking positions with maximal ambushes along the east-west trails in the area. Bravo and Charlie Companies were assigned the mission. Bravo Company would deploy near Plei Re and was given an operational box five by ten kilometers that stretched north and east of the village. C Company would have a similar area south and east of Plei Grap. Each company commander was to choose where to establish his forward positions and how and where to deploy the ambushes in his zone. The mission was to last five days depending on the level of contact and would be backed up by the ARVN Ranger battalion at Dak To as a QRF if the fighting got too heavy. A battalion of the ARVN 22nd Division would be on call as well to develop the situation if a major engagement ensued. The companies were to be inserted the morning of the 20th of May.

When Jim got the order he and SFC Rogers, who was scheduled to DEROS (Deployment Ends Return from Overseas) in 25 Days, along with 1SG Kue drew up the mission plan and selected their LZ for the combat assault. Rogers coordinated the helicopters and air support and 1SG Kue organized the platoons and oversaw the provisioning and ammunition draws.

After the plans were made for the operation Jim pulled SFC Rogers aside and told him he wanted him to stay at B-24 during the mission to coordinate any support B Company would need. Rogers protested, he could coordinate the support from the field and wanted to be with the company. But Jim didn't agree. "Roy you're a great soldier, but no sense pushing your luck. You're outta here in a few weeks and I want you going home in one piece. Besides, no one can help us better than you if you're here." Rogers felt left out, but he understood and appreciated his captain trying to take care of him. "Sir, you know I would rather be with the company, but I'll do what you want. I appreciate you looking out for me, but I don't think it's necessary," Rogers responded. "It's probably not, but I'd like you to hang in here anyway and run our support. I'll feel better about it if we work it that way." "Roger sir," was a disappointed Roger's reply.

By 2000 hours 1SG Kue had the company provisioned and ready to go. The combat assault would lift off at 0700 the next morning and 120 of the 141 men assigned to B Company would take part. 1SG Kue briefed Jim on the combat load he had assigned and told Jim he had added several additional claymore mines and hand grenades to each squad. "Agree, good job. If we spring some ambushes we might need all that. I also want the men to have 10 magazines each instead of eight," Jim told Kue. "Sir they all have eight now, but I ordered two additional cans of M16 ammo and two of M60 ammo for each squad since we won't be moving too much," Kue informed his captain. "Great, that should do it," Jim replied thinking he should have known Kue would be way ahead of him when it came to planning for an operation.

Jim spent the rest of the evening doing a detailed map recon and selecting where he would put the company NDPs and trying to figure out if he wanted to move each day or stay in the same place. He also tried to determine what routes the NVA might use to skedaddle back to Cambodia. He wasn't sure they would head directly back to Cambodia, they might go north along the border then into Laos. Hell, they could have already made it across the border if they force marched, but then again, they probably had lots of wounded which would slow them down. In any event, B Company would get out there in the morning and lay in wait for any NVA that entered its area of operations (AO).

At 0600 the next day Jim moved with his gear to the airstrip where 1SG Kue already had the 120 men designated for the mission organized into eight man sticks to board the helicopters when they arrived. There would be eight aircraft in the assault group requiring two flights to insert the company in the LZ. Jim would be on the third aircraft of the first flight with his two RTOs, Ren his bodyguard, and three soldiers from 1st Platoon. 1SG Kue would be on the first aircraft of the second lift. There would be two cobra escorts to cover the assault since the LZ was out of artillery range. The II Corps FAC would loiter over Kontum while the company was inserted in case any fast movers were needed to support the assault. Jim was calm and knew the company was ready, he'd be happier when everyone was on the ground.

The combat assault went in just north of Plei Re on a four ship LZ. It took almost three hours to move the company and get everyone on the ground. While the assault was unopposed without a doubt every person within 15 kilometers knew there was a major insertion and troops were now on the ground. Charlie Company was conducting their own combat assault into an LZ 15 kilometers south of the B Company location. While helicopters provide amazing mobility in all types of terrain the major drawback was that everyone knows you're there.

After the airlift was complete the company began moving to the northeast in combat column to where Jim wanted to set up the company's initial position and day one NDP. His plan was to put the company on defensible terrain near the center of his operational area and send out ambushes from there in the afternoon and evening. He'd rotate the ambush teams and change their locations daily. Every two days the company would move to a new NDP so their location didn't stay fixed, hopefully providing less of an opportunity to be targeted and attacked.

The terrain north and east of Plei Re was low mountains and hills running generally north and south. The mountains were mostly jungled with tall trees and intermittent, sometimes dense, ground cover. There were occasional open areas of tall grass and wide bushes. The streams were intermittent between the hills and dry or with low water even during the rainy season.

Most of the significant north-south movement of NVA units was done on the Cambodian side of the border using the Ho Chi Minh Trail, the sophisticated network of roads and trails that began in North Vietnam and ran through Laos and Cambodia. At various points along the Ho Chi Minh trail were infiltration routes to the east into South Vietnam. One of the major infiltration zones was in Kontum province where there was little population along either side of the border.

There were several significant east-west trails in the B Company AO, but only one road, an unimproved dirt road identifiable on the map as DT674. It ran east and west from Kontum City to Plei Re and was originally constructed by loggers to use when harvesting the hardwoods that grew in groves along the Vietnam-Cambodian border. At times the NVA took full advantage of this road to move vehicles and equipment, mostly at night to avoid American detection. On the Vietnamese side of the border the NVA troop movements into the south used the east-west trails. However, the useful trails in this area of western Kontum were fewer as you got closer to the border making them textbook locations for ambushes.

About 1500 hours, the first day on the ground Jim moved the company to a small hill top near the center of his AO and about four kilometers north of DT674. As the company started to set up it began to rain lightly. The rainy season was just starting. Rain and wet weather made soldering miserable and movement on wet roads and trails more hazardous. The rollercoaster hills and jungle added to the misery for the soldiers on both sides.

Jim picked out a location for his command post (CP) between two large mahogany trees and his RTOs began to set-up communications and do the routine checks as Ren started to dig a position for the captain and himself. Jim sat by one of the tall hardwood trees, put on his rain jacket, and began reviewing his map. He began picking out where he wanted to set that night's ambushes. Four squad size ambushes would be deployed that night. Tomorrow a platoon size ambush would be set along the western part of DT674 and four other squad size ambushes along the most prominent trails in the area.

Jim tried to protect his map as the rain started to fall a little harder. It was 1600 and he estimated it would stay light until about 1800, but sparingly so because of the dense overhead canopies and jungle that blocked much of the ambient light. The rain didn't help either.

Jim called in the platoon leaders and gave them their orders for the evening's ambushes and instructed them to have the ambush squads in their assigned positions NLT 1745. They were to coordinate re-entry points to the company perimeter directly with the squads in case they had to withdraw into the company perimeter quickly. They wouldn't need LPs out tonight because the ambush squads were out and they could give any early warning if someone was approaching the NDP. Shortly after the platoon leaders left to return to their positions Jim told

1SG Kue that he wanted to walk the perimeter to check the defense. The 1SG rogered and said he would be ready to go with him in five minutes. As he waited for the 1SG, Jim took out the indigenous ration that he always kept in his left field pants pocket and had a cold rice and fish dinner.

Upon the 1SG's return he and Jim walked the perimeter and checked the company's defensive preparations: the crew served weapons positions, platoon tie-in positions and generally where the men were setting up. It all looked good. B Company was a veteran group and Jim and the 1SG's inspection was just a formality, everyone knew what to do and was busily digging in and doing their jobs. After walking the perimeter, they returned to the company CP. Jim asked the RTOs about commo with B-24 and the fire support net (FSN). Communication with B-24 was good and on the FSN they had a good link with the day time FAC, call sign Rock'n Rooster, who advised he would be going off station shortly and the night FAC would come on the net - Arizona HellCat again. The RTO could check in with him to confirm commo at 1800 when he was on station. "Good work, let me know when Arizona is working," Jim said. "Yes, Sir," was the reply. Jim was pleased, his RTOs were as professional as the rest of his Hmongs. It was easy commanding professionals, he thought to himself. It was about 1700 and a light drizzle was still falling.

At 1715 Jim told 1SG Kue he was going outside the perimeter to take his daily "constitutional" and would be back shortly. Ren grabbed his weapon and rucksack and followed his company commander as he made his way to the 1st Platoon CP and told the platoon leader he was going to go outside the perimeter in front of his position for a few minutes and he would shine his flashlight at his position when he was coming back in. The platoon leader and his RTO and the other two soldiers in the platoon CP nodded their heads and smiled. It was good to know that even the big Americans had to take a shit every once in a while, they thought to themselves. Jim and Ren looked outside the perimeter, it looked clear as the rain began to fade. Jim picked out a large tree a ways out and they started walking past the perimeter and down the slope the short distance to the selected tree.

At the tree Jim found a log and unbuckled and unzipped his pants and sat down with his ass overhanging the log to relieve himself. One of life's small pleasures, he thought to himself as he did his business. Ren knelt down a few meters away looking down the slope of the hill, but he didn't see anything.

Jim was tidying himself up when the first mortar rounds landed about 25 meters away, between where he was and the company perimeter. The explosions were shocking as neither he nor Ren heard the rounds fired or coming in. Usually you can hear the BOOM - BOOM as mortar rounds leave their tube and a low whistle as they fall. But not this time, the first sound they heard was the explosion. It was close enough to knock them back and scare the hell out of them. Luckily neither was hit. Jim quickly put himself back together, grabbed his rifle and hugged the ground as the mortar rounds kept falling. They didn't seem to be landing inside the perimeter or to be adjusted, but the barrage lasted for several minutes.

Then suddenly, Jim and Ren heard small arms fire, the distinct sound of AK47s and M16s with a machine-gun also engaging. It was coming from the company perimeter on the southeast side, to the right of Jim and Ren's location. Jim and Ren didn't see anyone so they just stayed down behind the two mahogany trees keeping a careful watch. Clearly, the NVA knew where B Company's position was and they were not only lobbing mortars at it, but were also launching a ground assault. The engagement came as a complete surprise.

Jim was confused, how did the NVA know where B Company was? They hadn't seen anyone all day, and how did they get mortars in place to fire on B Company's position when the company had just moved there? They must have had trail watchers out — the NVA often used sympathetic locals to guide them and watch trails reporting if they saw any movement on them. This must be what happened. But how could the NVA launch an attack so quickly? The company had just taken up their position. Bewildered, Jim had more pressing issues to figure out, like finding a way to get himself, and Ren back inside the B Company perimeter without getting killed. He'd think about "how this happened" later. Best we lie still for a while and when the shooting and mortars stop maybe we can make our way back inside, Jim thought to himself.

After several minutes, the mortars stopped and the gun fire became more sporadic. Jim figured then was as good a time as any to make a break for the perimeter. He motioned for Ren to come closer and pointed towards the perimeter. Ren nodded. Jim grabbed his flashlight off his web gear and started to get up when Ren let loose with a volley from his M16. Whoever he was shooting at returned fire fivefold. Jim still didn't see anyone, but someone must be off to their right-front towards where they first heard the gun fire. He thought it had to be the assaulting force shifting his way to find a better approach for attacking the perimeter. Whoever was shooting at them stopped firing and so did Ren. Jim peered around the tree to see what was going on. About 70 meters away was a group of several NVA, combat loaded in khaki uniforms and helmets with rucksacks. They weren't local VC and they were headed right for him and Ren. Jim let loose a burst from his rifle at the approaching squad and so did Ren. The NVA took cover and returned fire, although it was not well aimed.

Things were serious now. The NVA knew where Jim and Ren were, had an advantage in numbers, and Jim and Ren were too far in front of the company perimeter to get back inside safely. Worse, if the bad guys assaulted Jim and Ren there was little doubt they would win, there were just too many of them. Jim and Ren had only a few minutes to think of something before the NVA realized there were just two of them and came after them then they would be in a world of hurt - probably killed!

The squad of NVA Ren saw had been maneuvering to find a better position from which to attack B Company's perimeter when, by sheer chance, they ran into Jim and Ren. They were the lead part of the unit that had been stung significantly the previous days during the attack on Plei Kleng. A third of their company had been killed or wounded in that fiasco. They had spent the past night after withdrawing from Plei Kleng licking their wounds and caring for their many wounded on a ridge about 1500 meters to the southeast of where B Company was setting up its NDP. A Montagnard trail watcher had alerted them to the location of B Company, but they already knew something was up after they heard the helicopters coming and going to their south all morning. All they were trying to do was get back to the relative safety of Cambodia, but now they had to deal with someone trying to cut them off.

Jim and Ren didn't have much to put up a fight with, especially against several attackers. Ren had his rucksack jammed with eight magazines of ammo, and a claymore along with some wire, a poncho, a few personal items, and a ration. He had two fragmentation grenades and one white phosphorus (Willy Pete) grenade on his web gear along with a knife and first aid pouch. Jim had only his web gear with his Randell knife, a flashlight, first aid pouch and his rifle with two magazines taped back-to-back. Jim assumed 1st Platoon, where he and Ren had left the NDP, would be under assault shortly so he and Ren probably couldn't expect any help from them. No, Jim and Ren were pinned down and essentially on their own. They'd have to figure their own way out of this one.

Jim told Ren they should run west away from the NVA and find a place to hide for the night. They would figure out how to get back into the perimeter in the morning. When he started shooting at the NVA providing covering fire, Ren should throw his Willy Pete at the NVA so the smoke would hide their movement. When the white smoke rose and obscured their position Jim would unleash another volley of fire toward the NVA and then Ren should run back about 50 meters or so, find some good cover, and set up to support Jim when he moved back. Ren should yell "Jim" when he was set up, then Jim would run back while Ren covered his move. They would continue that leap-frogging back to the west until they broke contact with the NVA. They could then pick up and run west together to try to put some real distance between them and the NVA and find a good place to hide for the night. Ren nodded, he understood and said, "Yes, sir" and took out the phosphorus grenade and made ready to throw it.

When Jim let loose with a burst from his M16 to get the NVA to stop and put their heads down, Ren threw the grenade right at them. It landed about 20 meters ahead of their position detonated and began spewing dense white smoke that drifted up between the bad guys, Jim and Ren. Jim told Ren to wait a minute and let the smoke rise a bit more and when he fired again to take off and find the next position. A minute later the white smoke had filled the air and with the trees and underbrush obscured everything to their east. Jim looked at Ren, nodded, and fired a deliberate volley through the white smoke towards the NVA. Immediately Ren took off running. After a minute of firing intermittently Jim heard Ren yell "Jim" and he stood-up and ran back towards Ren.

Unfortunately, when Jim got up one of the NVA clearly saw him. "It's an American," he yelled out and he and several of his comrades started firing in Jim's direction, but ineffectively. Jim zig-zagged back to Ren going past him about 30 meters then taking up a position behind a tree. "Ren," he yelled and started firing high over Ren. He couldn't see anyone but he wanted the NVA to stay in place and keep their heads down as Ren made his retreat.

Once he was informed the ARVN were setting up a position close to his company's withdrawal route and possibly blocking its path back to Cambodia, Captain Semal Dembo, the company commander of the NVA 24th Regiment's 2nd Company, chose to conduct a hasty attack on them. He wanted to attack quickly before they had a chance to get their defense organized and dug-in. His main objective was to pin them down, perhaps diminish them a bit, so he could be sure they couldn't cause him any problems as he moved what was left of his ravaged company past them into Cambodia. Carrying several badly wounded and with more than twenty ambulatory wounded his movement was slow. He figured it would take him another full day at least to get his wounded and everyone else in the battered 2nd Company back across the border. He didn't need any harassment from the ARVN.

To bolster his pinning attack, he had set up his three mortars in a small clearing well to the southeast to provide some fire support. He didn't exactly know where their perimeter was, but knew from experience they would be on the high ground so he fired his mortars where he thought they might be. After the short barrage he launched an hasty attack from the south. He didn't know a Mike Force company was his target. Captain Dembo really didn't intend to try and overrun the ARVN, he just wanted to punish them a bit and fix them in place so he could continue his retreat.

Captain Semal Dembo was black as the ace of spades. He wasn't Vietnamese, he was an officer in the Angolan Popular Movement for the Liberation of Angola (MPLA) rebel army. Dembo was 32 years old and from a small village in north Angola near the border with the Congo. He was a veteran guerrilla fighter having fought as a soldier in a local rebel militia since he was sixteen and with the MPLA in one African sub-Sahara conflict or another for the past decade. He really didn't know anything else. He had impressed the MPLA leadership and they sent him to Cuba for training, and then Mozambique before making him an officer following his return home. During the time he was with the MPLA it had become the dominant pro-independence political and militia force in Angola. They had been fighting the Portuguese for over a decade trying to force the Europeans to grant Angola independence.

Jose' dos Santos, the leader of the MPLA, wanted to show solidarity with other communist movements and garner their support for the MPLA so he sent Captain Dembo and several other Angolans to Vietnam to support the North Vietnamese insurgency. Captain Dembo was one of the "advisors" and had been in Vietnam for about 16 months. He wasn't fond of Southeast Asia, but he hoped his foreign exploits would earn him a higher position in the Angolan Army once the MPLA gained Angola its independence.

The past several days Captain Dembo had been leading the assault on the Special Forces Camp at Plei Kleng. The attack wasn't successful in itself, in fact it was a disaster, but the mission was accomplished because it tied up enemy forces so they couldn't be re-deployed to reinforce the defenders in Kontum, one of the NVA's prime urban objectives for Phase II of the North's Tet Offensive in the Central Highlands.

When one of the NVA squads spotted Jim during their hasty attack they immediately started shooting at him and sent a runner to their company commander to report what they had seen. Captain Dembo quickly came over to the squad's location to assess what was going on for himself. Before he moved he ordered his second in command to keep firing at B Company positions, but not to launch another ground assault. He wanted the majority of his company to keep moving — throughout the night if it could — into Cambodia. The rain on trails and carrying a number of severely wounded made movement slow, but the sooner they got into Cambodia the better.

When Captain Dembo got to the NVA squad's location they told him what had happened and that they had seen a big white guy run to the west with an Asian guy. They fired on them, but didn't think they hit either. They thought the white guy was probably an American - he was very tall. Dembo told the squad to get after them and he would go with them to try and capture the American. The squad fully understood the opportunity, to capture an American or even kill one was a big deal. They quickly got up and started to move toward the last location where they had seen Jim and Ren run down the gentle slope to the west as the rain started to intensify.

Jim and Ren were well away from the NVA squad when they stopped to assess things and try to figure out how they could get back to the B Company perimeter. Jim's plan was to separate themselves from the NVA then find a good concealed spot to hide for the night. It was getting towards dusk and raining on and off and he didn't want to stumble around in the rain and the dark into more NVA or get shot by his own troops. In the morning they could re-assess the situation and try to figure out a way to get back to the company. With any luck the NVA wouldn't come after them and concentrate on their attack of B Company.

Jim knew the company would be okay in 1SG Kue's experienced hands. But he still wondered about the attack. The firing had all but stopped as he and Ren retreated; he wasn't sure if the engagement was a serious assault or just a small attack to keep B Company away from a bigger NVA unit that was trying to escape west to Cambodia. He knew a large NVA force had unsuccessfully attacked Plei Kleng and been severely pummeled. His mission was to try find them and finish them off as they retreated to Cambodia. The folks shooting at him were probably part of that unit, but none of that mattered now. Jim's immediate concern was to figure out how to get out of the mess he was in and back to B Company.

After ten minutes of sitting and listening, Jim and Ren could hear the NVA as they were moving closer toward them. Damnit, Jim thought to himself, I wish they would have stayed with their unit. Now we have to give these guys the shake or we'll never make it back to the company. Jim told Ren they'd have to move again by "leaps and bounds" to cover each other, but once they broke contact they would move together. They'd head west, then when they had dropped the NVA turn north to find a place to hide, he didn't want to get too far from the company.

Jim waited another minute while he and Ren looked around. Seeing no one, he rose to a crouch, nodded at Ren and then jumped up and started running west along a little stream on the south side of the hill where B Company was setting up. He didn't think the NVA could hear him move as it was starting to rain harder and the light was fading to dark. After moving about fifty meters he stopped, found good cover and turned to wait for Ren.

Ren kept watch from the last position, weapon at the ready. After a few minutes, the coast seemed to be clear, so he jumped up and started running to where he thought Jim was. Ren was just in front of Jim's position when an unseen NVA to his north spotted him and started shooting. Jim returned fire as Ren dove into where Jim was crouched behind a tree. But he didn't get up. When Jim looked at him he could see he was dead — he had been shot in the head. Ren was a good man, but Jim didn't have time to mourn him now, that could come later, right now he was in a fight for his life.

Jim had a big problem, it was just him and what he thought was a squad of NVA who were closing on his position - probably within a 100 meters. He had to get out of there immediately or he would get pinned down and unable to move at all, then it would be all over but the shouting. Jim didn't like the idea of getting killed in the middle of nowhere or even worse rotting in a North Vietnamese prison camp for the rest of his life. He had to get out of there. Quickly, he bent down and took Ren's rifle and stepped on the barrel bending it and grabbed the two grenades off Ren's web gear. He knelt behind the tree and peeked towards the NVA. They didn't seem to have pinpointed his location but he could hear them moving forward, more cautiously now.

Still behind the tree, Jim pulled the pin on one of the grenades and held it, not letting the safety spoon flip-off. He waited another minute until he could see the lead NVA about 20 meters away. When two of the NVA bunched up to move around some bushes, Jim let the spoon flip off the grenade, counted to two, and threw it right at the two NVA. It hit just in front of them and exploded immediately. Jim could hear one of the NVA scream as he grabbed Ren's rucksack and took off running full speed west at a zig-zag away from his pursuers. The NVA didn't open fire after the grenade detonated which surprised Jim, maybe he got several of them and maybe they didn't see him sprint away. But in any event he wasn't stopping as the rain started again coming down a little harder now.

Jim sprinted as fast as he could until he figured he was out of range of rifle fire and couldn't be seen in the bushy terrain. At the bottom of the hill he was descending he stopped when he came to a trail. It led northeast. He could move faster on the trail, but would leave clear tracks that if the NVA got to the trail could be easily followed, probably even at night. But Jim took it anyway, he figured faster was better. Going as quickly as he could he kept moving for the next half hour. Then he abruptly jumped a few feet off the trail to the right of his footprints so he wouldn't be so easy to track and started moving up the small mountain on the right. He stopped mid-way up. There was an opening by several mahogany trees and he could just barely see the trail he had been on as it meandered around the mountain from the northwest. It was almost completely dark now and soon he wouldn't be able to detect anyone moving on the trail so he decided he'd just hunker down where he was and wait until morning to make his next move. He dug into Ren's ruck and found his poncho and put it on as the rain started to intensify.

When one of the NVA caught sight of Ren running, he was about 75 meters away, he fired at him immediately. He didn't know if they hit him or not as visibility wasn't good because of the rain. His comrades moved up to be online, but they didn't see Ren or anyone else. When Jim returned fire they all quickly took cover, but didn't shoot back because they couldn't see anybody. They stayed down and watched for a while hoping to locate where the shooting was coming from so they could attack the retreating American and his Asian buddy. After a few minutes seeing no movement and not hearing anything, Captain Dembo the company commander who was now running the squad, had them cautiously move forward on line, keeping a sharp lookout. He didn't want to be ambushed.

After advancing about 50 meters a hand grenade suddenly exploded in the center of the squad and two men were wounded, one seriously.

Tittsworth

There was no follow-up fire. At the blast the squad immediately took cover, but they didn't shoot because they still didn't see anyone in the dense underbrush and failing light. While a couple of guys tended to the wounded the rest of the squad covered them and kept looking forward hoping to see where the grenade had come from and catch a glimpse of the American or his partner. They weren't sure where the grenade was thrown from - but it had to be ahead of them and not too far away because of the dense terrain.

The NVA squad held in place for a while silently trying to look and listen. Dembo had the two wounded treated as best they could be under the circumstances and send one man back to the company to have help come forward and assist with the more severely wounded man and move him back to the caravan of wounded they were evacuating to Cambodia.

Shortly, after help arrived Dembo ordered the five men left in the squad to move out and continue the pursuit of the American. In short order they came across Ren's body and were surprised they had hit him, a lucky shot to be sure, but that meant there was now only the big white guy left and they had lost track of him. Dembo was determined to get after him, he was too big a prize to let get away.

In the fading light the NVA could see the dead man was a Hmong — interesting. That told Dembo that the company he had attacked was either a local militia or a Mike Force company and not an ARVN unit. The white guy was surely an American advisor, probably a Special Forces guy. He noted the dead man's rifle was bent and there was no gear around him. He assumed the American must have taken it, if he even had any. Why were the two of them outside their unit's perimeter? That was strange he thought, but they were, and now the American was on the run alone and would soon be his captive. Dembo didn't think he could be too far in front of them in the rain and the dark so he had the squad move out smartly, but cautiously, they'd keep after him for a while and see what developed. He probably wouldn't get too far as the darkness would slow him down and the rain make him easy to follow.

After the NVA quickly searched Ren's body, Dembo sent a runner back to his company to reiterate his previous orders to his second in command — to keep the company moving and not stop until they were safely across the border. He had also directed him to keep the unit they had attacked pinned down by fire until the main company had moved well past them. Then he could pull everyone back and get them headed to Cambodia as well. Dembo would stay with the squad pursuing the American and would join the company in the Cambodian base area once they captured or killed him.

The team with Dembo was now six; himself, his interpreter, a pointman/tracker, and three soldiers. He was confident that would be enough to hunt down the lone American. He'd give chase for a while and if they didn't get him they'd break off and head back to Cambodia.

The squad moved out and tried to quicken their pace, but the jungle and darkness was hindering their movement. After a while they reached a trail that headed northeast and even in the now darkness found footprints heading that direction and began following them. After several minutes they hadn't moved very far on the trail when it started raining harder and became very dark. Captain Dembo was concerned they might get ambushed so he had the squad stop, move off the trail, and find a place to hunker down for the night. They'd take up the chase again at first light. In the mud the big American would leave a good trail and be easy to follow. They wouldn't find the guy in the dark anyway and it was more dangerous at night, so it made no sense to exhaust themselves and get even more drenched for no reward. Just off the trail they found some drier ground and settled in for the evening. No need for security, just hunker down, try to stay warm and dry, eat what they had, and rest. Tomorrow would be a hard day.

As Jim sat in the folds of a large mahogany tree under Ren's poncho he went over again what his options were as he went through Ren's rucksack. He felt bad that Ren had been killed, but he didn't dwell on his death. He was a fine soldier and way too young to be dead, but he was just one of any number of good soldiers and young men who would lose their lives in the war. It was too bad, but it couldn't be changed. Jim had to focus on his own survival. He didn't know how many NVA were chasing him or who they were, he had only seen a few of them when the skirmish first started. He thought it was maybe a squad, clearly, they had seen him and Ren and knew it was just the two of them. They had most likely found Ren's body and now knew Jim was all alone. They probably thought they could capture him if they pressed him, figured he'd be running and might even be lost. What Jim needed to do was take stock of what assets he had and get a plan together to get back to the company. He'd have to do that in daylight, it was just too dangerous to try to rejoin them at night, especially after they had been attacked. So now he'd see what he had, try to re-focus and prepare. Tomorrow would be a hard day.

After going through Ren's ruck Jim had: one claymore mine, some wire, a grenade, seven magazines of ammo, plus the clip and a-half in his rifle, and a full indigenous ration. There was a half-full canteen attached to the rucksack. He'd toss out Ren's few personal items, no sense carrying more than he had to, no telling how long he'd be out here. Thankfully Jim also had his map, still in his right-side pants pocket. He was wearing his web gear with his Randell knife on his left shoulder harness, first aid pouch on the belt, flashlight on the right. He still had the half-eaten rice ration he carried in his own left pants pocket, a plastic spoon and a half-pack of Clove gum in one shirt pocket. He loved Clove gum, it took the bad taste out of your mouth when you were in the field. A small packet of toilet paper and a P38 can opener was in the other shirt pocket. So, he wasn't without capabilities, could fight and survive and perhaps provide a surprise or two for his pursuers.

Under the poncho Jim used the flashlight to study his map trying to figure out exactly where he was and where he should go in the morning. He thought he was about eight to ten kilometers north of Plei

Re and about three, maybe four kilometers northwest of B Company's position. While he wasn't sure what 1SG Kue would do in the morning, probably send out a patrol to try and find him and Ren. He might also put out a few ambushes. Jim assumed the company would all stay within the NDP tonight since they had been attacked and they knew there were bad guys in the area. Too dangerous to try and put out ambushes or even LPs. Unbeknownst to B Company, the NVA had dismantled their mortars after the initial barrage and had them start moving toward the border with the rest of the company, so there was no threat of additional indirect fire attacks. If they moved all night without interruption the NVA 2nd Company would be just about to the border by morning. Sometimes you did get lucky and they needed some luck after the disastrous attack on Polei Kleng.

After studying the map under his poncho, Jim decided he would stay put for the night. In the morning he would parallel the trail in front of him to the east for a while, then stop and make another assessment of his situation.

The jungle was thick in the Chu Mom Ray forest and would be to his advantage for losing those chasing him. If he could, he would try to make contact with B Company, although in the jungle highlands he wasn't sure exactly how he could safely do that, but that was his first choice. If he couldn't get back to B Company he'd try heading east and then go south and cross DT647, the logger's road. He could parallel that road east toward Plei Kleng until he reached someplace safe. But his first priority was to get away from any NVA chasing him. After his map recon Jim turned out his flashlight, rubbed the Jade elephant around his neck for luck, leaned his back against the tree and thought of Dara while listening to the rain.

The rain was steady most of the night ending just before daybreak. The heavy poncho had kept the rain off Jim during the night and all in all he had stayed as dry and warm as could be expected. He woke up surprisingly refreshed. Just after he came out from under his poncho and started to eat the last of his cold rice meal, the clouds started

211

clearing and the sun was starting to come out. Might be a nice day for a hike in the jungle, he thought to himself in a poor attempt at humor. As he ate the last of his cold rice he looked down the mountain towards the trail he had followed the previous evening. The view was captivating with the deep green jungle and tall hardwood trees, the clouds of fog were slowly rising from the valley floor. Everything looked peaceful and quiet. But it was a misnomer, beauty doesn't make war go away.

The rain left everything wet and the ground muddy and even slippery in places, especially on the dirt — now muddy trails. Jim's plan was to stay off the trails when the terrain allowed it, he'd just use them for navigating. Once the NVA picked up his footprints on the trail he knew it would be easy for them to track him. But knowing where he had been and his direction wasn't the same as knowing where he was, or where he was going, or even being close to him. The muddy trail would not make catching up easy either.

As he was finishing his rice Jim noticed movement back down the trail. It was the NVA squad that was chasing him. Now he could see what he was up against. He counted six men moving in file, seeming to keep a sharp watch but moving along smartly. As they moved farther up the trail he could see the third guy in line, he wasn't wearing a hat, and was as black as the ace of spades! So it was true, there was a black man leading NVA in the Highlands. He was somewhat shocked and wondered if it was an American? Surely no American would become a traitor and lead the NVA against his own country. But clearly it was a black guy with the folks chasing him and he seemed to be in charge by the way he interacted with the others. This made Jim even more determined to make it back and report what he had seen.

The NVA had spent a cold night just off the trail. Like Jim they were glad the rain had stopped and the sun was coming out. They knew their prey would be easier to track on the wet ground even though the mud would slow their movement, it would slow his too. When they moved back to the trail they easily saw the footprints Jim left behind the previous night. Captain Dembo was now sure they were only chasing one man and he chastised his men to pick up the pace. He knew if the guy had moved all night they had little hope of catching up to him, but if he made the mistake of stopping to hide, and get out of the rain, then they might have a chance to catch up to him. Capturing an American would be a feather in Captain Dembo's hat and he urged his men to move quickly, but still be cautious.

They were still about 1000 meters away when Jim picked them up, moving in file at a steady pace but not overly fast. The lead guy was looking mostly down at the trail following the footprints and the others looking around to their flanks and up at the hills. They were not very well spread out.

There were only six men chasing him. That was too many if he had to stand and fight. He also didn't know how long they would come after him before they gave up the chase. They had to be thinking about B Company being in the area and six men didn't want to run into them or one of their patrols or ambushes. If they were the remnants of the force that attacked Plei Kleng their full unit didn't have a lot of combat power as their nose had been pretty bloodied during their assault on the camp. Jim guessed these guys were a squad sent off from the main unit who were more than likely heading back to Cambodia. But he had been seen and so this small contingent was probably sent to try to catch an American while the rest of the unit fled to their base camp across the border. It was a good analysis.

Jim stayed put for a while as he watched the NVA move along the trail. They would soon be at the point where he had left the path and headed up the mountain for the night. It would be easy for them to find that spot. He thought it might be best if he took off now and ran along the side of the mountain to get farther ahead of them before he got back on the trail to make better time. Even though it was muddy he could move much quicker on the trail. If he did that, kept going, and didn't run into anyone, he was sure he could probably get to safety without coming into contact with them again. He could also run set up a little surprise for the boys in khaki further up the trail. But what could he do now that might slow them down or maybe even turn them back? Maybe if he killed or wounded one of them it would be a good signal that he was not going to be taken easily if they did catch up to him. A good punch in the mouth might be convincing.

Watching the NVA move, Jim could see the second man in line frequently turned around and spoke with the black guy and then spoke to the others. It looked like he was perhaps interpreting for him. If Jim could kill or wound him that would disrupt the black guy's ability to communicate with his men and would surely slow them down, if not turn them back. He decided to try and kill the second guy in line.

The point on the trail where Jim had turned up the mountain was about 100 meters downhill from his current location. What he needed to do was move down the mountain east of that point and find a good hide location with a clear view of that spot. He suspected when the NVA got to the point where his footprints stopped and went uphill they would stop and look around and the black guy would have to tell everyone what he wanted done next. It would be a perfect time to take a shot. If he could get a first round hit on the interpreter guy or even the black guy, the rest of the squad would most probably duck down and try to determine where the shot came from. He could see how they handled the situation and still have time to take off and put some distance between them and himself. He'd give it a go.

Jim moved down the hill and east a bit and to where he was about seventy-five meters beyond and above where he had gotten off the trail the previous night. He would be to the left of the NVA if they tried to follow his tracks up the mountain. He found a bushy spot in a grove of trees with an unobstructed view of the point where he exited the trail. The trees would give him cover and protection if they tried to shoot back and the underbrush was not so dense so he could scoot-out quickly and run away after the shot if he had to. He decided to try and shoot the interpreter from there.

Captain Dembo wasn't happy with the pace of his squad's movement. He told the soldier who was the interpreter, and spoke Spanish, the language they communicated in, Dembo didn't speak any Vietnamese, to tell the point-man to pick it up. He knew that if they didn't start to catch up to the American today he would probably get away. The interpreter passed on the message and the pace of the squad started to pick up — but it was at the expense of security.

Shortly after he pushed the squad forward, the point-man stopped and pointed to some footprints in the trail, and then to where they led up the hill to the right. He told the interpreter he thought the American had left the trail there and went up the mountain. The interpreter waited for Captain Dembo to come up and passed on the message. Dembo pointed up the hill and told him to tell the point-man to take two other guys and follow the tracks up the mountain and see what they found. He didn't think the American would stay off the trail long because it was headed east where he needed to go. But if the American had chosen to go cross-country Dembo wanted to know it now. He and the interpreter would stay there with the last man and watch the trail.

When the interpreter turned to pass on Dembo's orders to the point-man, Jim shot him in the chest just below the right shoulder. The high velocity bullet from close range slammed into his chest, tumbled when it hit his ribs, and blasted out his back. He went down like a sack of potatoes without a sound and started to gargle blood from the one-inch hole in his chest. At the shot the rest of the squad hit the deck, and because it was only one round out of nowhere, they started frantically looking around and up the hill trying to figure out where the shot came from. They didn't shoot back.

When Jim saw the man fall and everyone else hit the ground he watched for a minute and then slowly and quietly backed up to the far side of the grove of trees he was in and began walking swiftly along the side of the hill. The NVA never saw him. When he felt safe he went down the hill a bit and looked back down the trail to see what the NVA were doing. Because of the bushes along the trail he could only see a couple of them. The black guy and another man were bending down, probably tending to the man Jim shot. The other person he could see was looking around, up the mountain and like the others trying to understand what had just happened. Mission accomplished, Jim thought to himself.

When his interpreter was shot Captain Dembo automatically hit the ground and scrambled behind a tree like everyone else. He had just seen his main guy get flipped backwards and splayed out on the trail as he bled to death, his lung ripped open by an M16 round. The rest of his team, like him, stayed hunkered down behind cover in case there was more shooting - but there was only that single shot. No one saw anyone or heard anything but the wind blowing the tops of the hardwood trees. "Chinga," which was Spanish for Fuck, Dembo cursed when he saw his man lying there dying. He crawled over to him, but there was nothing he could really do. The guy was gasping for breath and then he stopped and was quiet. Now what would he do? He couldn't really talk to his guys now and they couldn't talk to him. He was really pissed off now, he'd find that goddamn American and kill him himself. He just shot his man so he had to be close.

With the interpreter dead soon after he was shot, Captain Dembo had to decide what they would do next. He was angry that the American had killed his man. Probably the smartest move would be to call off the chase and head to Cambodia and fight another day. But this was just one fucking American and if they caught him, he would be a prize and Dembo wanted to torture him before he killed him, just like he had many of the government soldiers he crossed paths with in Angola. No, fuck it, they would move on and get the American if it was the last thing they did. He'd at least give it until one more day.

It took the NVA a little while to get themselves together, go through the dead man's stuff, and place his body off the trail where they could find it later and take it back to the base camp. Those tasks done, they were now ready to get the American.

The men really wanted to go after the American, they were pissed-off. He had killed their buddy and they knew he couldn't be far off and he was only one guy. They would hang with their captain to avenge their dead buddy, at least for a while.

Ten minutes after the interpreter died the squad sent three men up the mountain following Jim's footprints to where he spent the night, then followed them to his ambush position. They saw that when he left there he was paralleling the trail, so they went back down the slope and awkwardly got across to Captain Dembo that the American had come back down to the trail and was probably in front of them heading east. Dembo nodded, he understood, and pointed down the trail and pumped his fist signaling to head down the trail and go fast. He also pointed to his eyes and then the jungle to indicate everyone should keep a sharp watch. The four remaining NVA nodded, formed up in file with Dembo third in line and moved out at a quicker pace down the trail. We'll catch that son-of-a-bitch, Dembo thought, and when we do he'll be sorry he ever fucked with us.

Jim was well down the trail by then, maybe 1500 meters away. He figured if the NVA continued following him they would be a little more cautious after he had killed one of them. He also guessed they would be having a harder time communicating with the interpreter dead or at least out of commission giving him an added advantage. More confident now knowing what he was up against, he decided to set up a lethal surprise for the kaki squad. He estimated he'd have about 30 minutes before the NVA arrived to get his trap set and get to a safe place where he could watch and enjoy his dirty work.

When he reached a sharp bend in the trail where it took a hard turn to the southeast, the trail began to narrow significantly making it an ideal place for an ambush. There was a good chance his chasers would bunch up after making the turn and be perfect targets. If he set the claymore up as an automatic ambush he could probably get most of his pursuers in one fell swoop, but he had to find the right place to put the claymore.

As he moved down the trail after the bend he pulled branches and leaves off trees and threw them on the trail. He also kicked deadfall and sticks onto the trail. He wanted the NVA to be used to seeing debris on the path and not just mud puddles and soggy dirt with his tracks. As he continued to move a little further the trail flattened out and narrowed even more. This was it, the perfect place for a claymore ambush.

A little further down from the narrowest part of the trail Jim found a tree that had two thick bushes on each side and a lot of ground clutter in front. It was about 80 meters past the sharp right turn, enough space to ensure all of the NVA were around the bend when the claymore detonated. Jim laid down behind the tree and sighted the mine so it would explode down and across the center of the trail. After aiming the mine Jim ran some of the green camouflaged wire Ren had in his rucksack in the grass just off the side of the trail back for about 10 meters. He ensured the wire was well down in the grass and not visible. He used a stick stuck in the ground to make a left turn with the wire stretching it across the trail, anchoring it on the far side with another stick. Jim then pulled the wire taunt, to about an inch off the ground. Beyond the tripwire Jim placed several long sticks and branches and one larger, longer branch about six inches before the wire. When someone stepped over the larger branch they'd most likely step on the wire and detonate the mine.

After Jim set the tripwire he went back and armed the mine. The trap was set. He gave the kill zone one last look to be sure the trail looked normal, the wire hidden, and the claymore camouflaged. It all looked good. Then one last trick.

About three meters past the tripwire, off the right side of the trail, Jim placed a piece of shiny aluminum wrapping from a stick of his Clove gum in plain sight. It was intended to catch the eye of the lead man and take his eyes off the trail making it more likely he'd not see the trip wire. The trap was now set. Jim took off further down the trail making sure he left easily seen footprints.

About fifty meters further down the trail Jim jumped off on the north side and continued a little further east until he found a place with good cover and concealment and a direct view of the ambush kill zone. He was about 70 meters away from the ambush and could easily run east concealed by the jungle if something went wrong. All that was left was to wait and see if his trap would provide the NVA with the deadly surprise he was counting on.

He didn't have to wait long to find out. Fifteen minutes after he took up his hide position he saw the NVA point-man round the bend in the trail. The lead man stopped and looked down the trail and to each side, saw nothing, and then started moving forward again. He was thirty meters away from the tripwire. A few meters behind him came the second soldier, then a few more meters back the black guy, and just behind him the two other NVA. All five were now walking in a 15-meter file straight into the ambush. Then suddenly the black guy stepped off the trail and sat down on the uphill side to re-tie his boot. One of the trailing soldiers came up to him and sat down as well. The point-man stopped in the middle of the trail and turned around and waited. After adjusting his boot, the black guy gave a signal to move ahead, the file re-formed and the point-man started moving again — he was ten meters from the tripwire.

As he started to move forward the shiny gum wrapper caught his eye. It was out of place in the jungle, someone must have dropped it — the American! As he stared at the shiny paper on the side of the trail it started to sprinkle rain again and everyone stopped for a second and looked up trying to figure out if the rain was serious or just a passing shower. As everyone stood there in the rain in the middle of the trail, the black guy abruptly stepped off the trail again just as the point man turned, stepped over the large branch in the trail and onto the tripwire detonating the claymore with a single deafening - BOOM! Instantly, the steel pellets raced down the narrow trail in an expanding cone four times faster than the speed of sound. In addition to smoke, the explosion churned up debris and mud and flung them all down the trail sweeping over the wet ground and raising a fog making it hard to see anything.

The point-man and the second soldier in the file were immediately blown away in the blast, torn apart like ragdolls, dead when they hit the ground. The number four man was peppered with pellets and dropped to the ground where he would die within minutes.

Luckily Captain Dembo had stepped off the trail and out of the kill zone to take a piss when the hail of supersonic pellets came exploding down the path. Only two pellets hit him, finding his left thigh after ricocheting off the tree in front of him. He was stung, bled a little, but wasn't seriously injured. He felt like he had been shot by a pellet gun. He easily popped one of the steel balls out of his thigh, the other one was further under the skin and stayed in his leg. The small wounds hurt but didn't seem to hinder his movement much. Fortunately for him the tree in front of him had absorbed most of the blast's energy, pellets and debris flying towards him.

The last guy in the file wasn't so lucky. He had turned to look at Captain Dembo when he stepped off the trail and was standing sideways in the middle of the kill zone when the mine went off. He was immediately peppered with claymore pellets on the left side of his body. He was a mangled mess and had taken several pellets to the head. If he got proper medical attention quickly he might have made it, but that was impossible in the middle of the jungle. When the smoke and fog cleared Captain Dembo moved over to where he was lying on the trail, saw the blood running down his face and out of his ears. His smashed helmet lay crumpled several meters behind him. Dembo knew immediately there was nothing he could do for him, he would not survive. After caressing the dying man's forehead, he moved down the line to each of his fallen men and found the same result - blown to bits or so badly mangled there was no hope. He was shocked that he had escaped the ambush with only a few pellets and scratches. Not my time yet, he thought to himself as he stood up and stared down the trail. He saw nothing, but his anger grew.

As he looked down the trail Captain Semal Dembo realized the hunt for the American was over, the American had won and would escape. He thought now he might even become the hunted. These fucking Americans, they have everything and they still can't win wars, he said to himself. If I had half their capabilities I would have won this war a long time ago. I only wish I could get my hands on this filthy American who killed my men. I would show him no mercy. But he knew that probably wasn't going to happen. The best he could do now was try and make it back to the base camp in Cambodia. Maybe he'd get another shot at the American in the future. He hoped so.

Jim watched with some satisfaction as the claymore did its nasty work. He saw the NVA squad go down, but in the fog and smoke and the cloud of debris, he lost track of the black guy. He didn't know if he was hit or where he was. When the smoke and fog cleared he could see four NVA lying on the trail, none were moving, but initially the black guy was not visible. Jim wasn't sure what he should do, take off running, or try to move closer and find the black guy? He chose to just sit tight, remain out of sight, and keep watching for a few more minutes to see what would happen.

As Jim continued to watch the dead bodies the black guy suddenly came into view. He was apparently unhurt by the claymore blast. He moved to the last man in the file and bent down. After a few minutes, he stood-up and moved up the trail checking each of his crumpled men. He didn't appear to do anything but bend over and look, so Jim assumed his guys were too far gone to help. Then he stood straight up right in the middle of the mangled bodies and stared right down the narrow trail towards where Jim was hiding. His left pant leg was torn and bloody. The look on his face was one of anger and contempt. Jim figured he had only been lightly wounded and was probably cursing him under his breath, wishing he could get to Jim so he could avenge his men. Perhaps, Jim thought, but not today. It's my turn for revenge.

Tittsworth

Jim stayed quiet in his hide place and stared back at the wounded black NVA, starting to think about how he could take him out.

The wounded NVA captain knew he had to head back toward Cambodia ASAP. There wasn't anything left to do there except gather the ID cards from his dead men. At least he could report that they were dead, not like so many other small units that went out but never came back and no one ever heard from them again. No, he would report his men were dead, that they died fighting. It might give some solace to their families. But first he had to make it back himself.

As Jim watched Captain Dembo remove the ID cards from his men and put them in his pocket, he decided he had to kill the guy. If he just ran back and reported he saw a black guy leading NVA troops nobody would probably believe him after all the rumors going around for the last several months and no one reliable ever reported seeing a black guy with the NVA, let alone one leading a unit. No, Jim had to have solid proof he fought a black man who was leading NVA troops.

Jim also decided he wasn't going to try and capture the black guy, that was too risky. He'd just kill him and get something that he could take back to B-24 to give to the intel folks. But how could he do that? The great irony was the two warriors were only about 80 meters apart as they both were trying to figure out what they would do next.

Captain Dembo knew that he had to move and get the hell out of there, but after he collected the IDs from his men he sat down on the side of the trail in a funk. Clearly their luck had run out and they ran into an ambush. There had not been any follow-up gunfire after the mine detonated suggesting that whoever set the mine was probably long gone. But the ambush had been effective and his men were dead. He was damn lucky to still be alive. Not my time yet, he said to himself as he surveyed the mangled bodies of his squad. He wondered if it was the American he was chasing who set the mine? It might have been, or more probably, they had just run into an old stay behind ambush left on the trail by some long gone unit. It didn't really matter, the deadly encounter did its job, his squad was gone.

Dembo suddenly felt exhausted and unfocused. He needed to get his wits about him. He had to start backtracking down the trail until he reached one of the designated rally points north of Plei Re where he could link up with 2nd Company or another unit and move back to base camp. Or was it too dangerous to stay on the trail? His 2nd Company should be close to or even over the border with Cambodia by now, even with all the wounded, if they had kept moving like he had directed. That meant the ARVN unit, or whoever it was they had attacked yesterday, was not engaged and they might be patrolling in the area and worse setting ambushes. He decided it would be better if he stayed just off the trail but paralleled it until he reached the rally point. His leg hurt but he could still move, he thought he best get going before his leg really started to bother him. He had to focus, the main thing was to get back to his unit, get some medical attention, and live to fight another day.

Jim knew the trail was a looping path that went basically east-west around the mountain. The high ground was on the south side of the trail which eventually hooked into the DT674 road just outside of Plei Re. Somewhere north of there must be the route the NVA were headed for that would take them back into Cambodia. He figured the black guy knew that and would more than likely head in that direction now that all his men were dead. What could Jim do to intercept him – stop him – before he reached safety? Perhaps he could attack him from where he was now, while he was still digesting the death of his men and maybe not fully focused on his situation. Clearly, he didn't know Jim was only 80 meters in front of him, well within rifle range. If Jim could get a good shot at him he could take him out now, then he wouldn't have to chase him which presented a number of risks. He had a critical decision to make and had to make it quick.

Jim chose to keep a close watch on the dead NVA for a while and if the black guy showed himself again, and he had a clean shot, he'd take it.

If he didn't and the black guy started retreating back down the trail, Jim would run over the top of the mountain to try to get in front of him and take him out in an ambush further down the trail closer to Plei Re. That is assuming he didn't run into anyone. Jim guessed the black guy would be making the choice for him by what he did next.

Jim also didn't know what B Company was doing? They had orders to find the fleeing NVA force that attacked Plei Kleng and engage and destroy them. Yesterday, just by chance, the NVA had run into B Company as they were retreating and had launched that hasty attack as the company was setting up its NDP. Bravo Company was caught off guard, but that engagement was defensive and not decisive. Today B Company might go back on the offense and send out patrols and set ambushes as was originally planned. Jim had to be careful if he went over the mountain, he didn't want to run into a friendly ambush. No, his best course of action would be to engage the black guy now, where he was, at his first opportunity before he started to move.

After several minutes Dembo got himself together. He decided, at least for a short distance, he would move west on the trail. There wasn't a high likelihood that someone had moved in behind him, but the explosion was loud and if anyone was around they surely heard it and might come to see what was going on. But he had to take the chance he wouldn't run into anyone so he could move faster.

It had stopped drizzling just before the blast, but Dembo expected it would rain on and off throughout the day. He also calculated he was about 6-8 kilometers from 2nd Company's designated rally point north of Plei Re. He'd make for that, and probably could get there by the afternoon if he didn't run into any other problems and his leg held up. But first he would move his men's bodies off the trail and mark the location, perhaps their bodies could be retrieved later. It was a respect thing, he cared for his men even though they were dead. It was the least he could do for them. He took a long drink from his canteen and stood up.

When Captain Dembo stood up Jim saw him immediately, but didn't shoot. Dembo began looking around for a place to put his dead soldiers. He picked a large tree on the North side of the trail that would be easy to spot if someone came back to get the bodies. Then he drug one body off the trail, then another and another until all four were laid out next to the prominent tree. He looked at his four dead men one last time and saluted. When he turned and stepped back on the trail Jim shot him.

Jim's shot hit Dembo just above the hip on his right side at a glancing angle. When the bullet hit Dembo he staggered back and tripped into a bush on the opposite side of the trail from his lifeless men. The bullet passed through his right side without hitting anything critical, but he was hurt and starting to bleed. Instinctively he knew he couldn't just lay there, he had to get to cover, he was under attack. He rolled behind a large hardwood tree and assessed his wound. It was serious, but not dire – they had just winged him. He was bleeding, but not too much. The shock of the striking bullet caused immediate swelling around the hole in his side helping minimize the bleeding. The wound stung like crazy, but he had held on to his rifle and his pistol was on his belt, so he was armed and could still fight. And, although painful, he could still move.

After a minute Dembo came to his full senses and, like the seasoned warrior he was, tried to figure out what would happen next. He didn't know where the shot had come from – up the trail, but where? Clearly, someone had been observing him, the American no doubt. He had to quickly figure out what he needed to do to defend himself – it was a question of survival and he wasn't in the best of shape, nor near any help. Staying under cover was the first thing, so he stayed behind the hardwood tree and tried to figure out what he would do if someone rushed him. Fucking fight!, he said under his breath as he began tending to his wound.

Jim had jerked the shot. He was confident he hit the black guy, but didn't know if he had put him out of action or just winged him. He wasn't sure what to do next. He knew it was just him and the black guy now in a life and death struggle, and he had landed the first blow — a clear advantage for him. He saw the black guy go down and then scramble behind a tree, but didn't know how bad he was hurt and now couldn't see him. He also didn't know if the black guy knew where he was, if not, another advantage Jim. But what now?

Jim had the advantage, he wasn't wounded and his enemy didn't know where he was — but he had to assume the black guy was still armed and dangerous. He'd just stay concealed for a while watching to see if the black guy tried to move. If he didn't Jim would have to go get him at some point. To do that he'd back out of his position, cross the trail farther east, remaining out of sight, and move as quietly as he could to the high ground south of the trail, above the big tree where he last saw the black guy. He'd then circle back west, taking it slow and careful, and see if he could locate the guy and get another shot at him — if he wasn't already dead.

Captain Dembo stayed behind his tree putting pressure on his wound. He had a bandage, but it didn't cover both the entry and exit wounds. He'd just have to hope the swelling and pressure would work until he could get himself out of there, back to Cambodia and to a medic. He was wounded, but now his senses were also heightened. As he kept pressure on his wound, he listened intently for any sounds that were out of the ordinary — like a person moving. Thankfully the rain stopped, so it wouldn't drown out the sounds of someone moving in the jungle. As he sat there putting pressure on his side, he occasionally peeked around the tree and looked up the trail to see if anyone was there or he could identify where the shot had come from. When he did look up the trail he didn't see anything unusual except a piece of silver paper on the side of the road that someone had carelessly dropped. He didn't know if there was someone still watching him, but he assumed someone was. It was probably that fucking American.

After about ten minutes Dembo figured he had to get a move on and head back to Cambodia while he could still walk and it was light out. His side was starting to throb and hurt more, although the bleeding seemed to have stopped. He could barely feel the pellet in his leg, but his leg was starting to stiffen up. He had to go now before things got worse. Slowly pulling himself up, he looked around one more time and then started to slowly pick his way west just off the south side of the trail. His side was really hurting now and he wasn't sure how far he could go, but he was moving and no one was shooting at him. He had a chance.

Jim watched as the black guy got up and started to slowly move back the way he had come, but just off the south side of the trail. He didn't have a good shot at him, the tree and too many branches were in the way. The black guy wasn't going anywhere fast, but he was moving. Jim could see his rifle slung over his left shoulder. He didn't have his rucksack. Jim decided to circle around and try to get in front of him. He'd follow his previous plan and quietly move back from his hide position, cross the trail to the south, and move up the slope of the mountain until he was about 200 meters or so above the trail. From there he'd turn west and move as quickly and quietly as he could, paralleling the trail up high, while watching below looking for his wounded target.

The jungle was intermittently dense along the side of the mountain south of the trail. The jungle there was characterized by tall broad-leafed hardwood trees and semi-evergreens with intermittent bushy undergrowth, occasional vines and ground cover grasses where the light reached the ground. It made moving in a straight line difficult and seeing very far ahead nearly impossible.

Once he got up Jim moved quickly, but tried to be as quiet as he could. On the mountain he kept the trail below him to his right to guide him. After he had moved along the mountain side for about ten minutes he stopped and listened. He thought he heard movement below him. He scanned the area between himself and the trail several times looking for the wounded black guy before finally spotting him about sixty meters behind and below him, limping along still just off the trail on the south side. He was not looking around, just seemingly focused on moving west as quickly as he could go – which wasn't very fast – he held his side as he walked. Jim stayed put behind a tree and watched him move for a while. It was clear he was hurting, his rifle was still slung and he wasn't tactical at all, just trying to move steadily west as he pressed his right hand to his hip. That must be where I got him, Jim said to himself, Well you're mine now dude!

Considering he had been shot Dembo thought he was doing pretty well. His side was growing more painful, but the bleeding had almost stopped. He could feel the pellet in his leg, but he was moving pretty well and he was putting steady distance between himself and the ambush site. He was concentrating on moving and not looking around too much. He stopped every few hundred meters to look and listen and assess his wounds. He hadn't seen or heard anything but the trees rustling, so he kept going. Maybe whoever shot him thought he'd killed him and took off. He hoped so. He'd stay off but parallel the trail a little longer, then hop back on it and try to pick up his pace. At the rate he was moving, he wouldn't get to the rally point until late afternoon or early evening. But if nothing else happened he thought he could make it.

Jim watched the wounded NVA move for a minute and decided to go further up the mountain where he'd have even better cover so he'd be sure to be out of sight. He could move a lot faster than the black guy so if he wasn't detected it should be no problem getting well in front of him to set another ambush. As Jim watched the black guy leaned against a tree and took a long sip out of his canteen it started to rain again, lightly at first and then more steadily. Good for me, Jim thought, he won't hear me at all now. Then he quietly backed out of his position and headed even further up the slope moving faster so he would have more time to find a good ambush site.

Captain Dembo stopped by a huge tree and took a swig of water out of his nearly empty canteen. He was really thirsty, he'd have to fill his canteen at the next stream he saw. As he drank he looked around as the rain began again, but he still didn't see anything or hear anything but the rain hitting the trees. Suddenly he was feeling heavy and tired. He'd go a few hundred meters more and then rest a bit. Then when he started out again he'd get on the trail and try to pick up the pace. Hopefully the rain would stop by then, the trail was already wet and muddy and he didn't need it to get worse and slow him down even more.

Jim was on a mission and it didn't take him long to get well in front of the limping Captain Dembo. The rain was helpful and covered-up any noise he was making as he moved. He went what he thought was about 500 meters and then came down the slope to where he could see the trail. The trail was getting wider at that point and sloping down a bit as it continued west. It was also getting muddier by the minute as the rain was steady now as a squall of clouds passed overhead.

Jim picked out another big hardwood tree in a grove of about eight where he could hide and still have a decent view out to about forty meters of both the trail and the jungle next to it. He expected the black guy to be coming his way shortly just off the south side of the trail like he was when Jim last saw him. But if he was on the trail that would be okay too, he'd still have a good shot at him.

Down near the trail the underbrush was not as thick as higher up on the mountain. When the black guy came towards him, Jim would wait to shoot him until he got close, maybe 30 meters, so he would be sure not to miss this time. His plan clear and happy with his position, Jim took his ruck off, set it behind a tree and sat on it so he was off the wet ground. The mahogany tree was wide and offered good concealment as well as protection. He adjusted himself, so he had a clear field of view towards where he expected the black guy to be coming from. He held his rifle under his right arm so he could quickly get in a firing position and finish the black dude off once he got close. All he had to do now was sit there and wait for his prey to come to him. Then it started raining harder.

The hard rain was pissing Captain Demo off. He was already soaked and wounded and in pain. He never wore a hat so the rain just rolled off his black head and down his face. It was irritating and added to his misery. He estimated he'd come about 400 meters since his last stop and he thought he'd probably lost anyone who was looking for him. Actually, he didn't think anyone was, but he had to be cautious. He picked out a big tree in front of him just above the trail and moved to it and sat down on a log next to it. I wish the damn rain would stop, he said to himself, I'm miserable enough. And as if on command the squall passed and the rain stopped. "Damn Right," he said out loud in Portuguese, his second Angolan tongue.

Dembo was sitting on the west side of the tree, away from the direction he had come. After finishing what was left of a cold rice ball he had in a plastic bag in one of his pants pockets, he drank the last of his water, put the canteen back in its pouch and stood up to take a piss. When he got up Jim saw him.

Jim was about 50 meters away, slightly uphill and he had a decent shot. He decided to let him finish pissing and when he turned around he'd shoot him in the head. It would be quick and the end of the story. Jim would search him and take something to prove he had killed a black guy, jump back on the trail and head east. He wasn't going to try to make contact with B Company. It was just too dangerous. He figured heading to Plei Kleng would be the safest option now. He might have to spend one more night in the jungle, but he could make it to Plei Kleng the next day if he kept moving. That was assuming he didn't run into any surprises.

When Captain Dembo finished relieving himself and started to turn around, he saw Jim raising his rifle out of the corner of his eye and instantly dropped down just as Jim fired several shots at him, all of which smacked into the hardwood tree harmlessly. Dembo grabbed his rifle, and crawled around to the far side of the tree. Bring it on, goddamn it, he thought, let's get this over with, I'm ready! And he was. To prove it he fired a few rounds back at Jim to let him know he could still fight. They were high and ineffective. Jim never took his eyes off Dembo's tree.

For some reason Jim had been slow to engage Dembo. By the time he raised his rifle and looked through the sights and fired, Dembo was dropping down, grabbing his AK47 and crawling behind the tree for cover. Jim had no real shot now and the black guy now knew he was there and where he was – behind a mahogany tree 50 meters to his left front, a little up the hill. After a pause Jim fired at Dembo a second time, spraying the tree where he saw Dembo duck with M16 rounds. Jim kept his rifle aimed at the tree and was prepared to fire again if Dembo stuck his head out, but he didn't. In fact, after initially returning fire Dembo had crawled back to another, bigger tree directly behind the one he'd peed on. Jim didn't see him move.

When Dembo got to the next tree, he took up a firing position and waited. He assumed, correctly, that Jim would come at him. He just didn't know when or from where. He knew Jim was ahead of him and above him, but couldn't see him. Jim had ducked back behind his own tree when Dembo returned fire. When Jim fired at him again Dembo didn't move or respond, he just stayed slumped down behind his tree. He knew the American still had an advantage being above him on the slope, but felt he'd probably be safe behind the big mahogany tree.

Jim didn't think the black guy would try to attack him. He was wounded and not able to move well or quickly, although he could still get around and was armed and dangerous. Most likely he would be a defender and let Jim initiate the action. Jim had to figure out how to get him out from behind the big hardwood tree - they were like leafy steel bunkers, rifle bullets hardly dented them. Jim thought for a minute and it came to him – he'd use the grenade he had in his rucksack.

Jim dug the grenade out of his rucksack then quietly moved a little higher up the slope. He'd try to move to where he could get a better view of the area where Dembo was hiding. He would then fire a few rounds in his direction to cause him to keep his head down while he moved closer to throw the grenade. He'd try to throw it beyond the black guy's tree so the explosion would be on the far side and hopefully splatter him with shrapnel. Jim could then maneuver around to where he had a clear shot and finish him off. No prisoners today!

Dembo was sitting tight, but staying vigilant. He figured the American who had killed his men and shot him would try to make him come out from behind his tree somehow, so he kept his rifle at the ready to fire back if attacked, but he wasn't moving. He was tired and weaker now, but he could still fight. He figured the next few minutes would determine who would win the battle. He was right.

The rain had stopped as Jim started moving back up the slope to maneuver around to where he could throw his grenade accurately. He didn't want to throw it very far or through bushes or branches that might knock it off target. As he moved the wind suddenly picked up a bit and the rustling of the trees made an eerie sound and shook the water off the leaves and branches so it seemed like it was still raining even though it wasn't. This was to his advantage as his target probably couldn't hear him moving.

Jim didn't have eyes on his target, but thought he knew the tree where he was hiding. As he came cautiously back down the slope he moved with his rifle at the ready. When he got as close as he deemed safe he fired a burst at the tree where he thought the black guy was hiding hoping it would cause him to move. It didn't because he wasn't there.

Behind another big mahogany tree a few meters away Dembo was starting to really hurt, his wounds were catching up to him. He wasn't sure where Jim was, but he believed he had good cover and he wasn't moving from behind it unless he had to. But when Jim fired at the wrong tree Dembo foolishly and weakly returned fire which wasn't even close to where Jim was. The returned fire was a huge mistake as it told Jim what he needed to know – the exact tree Dembo was behind.

Jim now cautiously moved to about 15 meters from Dembo and stood behind a tree. He took out the grenade and peered around the tree trunk to see where he needed to throw it. There was a gap between the tree where Dembo was hiding and a large bush. Jim pulled the pin and tossed the grenade under-handed into the gap and it bounced just before the target tree and rolled forward past it as Jim ducked behind his own tree for cover. When the grenade exploded Jim could hear a scream. Must have got him, Jim thought. Then, rifle at the ready, he again began to circle around to his right, slowly down the slope keeping his distance, trying to move to a position where he could get a clear look behind the big mahogany tree.

When Dembo saw the grenade roll past him instinctively he knew he had about three seconds. He immediately dropped down and curled into a ball at the base of the tree. When the grenade exploded it sprayed hot shrapnel 360 degrees and several of the projectiles struck Dembo in the back and legs. They ripped his flesh and left jagged wounds, but because he was on the ground and curled-up, he was again lucky, and the shrapnel hit nothing vital. However his ability to fight was severely diminished. When he was hit he had let out a scream at the pain of the hot metal ripping his skin and embedding itself in his body. Dembo was now physically beaten and the fight was out of him. His adrenaline rush was all that was keeping him going. He couldn't run away or even really put up much resistance - if he was to survive he had to try to trick his attacker, catch him off guard, and maybe he could get a jump on him, turn the table and get out of this mess. If not, he knew he was a dead man.

Shortly after the grenade exploded, as Jim started to circle around Dembo's tree, Dembo yelled out, "OKAY, OKAY," and got up to a kneeling position as best he could, still behind the tree. A few seconds later after catching his breath he yelled again, "OKAY, OKAY." Jim wasn't sure what was up? Was the guy trying to surrender? He kept slowly circling right and down to get where he could see fully behind the tree and his wounded prey. He was now only about 10 meters away, but there were still trees and bushes somewhat obscuring his view - so he kept slowly moving right, rifle raised at the ready.

Behind the tree while kneeling Dembo took his pistol out of its holster and put it in his right hand and he stood up, still behind his tree. He yelled, "OKAY, OKAY," a few more times and then threw his rifle out in front of the tree towards Jim. Jim saw the rifle come out and Dembo wave his left hand and again yelled, "OKAY, OKAY," the only English words he knew. Then he slowly stepped partly out from behind the tree. He held his left hand high above his head shaking it. He appeared to be leaning on the tree with his right hand, but Jim couldn't fully see it. When Jim looked at him Dembo stared back as if to acknowledge, so this is who I'm fighting.

It appeared the black guy might be trying to surrender, although Jim couldn't be sure. The guy was a mess, muddy, and his wounds had left blood stains on his uniform, torn badly on one side from the grenade blast. Jim was still about 10 meters away, just to Dembo's left, rifle up, pointed directly at the wounded black man. Dembo again said, "OKAY, OKAY," but in less of a yell and waved his left hand again as he stared at Jim. Jim could see the blood spots on his uniform were growing and his left hand shaking as he cautiously moved forward. When Jim was about seven meters away the wounded man seemed to turn to his right, step back, and drop his right arm behind the tree. When Dembo's right arm dropped Jim instantly saw the pistol, and as Dembo started to raise the gun Jim let loose with an automatic burst from his M16 that caught Dembo full in the chest before he could get the pistol up. When Dembo fired his rounds slammed into the ground well to the left of Jim. Jim's three round burst in the middle of Dembo's chest was fatal and punched him backward and he fell to the ground on his back where he would die.

After the exchange Jim quickly moved in on the downed black man prepared to shoot him again if he moved. He didn't, he only groaned as he attempted to breathe. Jim kicked his pistol away and looked to see if he had anything else. There was nothing. Dembo was taking his last gasp when Jim leaned against the tree and lowered his rifle. He'd done it, he'd survived and killed the mysterious black NVA.

Jim stayed there, back against the tree with Dembo's body for a few minutes gathering his thoughts. The last 30 hours had been quite the ordeal, but he had triumphed. Not much more to do now except to get back to B-24 alive. He didn't want to win the battle but lose the war. He still had a ways to go and there were still a lot of threats out there, but he had eliminated the main one.

After a while Jim got up and went back to where his rucksack was and brought it over by Dembo's body. He searched the dead man's pockets and took the ID cards of his men, his pistol and rifle, but he had nothing to identify him on his person. No wallet, no passport, no ID, no ration card. He had a map and a small pocket knife in a pants pocket, a few bills of North Vietnamese money wrapped in a rubber band and a packet of toilet paper both in a small plastic bag in his back pants pocket. Interesting, Jim though. He guessed it was a security thing, if he was killed the North Vietnamese didn't want him carrying anything that could identify him. So how could Jim prove that he killed the black guy or even seen him? "Fuck it," Jim said under his breath, and he removed the Randal from its sheath on his web gear, bent over and cut Dembo's right hand off. He then cut off a swath of cloth from the back of Dembo's bloody shirt and wrapped the severed hand in it and put it in his rucksack pocket. This ought to be evidence enough and maybe they can fingerprint him and find out who it is, but not my problem now, he thought.

Jim felt relieved, the tension of the last two days was lifted, but he was exhausted. He sat down on the other side of the tree to rest for a while and took out Ren's ration and ate the rice ball and the can of fruit. They tasted great. As he ate he took out his map and tried to determine exactly where he was. He figured he was about 20 Kilometers northwest of Plei Kleng and maybe 40 from Kontum. He decided that he would take a cross-country route directly to DL647 on the east side of Chu Mon Ray mountain. He would stay off the trails. It would be the shortest distance, and then he would follow the road west to the SF camp at Plei Kleng and find a way back to B-24. He figured if he didn't have any problems he could make it to Plei Kleng by afternoon the next day, which meant one more night in the Jungle. That didn't bother him, but he hoped the rain had stopped once and for all.

Fifteen minutes later Jim smashed Dembo's AK47 receiver, he wouldn't need it and Jim didn't want to carry it, stepped on and bent the the AK47's barrel, put Dembo's pistol in his ruck, pick it up, and headed for the top of the mountain so he could follow the ridge towards Plei Kleng. When he got to the top of the slope the clouds began to recede and it looked again like the sun would actually come out. My goodness what a fine day for a walk in the jungle, Jim said to himself with a smile as he made his way carefully east along the mountain top.

Two days later, Jim was back at B-24. He got a ride back from the team at Plei Kleng who had called ahead and let B-24 know that Jim was alive and they would be bringing him over.

Once he arrived at the B-24 compound Jim went directly to LTC Tower and reported in, filling him in on the last several adventurous days. Tower was genuinely glad to see him and expressed his worry that for a few days they thought they had lost him. He also filled Jim in on how B and C Companies had sprung several successful ambushes on NVA elements retreating from Plei Klang while Jim was on his walk in the woods. Both companies would be returning to B-24 the next day.

At the end of his report, Jim brought out the severed hand of the black guy. LTC Tower was a little taken aback that Jim had lugged the hand back to B-24. Tower had the battalion intel officer deliver it to the CIA's man in Kontum who said he would send it on and see if they could identify who it belonged to. The CIA had an extensive database of people who were part of various rebel and insurgent movements from around the world. This guy might be in it. LTC Tower told Jim that it was significant that he had proved there were third country advisors operating with the NVA. MACV would be very pleased that someone had actually verified it. Frankly, he told Jim he wasn't surprised.

Bravo Company returned to B-24 the next day around noon and 1SG Kue and the rest of the company were overjoyed to see Jim back at B-24. They were probably not as happy as Jim was. Jim's first concern was if the company had retrieved Ren's body. 1SG Kue said that they had, which put Jim somewhat at ease. He was concerned that the man who gave his life for him would be unaccounted for. Jim would make it a point to ensure his family was taken care of and tell them of Ren's bravery.

LTC Tower set up an informal briefing so Jim could tell his story to the entire leadership of B-24 at once. That way he would not have to repeat his story every time he saw someone. Jim was happy to do it and that evening gave an informal briefing at the team house. After the briefing LTC Tower told Jim he was putting him in for a Silver Star for his bravery and exploits. Jim was humbled and said he just did what he thought he was supposed to do. "No, Jim you did way more than that," Tower told him, "and I'm proud that I had the chance to serve with a warrior like you." "I'm the lucky one sir," Jim replied as Sergeant Rock brought them two more Ba-Muoi-Ba beers.

Three weeks later, the CIA sent a memo from its Vietnamese headquarters in Saigon to Nha Trang. The report said they had been able to identify the black man killed near Plei Re as Semal Dembo, a captain in the Angolan rebel group MPLA. The CIA had knowledge of him not only in Africa, but Cuba, and Mozambique and now Vietnam. He had been implicated in an attack on a Mozambique police station a few years prior in an attempt to break out several rebels that had resulted in five police officers and two civilians being massacred. That was the last sighting the CIA had of him. The CIA station chief put a hand-written note to COL Anderson on the memo, it said in part: "Looks like your Captain Tittsworth did the world a favor."

The report reached B-24 a few days later and its findings were announced at a meeting in the B-24 team house. LTC Tower, who would be leaving in the next few days for his new assignment at Fort Bragg, briefed the team on the CIA memo. Interesting, Jim thought to himself after LTC Tower's briefing, I'm just glad it wasn't an American.

A short while later, after several beers, as part of breaking in the newbies who had recently been assigned to B-24 some of the veteran SF sergeants broke out in a rendition of Mary-Ann Barnes. Jim just sat there smiling, popped a fried grasshopper, sipped on his beer, and enjoyed the camaraderie that only men at war can know.

Tittsworth

www.ingramcontent.com/pod-product-compliance
Lightning Source LLC
Chambersburg PA
CBHW051340020726
47501CB00007B/2187